The Storyteller
and Her Sisters

Cheryl Mahoney

Stonehenge Circle Press

Stonehenge Circle Press

ISBN-13: 978-1-68012-625-9

ISBN-10: 1-68012-625-3

First Edition

Quotes from Jacob and Wilhelm Grimm are taken from *Household Tales by Brothers Grimm*, from the 1884 translation by Margaret Hunt

Cover image courtesy of Diana Hirsch, via iStockphoto

Dedication

Unlike Lyra, I don't have any sisters—but I've known since high
school what it's like to be part of a close-knit circle of girls.
Thanks for all the laughter and support,
and for listening to my stories!

~ ◆ ~ *Part One* ~ ◆ ~

They went all the way down, and when they were at the bottom, they were standing in a wonderfully pretty avenue of trees, all the leaves of which were of silver, and shone and glistened...After that they came into an avenue where all the leaves were of gold, and lastly into a third where they were of bright diamonds.

Jacob and Wilhelm Grimm

~ ◆ ~

Chapter One

There are twelve of us, but most people think of us as one. For years we encouraged it. Our anonymity was our strength, and our curse.

I have eleven sisters, and all through my growing up, I struggled to define what made me *me*, not they or even we. It was no good discussing my appearance—we all looked much the same, with long gold hair and blue eyes. We styled our hair alike, and dressed alike. We did everything we could to ensure no one could tell us apart. For years, no one could, not even our father. Especially not Father. I liked to think our mother could have. Since she died when I was three, that was only an imagining.

Any significant difference, therefore, had to be inside. The truth was, we weren't at all alike. Atalya was afraid of everything; Alaina, of nothing. Amina loved to know the facts about everything, Acacia loved drawing, and Adalia loved to sing.

I tell stories. I read them, I invent them, I live them and breathe them and can no more imagine my life without them than I can imagine a life without eating. I *tried* to imagine a life without my sisters, but it was like imagining life without the sky. How can you imagine away something that has always been there?

I won't try to take them out of this story. I couldn't, because ultimately it is *our* story.

In order from oldest, we are Avira, Alaina, Adalia, Acacia, Anila, Adrina, Amina, Asasia, myself, Arayna, Amara and Atalya. My name is Alyra. Our parents had very little creativity when it came to names. It was a blessing in a way. If no one could remember our names, it was much harder to tell us apart. Amongst ourselves, we never bothered with the first letter. Mina and Lyra and Talya feel much more individual.

If this story was only about me, it would begin in a different place. It would begin the day my oldest sister Vira read me a tale, and for a few minutes I forgot that I was trapped in a castle, trapped as the ninth in a sisterhood of twelve princesses. For the first time I realized that stories could take me somewhere else, let me be someone else. I realized that stories had power.

Since this story is about my family, there are more appropriate places to start: two hundred years ago, when a wicked enchantress cast a curse; or a mere ten years before I was born, when a Queen fell in love with the chief of her guards; or when I was three, and that guardsman-turned-king learned his wife's great secret, and everything changed.

But I think the real beginning, for my sisters and me, was the day the Gate opened.

On that day, Vira, the oldest, was twenty-four. Talya, the youngest, was fifteen. I was seventeen. We are each spaced loosely a year apart, except for the two sets of twins, Nila and Drina, Rayna and Mara.

It was evening when the Gate opened, and though that evening proved momentous, the day that preceded it was only the usual round of embroidery, penmanship and dancing lessons—we were all excellent dancers. Anything we did had to be inside my father's castle. We were never allowed to leave. The day closed with supper in the banquet hall with Father. Such ran every day.

And in the evening, all my sisters were in our bedroom, brushing hair, pursuing hobbies, and chatting about a thousand different topics. Rather like most girls, I imagined—not that I had had much experience with a great many other girls. But I had read things.

Twelve of us shared a single bedroom, and there were days when it felt incredibly cramped. In reality it was a large room, long and with a high ceiling. There was a door at one end and a fireplace at the other, beds stretching in two rows down the length of the room. I suppose we didn't undergo much hardship in our living conditions—though I defy anyone to share a bedroom with eleven sisters for fourteen years and not come up with a few complaints.

Such as the problem of constantly being interrupted in the good parts of stories. On this evening, I was stretched across my bed, halfway through a story with the heroine just about to unmask the hero. Mina chose that moment to put down the book she'd been reading, sitting cross-legged on her own bed, and asked, "Has anyone else noticed what today is?"

"Tuesday," Talya said, hopping on one foot as she pulled a stocking on. Inevitably she tumbled back onto her bed, next to mine.

We didn't sleep in order by age. That would have been too obvious.

I didn't have to look up from my storybook to know that Mina was rolling her eyes. I could hear it in her voice. "No, I didn't mean Tuesday. I was talking about the date. It's the seventh."

There were several groans from around the room. "Oh, not this *again*," Rayna said, to the accompanying clatter of jewelry she was sorting at her dressing table. We all had just a little bit of our own space, if having our own dressing tables next to each bed qualifies. The compartment below my table was full of books. We each had a wardrobe too, but every wardrobe had identical contents. Anything that didn't fit into the wardrobes went into the large closet adjoining our room, and no one bothered if things got mixed together there.

Mina pushed on with her pet topic, over the groans. "We agreed. We try the Gate on the seventh of each month. And we especially have to this month. It's been exactly fourteen years."

If it was exactly fourteen years since the Gate last opened, then it was thirteen years, ten months, and some days since our mother died.

"Fourteen years and we've never been able to open it," Laina said. I glanced up to see if her expression matched her curt tone. I couldn't tell; she was leaning on the sill at one of the two narrow windows on either side of the fireplace, looking out over the moat. "I vote we give the whole business up."

"We can't," Mina said in her most scandalized voice. "It's a sacred trust. And I've spent years trying to understand it. We can't just give it all up now."

"So you can go," Laina said. "I don't feel like trekking down all those stairs in the dark, and then back up again to no purpose."

"And it's creepy down there," Talya put in.

I could see Laina's side, and Mina's too. There was something fascinating about the Gate...but we hadn't been accomplishing anything all these years. If it had been up to me that evening, I would have stayed on my bed reading, so it's fortunate matters weren't in my hands.

"Mina's right," Vira said, standing up from her dressing table in a sweep of gray silk. "We decided a long time ago, we always try on the seventh. And it has to be all of us. When we come up with a better way to escape from here, a way that succeeds, *then* we'll give up on the Gate."

When Vira put her voice in, we all knew we were going to visit the Gate that night. When our oldest sister said something, it happened.

The remaining complaints were really just for form's sake, and my sisters began drifting towards Vira's bed, the closest in its row to the fireplace. Mina paused by me, and shook my foot. "Come on, Lyra."

I still had my book open, though I'd been marking my place with my finger for several minutes now. "I'm in the middle of a story."

"So what? You've read it before."

Our castle library had seventy-one books of stories. I had read all of them. Repeatedly.

"That's not the point," I sighed, pushed the book aside and slid off the bed to follow Mina.

Once we were all clustered around her, Vira pushed against one bedpost and the bed slid several feet to the right. We'd never been able to work out how it moved so easily—none of the other beds did. It just always had. When it slid over, it uncovered a trap door beneath. Vira lifted the door, and the room's light fell onto the stone steps below. Sasia handed her a lit candle, and Vira led the way down the stairs.

Talya slipped her hand into mine and we descended together, at the back of the group.

There were 366 steps. I had mostly stopped counting them years earlier. Once in a while I checked again, in case the number had changed.

The steps went straight down, with a wall on one side and no railing on the other, so that I was always grateful for their width. Talya and I could easily walk side-by-side without tipping off the edge. The stairs ended in a dark tunnel carved from stone, not so narrow as to feel tight, but small enough for Vira's single candle to light it easily. Even though it was late summer up above, the stairs and the tunnel were always cold.

A hundred yards on, we reached the Gate. It was a great beast of iron bars and curling decorations, cutting across the tunnel, blocking the path to anything beyond it. Vira's candlelight didn't reach far enough to show anything except more tunnel on the other side. A lion's head loomed from the top of the Gate, and I had never been able to escape the feeling that it was looking at us. I'd never seen it move, unless you count one very disturbing dream.

For fourteen years, the Gate hadn't moved at all, not even the rational way gates are supposed to move when someone tries to open them. There was no lock, and apparently no need for one. The Gate simply hadn't shifted no matter how we pushed. Not even a wobble.

Until that night. I already told you it was the day the Gate opened, so you won't be surprised that Mina, the first to push, thought she felt it move. The rest of us gathered around, and the more of us who tried, the more it seemed to sway and give. Finally, when all twelve of us took hold of a bar and pushed, the gate swung neatly open, like two wings sweeping to either side.

You may not be surprised. For us, it could hardly have been more shocking if a blank wall in our bedroom had opened. Even though we had kept trying the Gate, we were very used to the idea that it was never going to move. I turned to Talya next to me and grinned, my stomach fluttering with anticipation. She bit her lip and gave only a half-smile in response.

"Now what?" Laina said, the first to break the silence. The amount of detail in our plans for this eventuality had about matched our expectations of it actually happening.

"Let's go back," Talya said, wrapping her arms around herself. "Let's close the Gate and go back. It's *dangerous* through there, you all know that."

"Our whole lives are dangerous," Laina said. I could see my own excitement reflected in the gleam in her eyes. "We have to risk this. It's the best chance at escape we've ever had."

"It may mean something that the Gate finally opened," Mina pointed out. "Magical things rarely happen randomly, and if a magic door opens it only makes sense to go through it."

"But you know what could happen," Talya whispered.

"We've talked about this from every angle for *years*," Laina groaned, "are we really going to do it again now? We've always agreed that it would be worth the risk if we ever had the chance. Besides, if it was all right for Mother, it can't be that dangerous."

"Laina's right," Vira said, raising the candle higher. "In all practical ways, we decided this a long time ago. So let's go on and see if it's how we remember it."

I didn't remember it, at least not with any certainty that I wasn't just imagining memories. But Vira had been ten years old, fourteen years before. She remembered.

We all passed through the Gate, Talya clutching my hand again, though even she had finally given a reluctant nod to going forward. I squeezed her fingers tightly. For me, it was anticipation, not dread. I had been hearing about this my whole life. I had always wanted to see it for myself. It was an adventure, like one of my stories. People in stories didn't turn back because the adventure was dangerous.

Beyond the Gate, after two more turns, the tunnel opened up into a broad cavern. Shortly beyond the tunnel's mouth stood the forest. The trees formed an orchard of orderly rows, and the trunks of every tree shone like moonlight, casting a shimmering light throughout the cavern. Above the trunks, the branches and leaves were silver.

I don't mean they were gray, or resembled silver, or were some variety of tree with silver in its name. I mean they were *silver*. They looked like some kind of elm, made of glittering metal.

This wasn't a surprise. Vira had remembered the trees, and so had a few others of my oldest sisters. Hearing about it and seeing it, that's two very different things. Somehow, I had never quite believed in this forest until I saw it myself. Talya's hand clasped tighter around mine.

We slowly walked down a wide pathway between two lines of trees, our footsteps making little impression on the cold silence. The trees grew out of the cavern floor, and if they had ever shed a leaf, it wasn't visible on the bare rock around them. Mostly I was looking up. I stared at those silver leaves above us, and almost without my noticing, my thoughts began to drift towards all that I could buy with just a few branches.

I wanted to keep looking at the silver trees, but at the head of our group, Vira kept pushing onwards. Long instinct made us all follow her, and soon the moonlight silver forest gave way to a brighter stretch of trees. These trees shone like sunlight. These trees were made of gold.

They glittered and shone and enticed. With a handful of these leaves, I could buy dresses and jewelry and shoes... I blinked, momentarily confused. I didn't even *like* shoes very much. It was Nila who was obsessed with clothes, not me. And yet I suddenly wanted gold, lots of it, to buy piles and mountains of beautiful things. So many beautiful things.

The gold trees ended too, and a third forest began. This one glittered like starlight. This one had trees made of diamonds. I looked at the nearest branch, seeing delicate sprays of flowers and buds, crusted with shining stones. A single branch had enough diamonds to make necklaces for all twelve of us.

With that kind of wealth, I could do anything. I could buy castles and horses and armies...and books, I could buy so many books...and entire countries if I wanted to...and I wouldn't need anyone, not Vira, not Mina, not Talya...

I was still holding Talya's hand. I looked down at our hands, and then at her face. She was staring up at the diamond trees with wide, blank eyes. I turned my gaze to the rest of my sisters. Vira and Laina, their expressions were grim. Mina and Rayna appeared confused, as confused as I was feeling. The rest looked entranced.

I was thinking thoughts that I knew I wouldn't think. Buying books, that was me. That was a constant wish. But buying armies, buying countries? And while I sometimes (all right, often) wished to not be dependent on my sisters, the thought had had a nasty undercurrent to it that I didn't recognize.

I *should* have recognized what was going on right away. Knowing the theory of something doesn't always help when experiencing the reality, especially when the nature of that reality is to twist a person's thoughts.

The forests were beautiful. And they were poisonous. And it was an indication of how strong they were that they had pulled us in, made me completely forget the danger for a few moments, even though we had walked into the forest expecting it. Vira had remembered the poison too. The results of that poison had reached into the world above, and made our lives what they were now.

We came out of the diamond forest, its light casting far enough to show us the shore of an underground lake. The water looked unnaturally black, though perhaps that was only the reflection of the cavern roof that I assumed was arching above us. The light from the trees didn't reach far enough to show it.

I had barely stepped out from beneath the last spreading diamond branch before I felt as though a pressure had lifted. My mind felt clear again. The only thoughts were my own. I still wanted to buy books, but I didn't feel any desire to buy armies. Or shoes.

I heard Talya inhale a long, shuddering breath, and watched the expressions change on my other sisters' faces. There was relief, surprise, horror, shock.

"Does anyone still feel an overwhelming desire to make extravagant purchases?" Vira asked after a long moment. Her mouth was set in a hard line, her eyes like stone.

There was a great deal of head shaking, some of it violent. Talya's hand tightened again on mine, and I can't say that I wasn't glad of the connection.

"Anyone feeling that murder would be a small thing if it got you what you wanted?" Vira asked.

More head shaking, and several exclamations in the negative. Murder had never crept into my thoughts, although for a period there I *had* been thinking that getting rid of my sisters would be a pleasant thing. It gave me a shiver to imagine my sisters thinking the same idea.

"I *said* it was dangerous." Talya's voice caught on something just this side of a sob.

"We didn't say it wasn't," Laina said. Her voice was perfectly steady, her arms crossed defiantly. "We said it was a necessary risk."

"And even if it was unpleasant, we all came through it." Vira looked around at us. She must have approved of what she saw, because she allowed herself a small, satisfied smile. "Mother always thought we'd be all right."

"Maybe so," Laina muttered, "but she also thought that about—"

"Never mind that now," Vira interrupted, head high and shoulders at a commanding angle. "What counts is that we all came out of the forest, and none of us appear to have lost our minds in the process."

We regrouped, took a few deep breaths, and started to think about what came next. For years we had dreamed of finding a way out of our father's castle. A tunnel, a passage, a portal that would transport us to another place. After all this time, anywhere seemed like it would be better than where we were now. Maybe in another place we could have a future.

We drifted across the shore, mostly staying in groups of two or three, no one too eager to get entirely by herself. Mina walked confidently towards the water. Without a better idea, I followed her, hauling Talya along. Mina usually had good ideas.

I sniffed the air as I walked. It felt like a completely different world down here. It was cold, like the tunnel, and smelled different too. I couldn't figure out what it reminded me of. Possibly the salted fish Cook made sometimes.

Mina was standing on the shore, hands on her hips, frowning over the waves that gently lapped the sand. "Is it me, or does the water look strange?"

"*Yes*," Talya said. "This whole place is strange, and I don't like it."

We ignored her second sentence. "It looks sort of black and shiny," I observed. "Which I guess water would, in the dark and with this lighting, but it looks, I don't know…*strangely* black and shiny."

"Not your most eloquent description, but agreed." Mina crouched down, the water's edge a foot from the toes of her boots.

My descriptions are better when I'm telling a story. I have to step into the right mindset.

"It might not be ordinary water," Mina continued. "A magical forest could easily have a magical lake. And magical water might be of use to us somehow." She stretched her hand out over the water, palm down. "It's not hot…doesn't smell either." She lowered her hand. "It feels sort of—oh!"

Mina had dipped her hand into the water. After barely a second she leaped backwards, not easy to do from a crouch. I dropped Talya's hand to catch Mina, and we nearly tumbled together across the sand. With a scramble and kicked sand, we managed to steady ourselves.

Mina was shaking her hand, and muttering, "Ow ow *ow*."

"What is it? What happened?" Talya asked, voice wobbling.

"It burned me!"

Even in the odd light, I could see that Mina's hand was an alarming shade of red. My own hand tightened on her arm, and I hoped the half-dozen stories that immediately came to mind about cursed water and withered hands were completely irrelevant.

"*Ow*," Mina muttered again.

I shook away thoughts of stories. "Sasia, come here—Mina burned her hand," I called, digging into a pocket for a handkerchief. Sasia would know what to do. She knew more than I would ever want to know about herbs and medicine; if we had a headache or a paper cut or a fever, she was the one to talk to. The handkerchief was the best I could think of. I didn't know what help it could be—Mina wasn't bleeding—but people in stories are always wrapping up injuries.

People in stories are also always ripping off bits of their clothes for bandages, but have you ever actually tried to rip a piece from a reasonably good quality garment, not to mention one you're wearing at the time? It's not so easy.

Sasia hurried over to inspect Mina's hand, and everyone else gathered around.

"It's not so bad, is it?" Talya said, voice too bright, while I peered over Sasia's shoulder to watch for signs of withering. None yet.

Sasia spent what felt like a long time inspecting Mina's hand, before finally saying, "It certainly could be worse. I don't think the burn is serious enough to scar, though there will probably be blisters. I have a jar of ointment in our room that will help, and the sooner I can get it on, the better."

"All right then, we go back for tonight," Vira decided.

"Oh, no, I'm all right," Mina said. "We should look around more..." She would have been more convincing if her voice didn't shake. I tried not to worry about that, to be glad instead that at least she was saying something besides 'ow.'

"We've all had enough for one night," Vira said. Sometimes she thought we were still children.

She was right about going back, of course; with Mina hurt we didn't really have much choice. And after all, even if we had found a path or a tunnel marked by a sign reading 'This Way to Leave Behind Everything You've Ever Known,' we were hardly equipped for following it. We weren't dressed for a journey, and we had carried nothing with us—although if we really had found a sign like that, it would have been hard to resist.

Despite our reluctance, we turned back towards the glittering diamond forest. I wasn't eager to go back through the forest either. No way around that.

I glanced over my shoulder as I walked towards the first trees, and for a moment I thought I saw movement, just on the edge of the light. It was a shadow among shadows, possibly a silhouette. I blinked, and when I looked again, I couldn't be sure that I'd seen anything. Even if I had, I didn't know if that was a reason to stay, or an even better reason to go.

Chapter Two

The magic forest was better and worse as we walked through it the second time. I expected the invading thoughts, which helped, but they were more detailed and specific, which didn't. By the time we got out of the silver forest, I knew exactly which books I would buy, if only I had just a few of the leaves glimmering around me.

We didn't talk much (an unusual situation in itself) as we walked. There was something so eerie and hushed about the surroundings. We never heard any sound at all in the forests or the tunnel, except whatever we made ourselves—very little. Some places just make you want to be quiet. And I had plenty to think about, to compare what we were seeing to stories I had read, to think about what it all might mean. To think about the hazards of an enchanted forest that twisted people's minds, bordered by a lake that burned anyone who touched it. On the other hand, magical things always had a dangerous edge, in every story I'd ever read. So while it sobered me a little, mostly I was just…fascinated.

I thought about our story, too, as we walked back through the tunnel towards the Gate. At the time, it was a story that still had too many holes in it, and not nearly enough answers.

On that night, the earliest starting point I knew for our story was ten years before I was born, once upon a time when my mother fell in love. No one in my father's castle talked about those early days anymore, but Vira had learned the story from Mother while she was still alive, and she told it to the rest of us. Mother didn't make a popular choice in her romance. She was the newly-crowned queen of Pareed, and he was the chief of the guards.

Father was young and handsome and could charm anyone. My mother used her influence and my father used his charm, and the queen married the guardsman. It became so obvious to everyone how in love they were that by the time Vira was born, everyone had grown reconciled to the guardsman-turned-king. That was convenient, since my father did quite a bit of ruling even while my mother was alive. She spent the next ten years having twelve daughters, which could rather distract a person.

There was something else distracting her. My mother knew about the Gate, the magic forest, and the dark lake. They were secrets passed through the family for generations; none of us knew how far back it went. Mother told her oldest daughters, who told the rest of us.

The Gate used to open for Mother, and she always felt that there had to be a purpose to the strange place. The Gate would only open to certain people; only someone of the right kind of mind would get through the forest. There was some task that needed doing on the lake, and the rest was there like a test to let only the right people through.

For eleven years, she didn't tell my father about any of this. It makes me wonder if, despite how much she was in love with him, she still sensed something. He knew she had a secret, that sometimes she would disappear and then return unusually thoughtful. At first he would laugh and say that women had to have their secrets. As time went on, he stopped laughing. Then he started asking why she did need to have a secret anyway, and didn't she trust him, and who would be better to tell than her own husband? And that perhaps there was something more sinister going on after all.

Finally she relented and agreed to tell him the truth. Vira was ten. I was three. Talya had just been born three months before.

Mother took Father to the room that would one day belong to my sisters and me. At the time, it was a guest chamber in a little-used wing of the castle. When she went there on this day, she took Vira, Laina and me.

I wasn't supposed to go at all, but the expedition interrupted a story that Vira was telling me, and I was so distraught that Mother agreed I could come on the adventure. Even then, I hated missing the end of a story. I don't think I remember any of what followed. I heard the account from Vira so many times, that I don't know what's my memory and what's only my imaginings of what she told me.

Mother opened the trapdoor, and we all descended the stairs. Father carried me. The Gate opened for Mother, and we went into the forest. I exclaimed over the prettiness of the silver, gold and diamonds, and showed little other effect. I think I was too young for the forest to know what to do with me. Vira said it made her think about candy and toys. Laina wouldn't say what it made her think about, and Mother never told anyone her thoughts.

We knew exactly what it did to Father. He was entranced, mesmerized, transfixed. He stared at the silver trees, fingered the gold leaves, ran ahead to look at the diamonds.

I had always wondered how hunks of metal, even if they were beautiful, could have such an effect. Now that I had been through the trees myself, I understood a little more, with an understanding that made my stomach churn.

As he looked at the trees, Father started talking about the incredible wealth, about the incredible things they could do with it. He said that Mother had been foolish not to make use of it, foolish not to tell him sooner. He started talking about plans, about how easy it would be to take the leaves, to wrench off branches, to tear up entire rows of trees. To take the gold and the silver and the diamonds back up into the light, to pour them into the treasury. A kingdom with this kind of wealth—that was a kingdom that had power. There was enough wealth to hire armies, to build up weapons, to go to war against our neighbors and win. To conquer the nearest countries, and then ones that were farther away, to build up navies…and on and on and on.

Mother told him he wasn't thinking clearly, that the trees weren't meant to be used, that there was something in them that was tainting his thoughts and making him say things he never would, believe ideas he had never had. She told him that what he was suggesting was impossible, unthinkable. That nothing good could come of wealth that poisoned people's minds.

He got angry. And he yelled and he ranted and he insisted that he knew what he was saying and she was blind if she couldn't see the possibilities. Vira says it was the first time she was ever afraid of him. I can't remember a time before that.

Mother got him out of the forest by telling him they'd go back later, bring people to help carry the wealth. We all passed through the Gate, and it closed behind us. It didn't open again for fourteen years.

It was Mother who carried me back up the stairs. Already, everything was changed.

She had hoped that, outside of the forest, Father would come back to his senses, turn back into the charming man she had married. He didn't. He wouldn't let go of the idea of the forest, of his dreams of the wealth and the power that could be had. He wanted to go back, to harvest the vast riches below us.

Mother wouldn't open the Gate for him. He pleaded, cajoled, and threatened. He hounded her and harried her and he wouldn't stop. Not even when she got sick.

There was a fever going around that winter. I can't say that Mother catching it was Father's fault. But he didn't help.

Less than six weeks after she let him into the magic forest, Mother died, leaving me and my sisters with just each other. And leaving all of us to desperately miss someone most of us couldn't even remember clearly.

As for our father, it didn't take him long to get the idea that perhaps Mother's daughters would be able to open the Gate. He dragged Vira down below one day and ordered her to open it. When she said no, he pushed her hands against the Gate. Nothing happened.

He never let go of the idea. He moved all of us out of our separate bedrooms into the room with the trapdoor. The new bedroom was locked at night. We were never allowed to leave the castle, even by day. For the court, he made up explanations about guarding us for our own good.

He was always very careful around the court, the nobility— anyone with enough power to start reminding people that he was only a guardsman who had married into the throne, that there were laws that would make it possible to quietly move him aside, in favor of the next blood heir. Losing the throne would likely mean losing the castle too, and with it the trap door, the Gate, and, of course, the forest. People besides us feared Father, but they feared him as a strong, fierce leader, not as a madman who shouldn't be running a country.

Father was even more careful to make sure no one ever knew about the magical forest below us. Unlike Mother, he didn't view it as a trust. He was afraid of anyone else stealing all that wealth.

It was a symptom of how much the forest twisted his mind that he never seemed particularly interested in *other* wealth. He ranted about all that he would do if he had the wealth of the magic forest, while it never seemed to occur to him to raise taxes to unreasonable levels, or to launch invasions based on what was already in the treasury. It was something we feared, but for fourteen years, it hadn't materialized. He was a good king in his policies and his rulings. The madness came out in his personal interactions. I couldn't remember a time when my father's only interest in his daughters wasn't their possible ability to open the Gate.

Father was never convinced that we weren't merely refusing, that we couldn't do it if we tried. He threatened and cajoled us too. Sometimes weeks went by when he never mentioned the Gate and the forest. Sometimes, it was a daily, constant topic, hammered at us every morning and every night for weeks.

With no options for escape all those years that the Gate stayed closed, with no one else around us believing in Father's true danger, we fought back the only way we could find. We defended ourselves in our anonymity. It's much harder to frighten or tempt someone if you know nothing about them. Father never tried to tempt me with books, because he didn't know that I loved them. He never tried to frighten Talya by putting her in a dark room, because he didn't know that she had a terror of the darkness. He didn't know that Mina knew more about his kingdom and its neighbors than anyone in the castle, or that Vira had a will like steel. He couldn't turn us against each other, because he couldn't tell which of us was which.

We dressed alike, we wore our hair alike, we spoke softly and kept our eyes down. No one could divide us, no one could target us. We trusted no one but each other. We were close to no one but each other. We protected ourselves, we protected our mother's secret, and we protected our country from the disaster that would come if Father ever got his hands on the tainted wealth he dreamed about. And we dreamed of some day when the Gate would finally open, finally let us do whatever task was needed, if there was such a task—or finally let us escape, putting the closed Gate forever between Father and us, and between Father and the twisted forest.

On the whole, our story felt more sobering than the ones I read about, and nothing in it made me happy about the prospect of going back through the Gate again, and back to the world I'd known all these years.

The tunnel felt all too short, and soon the Gate loomed above us. It opened on its own as soon as Laina touched it. I wasn't the only on with dragging feet as we slowly began passing through.

"What if it doesn't open again?" Rayna asked, stopping halfway through the Gate. "What if this was our one and only chance?"

"It will open again," Vira said. She was still on the forest's side, sending all the rest of us first.

"You don't know that," Rayna objected.

"It's going to open again," Vira said. "Mina was right when she said it's a sacred trust. Or something similar. There's a reason all of this is here, and there's a reason the Gate opened tonight. It wasn't just to let us wander around in the forest. Whatever's going to happen, it hasn't happened yet. The Gate will keep opening."

It wasn't proof. But it made sense. I so hoped she was right.

We straggled up the 366 steps, and when I stepped through the trapdoor into our bedroom, it hardly felt possible that the room was no different. There was still a fire in the fireplace. Rayna's clothes were still piled around her bed; she had been trying on different outfits, and she never picked anything up. My book was still on top of my quilt where I had dropped it.

There was some conversation as we got ready for bed, less than I might have expected. The mingled horror and fascination was still holding everyone mesmerized, and I wasn't the only one thinking hard.

We changed into twelve identical white nightgowns, pulled out hairpins, and turned down blankets. Everyone seemed eager to escape the chill of that cold forest beneath warm quilts. I was just sliding under mine when Talya perched on the end of my bed, sitting with her knees drawn up and her arms around her ankles.

I knew what she would say before she said it. "Lyra, would you tell me a story?"

I looked at her wide eyes. I could see the ghosts of the magic forest behind the blue, and I wondered what the forest had used to tempt my innocent little sister. Sometimes she seemed much younger than the mere two years of difference in our ages.

"I'd love to tell you a story." I wanted to keep thinking about what had happened, but I could use something to take away the icy touch of that dark lake and those glittering trees too.

Mina drifted over, white bandage on her hand stark against her pink skin, and sat next to Talya. I spun out an old familiar story I knew I wouldn't have to concentrate very hard to tell. It was about a girl who fell in love with a Beast, and in the end, her love turned him into a prince. I got it out of a book. In my experience, monsters most often stay that way. And men are just as likely to turn into beasts as to go the other direction. It's a comforting story anyway. Perhaps you know it.

After the story ended, after all the lights were put out and I was lying in bed, my thoughts went back to our own story. In particular, they circled around and around the Rhyme, the last and perhaps most intriguing piece of the puzzle. We had grown up hearing it, from Mother and each other, and we all had it memorized.

> *Twelve princes will in a castle wait,*
> *Until twelve princesses come through the magic gate.*
> *They'll walk where the metal forest stands,*
> *And cross the lake to distant lands.*
> *They'll dance until they wear their shoes away,*
> *And free the princes in a year and a day.*

It was obviously connected to everything below, but we didn't know where it had come from, or if it was poetry or a spell. A pretty story, or a magic key. Laina thought it was just a nursery rhyme, something some ancestor had made up. Mina thought it was significant, without having any clear theory on what we ought to do about it. If it *was* a story that was meant to come true, we had the setting only, not the rest of the pieces. Not the important parts, like a way to cross the lake (supposing we wanted to) or princes who needed freeing (supposing we wanted to do that either).

I had always hoped that someday we'd find those other pieces, that the Rhyme would play out just the way it sounded. Because that would mean there really was a purpose to it all. It would mean that

Mother was right about the forest wanting something, and that we were meant to fulfill it—because how many groups of twelve princesses can there possibly be in the family tree? It would mean that we had something else to protect, and something to look forward to.

And I really wouldn't have minded meeting a few princes.

Chapter Three

The morning after the Gate opened, the mesmerizing influence of the forest had passed—and there was talking. You might never have listened to twelve girls talking together, but probably you've heard three or four. Double the noise level for each additional girl, and you'll have some idea of what our bedroom sounded like as we were dressing.

The contrast was sharp when we fell abruptly silent. A small thing prompted the change, the sound of a key scraping in the lock on our door. You might wonder that we could hear it, over the sound of all our voices. It's like hearing your name spoken in a room full of conversation. The ear learns to catch certain sounds, and we had been hearing that key in that door every morning for nearly fourteen years.

We fell silent half a beat before the door opened and Father came in. He stood in the doorway, his gaze raking over us all where we sat or stood, hairbrushes still, unfastened jewelry dangling from hands, partially-made beds halted with covers half pulled-up.

I closed the book I hadn't been reading anyway, busy with conversation. They say, in the terribly practical books that Mina reads, that if you're ever so unfortunate as to have a large and hostile predator staring at you in the woods, don't move. Movement attracts them. My book closed and my father's gaze swept to me, piercing, hard, cold. It's not the sort of comment a girl ought to make about her father, but he had creepy eyes. I think he would have been handsome—certainly he was tall and broad-shouldered enough—but the eyes ruined the effect.

My stomach churned as he stared at me, and I strove to keep my face blank. It was all-important to act *normal*. Not that he would have found it strange to see one of us look afraid.

We all stood where we were. When the last of us—Laina—was standing, we said, "Good morning, Father." Our unison was perfect. We'd had every morning of nearly fourteen years to practice.

"Good morning, my dears," he answered. His voice was like velvet. It almost always was. None of us were fooled into believing that there wasn't steel beneath. "And how did you sleep?"

His eyes were still focused on me. I didn't make the mistake of thinking that meant I was supposed to answer. This was a ritual, and it wasn't my line.

"Very well, thank you," Vira said.

Vira and Talya—the oldest and the youngest—were the only ones of us he could reliably identify. He still didn't know anything about them, but he could pick them out of the crowd, most of the time. Sometimes I wondered if that was why Talya was so skittish.

Father finally looked away from me, turning his snake-gaze on Vira. "How pleasant. So there was…no excitement?"

She lied, and did it without even a quiver. "No."

His head turned back in my direction. I thought he was going to look at me again, my stomach clenching at the possibility. Instead, he stopped when his line of sight was on Mina. "You've hurt your hand…" He paused, searching her face, and we knew he was going to try a name. "…Adrina."

Off by one. Drina was a year older than Mina.

"I'm not Adrina," Mina said, and would have said it even if he'd guessed right. We always lied about our identity. "I spilled tea on my hand."

Out of the corner of my eye I could see Talya twisting one finger in a strand of hair, a sign of nervousness I desperately hoped Father wouldn't notice.

He crossed the room, footsteps heavy on our carpet, and extended his hand towards Mina, palm up. She lifted her burned hand and let him examine it, the red blisters showing at the edge of Sasia's bandage.

Sasia had already checked it this morning and been satisfied by the results; none of my worries about withering or other curses had materialized.

"Tea, you said?"

"Very hot tea."

"Really." He stared at Mina's face for a long, long moment more, his own expression intent and otherwise unreadable. Then he dropped her hand, turned, and walked to the door. "I'll see you all at breakfast." He didn't turn back around.

You could hear the exhales when the door closed behind him. Mina sank onto the nearest bed, mine. I looked down and realized that my knuckles were white, gripping the spine of my book. I unclenched them with an effort.

"He knows," Rayna said, voice flat, without doubts or hopes.

"He doesn't know," Vira countered. "He suspects."

"This is hardly evidence," Mina said, waving her burned hand. "I really could have spilled tea."

"But he does suspect." I stretched my cramped fingers, and told myself that if they were shaking, it was because of tight muscles and nothing else. "You could see he suspects. He wants us to get through that Gate so badly, he'll leap at anything that suggests we might have done it. He'll chase down anything out of the ordinary."

"And that's happened many times before," Vira said, taking on her most placating tone. "There's no reason to panic."

"Sure, he's suspected before," Rayna said. "*Before*, he was always wrong!"

In all the discussion that followed, between Father leaving and us going for breakfast, the one suggestion that didn't come up from anyone was that we shouldn't go back. Not even Talya said it, though I can't swear she didn't think it. We all wanted that promise of an escape too badly. None of the dangers, the forest, the lake, or Father's suspicion, were enough to make us give up that idea. If Father suspected something, that only made it more imperative that we find a way to leave, now.

And there may have been something more at work too. If you believe in Fate—if you believe we were meant to go down to that lake shore—then perhaps there was something drawing us there, even if we didn't know it yet.

That entire day was merely a prelude to the night. All any of us cared about was getting back down below the castle, and we didn't dare try it until nightfall, when the castle would be quiet and no one would question all of us being in our bedroom. The day crawled interminably. Father didn't say much at breakfast, but he *looked* at us. We retired from the banquet hall as soon as we dared, then had nothing better to fill the day with than sewing. We couldn't risk changing our routine. I did a little better than the others, because at least I got to read aloud while they sewed. No one got any decent work done and large stretches of time went to picking out crooked stitches.

I won't make you sit through the day, as I had to. I'll jump ahead to the evening.

After our door was locked and we were meant to be going to bed, we set about to go below instead. We tried to make better plans this time—like dressing more appropriately for the cold down there.

There was another, less practical motivation for changing clothes. For once, just for once, we didn't have to match. Try matching eleven sisters every day for your entire life. Anything can wait five minutes if it means you finally get to look different. I pulled my blond locks out of the twist we'd chosen as a style that morning, and wore a dark blue dress with gold bands on the sleeves. I loved the dress, and half my sisters hated it (meaning we rarely wore it). I was one of the first ones ready, and then had to wait around tapping my foot while the rest finished. Nila, who lives for clothes and hair, was the last.

Finally we got on our way, down the long stair and through the short tunnel. When we reached the Gate, we lined up and each grasped a rail. I held my breath as we pushed, only letting it out when the Gate swung open again as easily as it had the night before.

The sight of the magical forest was not the shock it had been the first night. It was still beautiful and mysterious. Still entrancing. Still poisonous. It still made me think about buying books and castles.

The shore was different. Or if not the shore itself, what we found there.

The night before, the shore had been empty—nearly. I know now that I really had seen a silhouette the first night, and on the second night, the silhouette turned solid and brought friends.

On the second night, there were twelve small boats pulled up in a neat row along the shore—twelve delicate-looking boats of pale polished wood, with arching bows and sterns, and a lantern hanging from the prow of each.

Standing in front of the boats, there were twelve young men.

They were beautiful. There's no point in being evasive on the subject; they really were, all tall with dark eyes, thick brown hair and strong features. I hadn't had many opportunities to meet men, but I knew enough to know what handsome looked like when I saw it. We were definitely seeing it.

My stomach turned over, my palms went sweaty and I told myself not to lose my head, because after all, I had read plenty of stories where handsome strangers turned out to be dangerous in the extreme. Though I had also read others that took the meeting of a handsome stranger and went in quite a different direction. A far more promising direction.

Once I got past looking at their faces, I managed to notice clothes too. They weren't dressed alike, though they were all in a similar style of dress shirts and jackets. I could recognize a well-cut jacket made of expensive cloth, even if I didn't know half of what Nila knew about clothing.

We all stared at each other for a moment or two, and probably we were all trying to work out the etiquette of what to say when you bump into a crowd of strangers while on what is clearly an enchanted beach. One of the men spoke first, starting with a perfectly ordinary "Good evening," and following it up with the more intriguing, "I think we've been waiting for you."

I leaped to a guess, looked at Mina and could see she had too. "Were you waiting in a castle, by any chance?" she asked.

The man who had spoken looked surprised. So did the others, but I was mostly looking at him just then. "Yes, actually."

My stomach had been fluttering with excitement for several minutes by now, and it was only increasing. "And would you happen to be princes?" I asked.

"Does it show?" another man said with a grin.

I flashed a grin back. "Lucky guess." Although in a way, it did show—in their clothes and their bearing. They weren't wearing circlets, but those were elegant clothes and they were wearing them very comfortably. "It's this rhyme we know."

More surprise from the princes. "You know the Rhyme?" the first man said.

"We know *a* rhyme," Mina said. "Do you?"

"I know lots of rhymes," the second one volunteered. "I know one important one."

So the long and the short is that we compared important rhymes. You remember ours?

Twelve princes will in a castle wait,
Until twelve princesses come through the magic gate.
They'll walk where the metal forest stands,
And cross the lake to distant lands.
They'll dance until they wear their shoes away,
And free the princes in a year and a day.

Theirs was the same. A few words varied slightly, like 'must' instead of 'will' in the first line, but it was plainly the same poem or spell or litany.

I think we all felt rather companionable after that. There's nothing like finding out that someone you've just met shares the same nursery rhyme—or something that's been passing for that. It makes you feel as though they must be all right. Finding out they may actually be figures in the Rhyme was hugely exciting. I'd always wanted to get into one of the stories I read.

We had barely begun on the subject of what it all meant (the first three lines we could pretty well see now, while the second three— tantalizing!) when Vira just had to go all proper and insist on introductions. Which I suppose was practical too, or would have been, if any of us had actually learned anything. No one ever learned our names on a single introduction, and for the first time we found ourselves meeting people in the same situation.

I learned all their names later, so I'll give them to you now, though at the time I could have hazarded a few at best. In order from eldest, the princes were Daemyn, Danton, Dacien, Dathan, Daylin, Dagan, Dastan, Darshan, Darnell, Darius, Dallon and Damek. You see why we didn't learn any names. They were twelve brothers and they looked it, which did not make matters easier. Their ages ranged from seventeen to twenty-six, with one set of triplets. They were all similar in height and build, and, of course, they were all handsome.

On the other hand, we were used to looking at the details in a face—the tilt of a nose, the setting of eyes, a dimple or a cleft chin, the thickness of eyebrows or the slope of a jaw. It was how we told each other apart, and it didn't take long before we could tell them apart too.

That came later. That first evening, we had a swarm of names and faces and even more questions.

Mina had been trying to work out different theories on the Rhyme (and the Gate and the forest) for years, so she led the conversation back that direction as quickly as possible. "The first three lines seem clear now—princes, princesses, the Gate and the metal forest. But the second half…"

"We have boats," Daemyn said. He had been the first one to speak earlier, and I might have guessed he was the oldest. He seemed to be the leader, and he had the same serious, responsible look that Vira often had. "Making crossing the lake possible."

I could think of worse ways to escape my father's castle than to sail off in a boat with a handsome prince. In fact, I would be lying if I said that I hadn't had various daydreams, building off of the Rhyme, that had looked a good deal like that.

"So much for line four," Mina said, "although exactly where we would be crossing to still seems like a relevant question. More importantly, what about line six? Is there something you need to be freed from?"

It would have been lovely if they said that all they needed freeing from was loneliness, and we all went away that night together and lived happily ever after. Of course it wasn't that simple. I hadn't expected it to be. The princes shuffled and exchanged looks and tugged on hair and finally Daemyn said, "I suppose we'd better tell you. You may want to sit down; it's a long story."

Chapter Four

"Oh good, I love stories," I said, gathering my skirt around me and plopping down on the sand. I was frankly delighted by the princes' promise of a long story. It had been ages since I'd heard a new one—one that I didn't make up myself. A true story was even better.

My sisters and the princes all found places in a loose circle, with women on one side, men on the other, and the princes told us their tale. It came out in fragments and pieces with frequent interruptions, so I won't try to tell it the way they did. Here, instead, are the essential points.

Once upon a time of uncertain distance in the past, there was an island kingdom called Marileigh. It was by all opinions a beautiful and happy place, which was probably true—although I imagine bias and nostalgia came into play too. It was a small and wealthy kingdom, whose chief export was cloth, especially cloth colored with a vivid dye made from certain fish in the surrounding waters.

The island was ruled by a wise king who had twelve sons. All was well until a fisherman caught a talking fish. He brought this marvel to his king, who had heard of such things in stories. The fish spoke to the king, and told him that if he was not returned to the sea, disaster would befall the kingdom. Not being a fool, and acquainted with such happenings from those stories, the king ordered the fish returned to the sea at once. And so it was done.

Unfortunately, the king was working from the wrong story. I can entirely see how this could happen; stories are woefully inconsistent at times. Unlike many talking fish, this one was not serene and benevolent and prone to granting wishes. This one was a wicked magician, who had been seeking to conquer the underwater territory of a powerful Enchantress. She had repelled him once, and transformed him into a fish. Returning him to the sea restored his powers (the princes didn't know why and neither do I, but magic is funny that way) and he attempted a second attack on the Enchantress. She defeated him again, with considerable damage to her followers and territory.

Enchantresses are not known for their forgiving natures—or for their rationality. The more magic a person has, the higher the probability seems to be that they'll be unstable. Or maybe it's just that unstable magical people can create very large splashes. This Enchantress destroyed the magician, and then sought out the ones who had enabled him to attack her again. She came to the King of Marileigh, arriving in the midst of a storm of unprecedented fury. She appeared in the throne room, ignored all explanations and apologies, and cast a curse over the kingdom.

The island was shrouded in mist. Boats would never find it. Any who sought to leave would be swallowed up in the fog, never to emerge. The people became ghosts by day, insubstantial as the mist, and only at night were they solid.

The King of Marileigh begged for mercy for his country. If the Enchantress wouldn't lift the spell herself, at least provide an opportunity for the spell to be broken. She agreed, at a price. She took the king's life, and in exchange gave his sons a chance to save themselves and their people. She told them the Rhyme, and one direction—to venture forth when the mist cleared.

The mist stood as a dark wall, sitting perhaps two hundred yards out from shore. Only a few hours after the Enchantress vanished, the fog shifted and an opening formed, appearing like a tunnel's mouth. The princes set out in their boats, and passed through the tunnel of fog. In the darkness, they couldn't tell when the fog walls turned to rock ones, eventually pulling up on a new shore.

The shore was lit by rows of glittering trees—the diamond forest. They explored the forest, until they came to the Gate. It didn't open for them. The forest, however, treated them just as it had treated us, invading their thoughts. Like us, they left the forest and had control of their minds again.

Their stay on the shore was brief. They found no princesses, or anyone else, and if the Rhyme was correct, the place to wait was the castle, not the shore. They returned to Marileigh, and the mist closed again behind them.

A new aspect of the spell came into effect that first night after they returned. A deep sleep fell over all the inhabitants of the island. And so time passed.

At intervals—and there was no way to judge how much time had gone by—the princes would awaken, to see the opening forming in the fog. Then they would go to the magical shore. Sometimes they explored. Sometimes they were more cautious, and only looked without coming ashore. Sometimes they saw at a distance a woman alone, or a woman with a child, but even though they saw different people on different nights, they never saw twelve girls together, and they never spoke with anyone.

They had come the night before we met them. We were already leaving by the time they reached the shore. They caught a glimpse of us—and I do think I caught a glimpse of at least one of them. We disappeared into the forest, but Daemyn reasoned, rather like Vira, that if it was all meant to be, it would be. They returned to their castle, and when they slept, they all agreed that it felt like a normal sleep, not the magical sleep they had been experiencing. They weren't surprised to see the fog open again that evening, or to see us when we came out of the forest.

That accounts for the past, and brings us up to the present in the story of my sisters and me.

Once the story had ended and we had made the appropriate sympathetic comments, we all turned to the question of the future.

"I think you've answered Mina's question about line six of the poem," Vira said, "but four and five are still obscure, about crossing the lake and dancing."

Daemyn ran a hand through his hair. "The rest have turned out to be literal. Our best guess is that those are too. We can take you across the lake; we have a castle, musicians; we can arrange for a dance. Many dances."

Mina's brow wrinkled in thought. "It's so obvious when you look at it that way. We go to the castle with all of you, dance each night for a year and a day, and at the end the spell on your country is broken. Simple."

"I think it's a very strange way to break a spell," Rayna remarked, flipping a long lock of hair back over her shoulder. "It doesn't have anything at all to do with the original enchantress. Why should she care if we dance?"

"That's the way enchantments work." I was leaning back on my hands, tapping my feet as I mentally reviewed tales of curses and spells. All of this was so *very* like a story! "I've read reams of stories where the enchantment breaks in some way that seems random. Like the girl who sewed shirts to free her enchanted brothers, that's a good one. Dancing is no odder than that. And probably easier. At least we don't have to chop anyone's head off, or kill a dragon. Those are standards too."

"Dancing's safer than killing a dragon," Rayna said, "but that's still a *lot* of dancing."

"And we'd have to come down here every night," Vira said, getting right to the heart of the matter, as usual.

"The forest *is* rather awful," Daemyn acknowledged.

Vira gave a slight shake of her head. "It's not that. It is awful, but that's not the issue. It's our father. If we're coming down here often, he'll…cause problems."

"He's insane," Rayna supplied.

"Rayna!" Vira hissed in exasperated disapproval.

"What? It's true," Rayna said, with an unrepentant tilt to her head. "They told us their story. Ours is that our father saw that forest once and became completely obsessed with getting to it again, so he can use the wealth to conquer the world. If he finds out we can get to it, he'll try anything to make us let him in."

Vira squared her shoulders, and when she spoke her tone was plainly trying to put this back on a diplomatic footing. "We're going to have to think about all of this very carefully, before we can commit to anything."

"Yes, of course," Daemyn said with a nod. "We aren't trying to force you into anything."

"It's just that our entire country will probably die if you don't get involved here," another prince remarked.

"Damek!" Daemyn hissed, exasperation an almost perfect match for Vira's.

I managed to swallow a grin. It was going to be fun, knowing other people with siblings. If we got to know them.

"It's true," Damek said, no more repentant than Rayna. "You want to be all polite and that's fine, but they can't just ignore the fact that if this doesn't work—"

"We are aware of the stakes, thank you," Vira said at her coldest. "We will keep your country's situation in mind. And we would appreciate it if *you* keep in mind that every time we open that Gate we risk letting cursed wealth fall into the hands of a madman intent on waging war, putting our country at risk too." She swept up to her feet. "I believe that is all we need discuss tonight. It's late, and we should return."

It was not the most auspicious note to end on. But there were twenty-four of us; we weren't all going to stay silent as we left, and there were enough pleasant farewells and good wishes that the atmosphere didn't seem nearly so fraught by the time we were entering the forest.

The forest that night steered my thoughts towards jewelry and dresses and perfume, and all the other things money can buy that would, in theory, attract a handsome prince. I had to admit with a grudging admiration that the forest was quick to pick up on changing circumstances. It wasn't that I had any particular interest in any particular prince—yet. I didn't know any of them. I had merely been presented with twelve handsome and presumably eligible young men. I suppose the forest only drew the obvious conclusion.

We didn't come to any conclusions ourselves that night. We talked until dawn, with nothing significant decided. It's not easy to reach a twelve-person consensus.

Father stared even harder the next morning. We still weren't giving him any proof—but there was an excitement in the air that our best efforts couldn't suppress.

I didn't have to waste time on sewing that day. That was one minor decision that we made during the night. Mina and I were off to the library to see what we might find out about an enchantress, twelve princes, and an island that had gone missing. Talya came along, because she was bored with sewing and because three princesses can blend together more easily than two, if the need should arise.

The library was my favorite place. It had limited competition, since I had never been outside of our castle. I think it would have been my favorite place anyway. It seemed in a way a wondrous thing. Every room in the castle had some purpose—rooms for sleeping, for eating, for sewing, for dancing. They were practical and tangible. I loved that there was a room simply to store information, ideas, thoughts…and stories. A room for thinking and for dreaming.

For all that it held, the library wasn't a large space, occupying the top floor of one of our towers. The tower was round and the room was an octagon, with shelves on all eight sides. The shelves were broken by four windows, one at each point of the compass. I liked looking out at the fields around our castle, at a world so much bigger than the one I lived in; on clear days, I could even see a smudge of the Fallaron Mountains in the south. A wide wooden table and four straight-backed chairs filled the center of the room. The library was so full of books that it smelled like them—and I swear I could still catch a hint of the hot cocoa I had spilled up there once when I was nine years old.

I knew all the story books intimately, and some of the history books that were written in enough detail to be stories in their own way. Mina knew the history books far better than I did, and had ranged across the others too, looking for facts and philosophies to explain the world. Today, we each went at once to our own particular sections to look for any kind of answers.

Talya perched on the edge of the table, idly swinging her heels, and watched us search. "Do you think you'll find anything?"

"Mina has a better chance than I do." I dropped three books on the table and went back to the shelves for more. "I doubt the princes' story is in any of my books. I'd remember it if it was. There are some similar stories I want to look at."

"I wish I recognized the name of their country," Mina said, already sitting at the table and paging through her first book. It was an enormous dusty tome; I tried to read it once and got only three pages in before giving up. The writing was as dusty as the book. "I don't understand why I *don't*. An island country, they must have been trading with other countries…we ought to know about them."

I opened a book and scanned down the table of contents. "Mina, even you can't know everything."

"I can try."

"Here's that story I was thinking of last night," I said, turning to the relevant page. "The girl who had to sew shirts to free her brothers, after they were turned into swans. I think I'd rather dance. Especially since she had to be silent for years too."

Talya shook her head. "Wouldn't ever work for us. Can you imagine Rayna being silent for years?"

"I can't imagine *you* being silent for years," I said, poking her shoulder with the edge of my book.

"You either," she countered. "You couldn't tell a story. It'd kill you."

"Probably," I agreed, putting the book down on the stack next to Talya and turning to find another. "Completing tasks is a fairly standard way of breaking spells. There must be dozens of stories with that premise. Girls have to sift seeds, or go in search of a magical object...although the quests are more often for the men."

"I'd like to go on a quest," Talya said, clasping her hands around her knees.

I pulled two more books off the shelves and raised my eyebrows at my sister. "No, you wouldn't."

"I'd like to go somewhere."

"All right, but not on a quest. Quests always involve monsters. And you'd probably have to be in the dark at some point."

Talya sighed with the incomparable drama of a fifteen-year-old. "It's not *my* fault I'm afraid of the dark. It's *your* fault, for telling me all those ghost stories."

I grinned, dropped the books on the table and reached out with one hand, fingers waggling. "Like the story about the little lost child who creeps up behind you in the dark night and—"

Talya snatched up the nearest book and rapped my wrist. "Yes, that one, ugh! Anyway, compared to all the things people have to do in your stories, I'd much rather dance with handsome princes. It sounds wonderful."

"It won't be." I shook out my arm and returned to scanning titles.

"Why shouldn't it be?" Talya demanded. "Didn't you think they were handsome?"

"Of course. Although you're too young to be thinking about that."

"Am not. Lots of the girls in your stories are sixteen when they get married."

"You're only fifteen," I pointed out.

"I'll be sixteen by the time we've finished dancing for a year and a day!"

She was right, of course. Except that imagining a sixteen year old girl in a story getting married was entirely different than imagining my baby sister getting married. Never mind that I was only two years older. It was a long two years. For now, I settled for saying, "We'll see. As to it being wonderful—well, it might be sometimes. But breaking spells is always hard. If it wasn't hard, it wouldn't work."

"I think I have something," Mina said suddenly.

I set three more selections on top of my growing pile of books. "That was fast."

"I was actually concentrating, instead of chattering about ghost stories. Here, look at this," she said, pointing to a paragraph. "I thought I remembered something in here about an island with cloth of an unusual color. The historian says the king had his royal robes made there."

I wrinkled my nose. "All right, it could be them. There could be dozens of islands that weave cloth, though. Sheep and islands kind of go together."

"Yes, only then see farther down here?" Mina's finger skimmed down the page. "The author's lamenting that the island can no longer be found. I remember now, I always thought he meant it metaphorically, that they had lost a treaty or something. Maybe it's literal after all." She made a frustrated noise. "He doesn't say enough. Not even the island's name."

Mina kept hunting for passages about disappearing islands. She dumped a pile of geographies on Talya and told her to compare maps. I kept looking for stories about overcoming curses.

Mina's first success was not so easily duplicated, but by late afternoon we were armed with a few more details. Mina found a handful of references to a disappearing island, usually unnamed, and with three different names on the occasions when a name did come up; one of them could have been a corruption of Marileigh. Our best guess was that it was an island in the Dyjon Sea. Talya found an old map that showed it, and more recent ones that didn't, though that might have only been proof of careless cartographers.

"It's on the other side of the continent," Talya said, staring at the map. "I mean, hundreds of miles away. And they row here?"

"It's magic," I said with a shrug. "We knew they couldn't really be rowing distance away. We're a landlocked country."

"I know, but…" Talya shook her head. "It's just funny to think about, you know?"

"The Rhyme does reference distant lands," Mina said. "And you said you wanted to go somewhere."

Our best proof, possibly, was that Mina found one reference to Marileigh by name, in a very old tome with barely-intact binding. It mentioned only that the king had a dozen sons.

"That's got to be them, right?" I said. "How many sets of a dozen sons can there be in one family tree?" They had to be at least as rare as, say, a dozen daughters.

Mina frowned down at the book. "Yes…so either this is proof that it's all real, or that the whole thing is a hoax."

I blinked. "Those are opposites. If it can prove either one, it means it doesn't prove anything. And anyway, why? All it seems to prove to me is that there really were twelve princes in Marileigh."

"Right," she agreed. "There *were*. Lyra, this book is almost two hundred years old. If they're written down in here…"

The miles hadn't bothered me. The years felt more disconcerting. "Oh. Well."

"So they're two hundred years old? That's *strange*," Talya said, shivered, and turned thoughtful. "They don't look it."

"Either they've really been asleep for two hundred years," Mina said, "proving it's true, or someone's been reading up on history and made the whole business up."

"You have a suspicious mind," I said.

She didn't deny it. "It goes with having an inquiring one."

"They're not *really* two hundred years old." It had taken a moment, but I had seized on a relevant story and had a better grasp on the idea. "I mean, if it's real, they sort of are, only not really. It's like the story about the sleeping princess. She was asleep for a hundred years, and she was still sixteen when she woke up."

"If we had thought about it, I suppose it's obvious they'd have to have been under the curse for a long time," Mina said, idly toying with the corner of a page. "If this is what it's all about—the Gate, the forest, everything—we already knew that all of that has been around for generations. Mother learned about it from her mother, who got it from hers, and so on."

I don't think we really thought it was a hoax, not even Mina. After all, they knew the Rhyme.

As to my research of the afternoon, the main detail I learned from all that reading up on curses was that everyone had to suffer to overcome them. Like I had said—it was never easy.

Chapter Five

We got our first idea of how not-easy it was going to be that same evening. Father came to our room to lock the door, as he did every night. Instead of simply locking it and going away, he came inside.

We all halted what we were doing. I looked around at my sisters, and wondered if it was as obvious to him as it was to me that we were all desperately impatient for him to leave. Toes were tapping, knuckles were white around hair brushes, eyes were shifting.

He closed the door behind him and stood in front of it, arms crossed. When the room was completely silent, he spoke. "You've been through the gate."

Talya dropped her comb.

Vira didn't rise from her seat at her dressing table. She coolly said, "You know the Gate doesn't open for us, Father. We've been over this again and again."

I didn't dare look at Mina, sitting next to me on her bed. I was afraid Father would see the look and make something of it. I wanted him to believe Vira. I desperately wanted him to believe Vira and stop asking questions and go away.

Of course he didn't. "But something is different." He stared hard at Vira. "You were in the forest last night."

"We were in bed last night," Vira said, "like every night."

"No. You weren't. I checked. I had a feeling, so I checked and there was no one here. The door was locked; you didn't go out that way. I went down the stairs below the trapdoor. No one there. You were on the other side of the gate." He smiled. I hated his smiles. "Really, Avira, did you think twelve girls could hide that they were excited about something? I thought you were smarter than that."

I'm convinced Vira always was the bravest of us. She never wavered, and she didn't then. "Very well. The Gate did open for us," she said, back perfectly straight. "That changes nothing. We won't open it for you."

His façade of calm evaporated. "Yes, you will! One of you will." He whirled, turning towards Rayna. "Will you?"

She shook her head. "No."

He turned again, towards Dalia. "What about you? Think what we can do with those riches!"

"No," she whispered.

Another turn, another demand, another refusal, again and again. Then he pounced on what I'm sure he thought was our weakest point. "And what about you? Little Atalya, will you let your father past the gate?"

I could see her lower lip trembling as she said, "No."

Father gripped Talya by the arm and leaned in. "Are you sure?"

"Let her go." I was only two beds away and I crossed the distance in a few steps. I put my arm around my sister and glared at my father. "She won't help you. None of us will."

He backed away. He didn't back down. "Are you all completely mad? Am I really the only one with any vision? There's a wealth below us such as the world has never seen. No one but me has any idea how to use it. Think of what you can do with that gold and those diamonds. You girls must want something. Dresses, horses, fine jewelry." His eyes were shining with an unholy gleam. "And we'll have power. I'll take that money and I'll use it, use it to build and to expand and to conquer. We'll be the richest, most powerful country in the world." A crafty edge came into his smile. "You'll be able to marry any man you want. You can simply command and they'll come running. Doesn't that appeal to you?"

He paced the room as he spoke, and he halted in front of Vira. She rose to her feet, chin high. "We're not opening the Gate for you. We never will."

He raised his hand, and I was sure he was going to hit her. Usually he was too restrained, too aware of how hard it would be to explain bruises to the council and the court. He reined himself in this time too, and instead pointed towards the door. "Then all of you can leave this room. You don't open the gate for me…you don't open it at all."

We spent that night locked in one of the tower guest rooms. There were eight beds, arranged in a circle in the round room, all the feet pointing towards the center. Most of us had to double up, and none of us slept much anyway.

As soon as Father was gone the clamor arose, echoing off the stone walls and only somewhat softened by the rugs on the floor. Most of the comments were along the lines of how awful this was, and were not helpful. My chief contribution was to observe that people in stories were locked up all the time, which I admit was not especially helpful either. I also noted that they always got out somehow. I didn't have an idea in that direction. The door was locked and the windows were too narrow to climb out, besides being a terrifying distance from the ground anyway.

When we finally calmed down enough to bring the conversation to a more coherent plane, Vira insisted that this wasn't entirely bad. Plenty of dissent rose from the rest of us gathered on the beds, which she talked right over. "We have an advantage right now because Father doesn't really have any idea what happened down below. He thinks he's hurting us by keeping us here."

"He *is*," Rayna said. "All those princes are going to think we decided not to come back." She kicked the footboard of the bed she was sprawling on.

"Maybe not, Rayna," Vira countered. "You told them our father was insane. They may guess more than you think. Whatever they do, *we* have to convince Father that we don't care if he stops us from going through the Gate. He's only keeping us here because he thinks it will make us let him into the forest. If he believes it isn't effective, he'll have no reason to keep doing it."

Mina nodded, sitting cross-legged at the end of one bed. "And he'll have every reason to let us go through the Gate. As long as we're opening it, he'll hope that he might find a way to duplicate what we're doing, or trick us into letting him through at the same time, or letting someone else through, or...all kinds of things. If the Gate isn't opened at all, he can't possibly get through it himself."

"Exactly," Vira agreed. "What we have right now is a stalemate. We just have to outwait him."

I leaned my elbows on the footboard in front of me and rested my chin in my hands. "In a way it's good that it happened now. We haven't started trying to break the spell. When we start, he really will be able to ruin everything by keeping us here." I could think of all sorts of parallels in stories. You can't stop an undertaking like this halfway through. If the Rhyme said we needed to dance for a year and a day, it meant every night. I thought all that through before I realized what I'd said: when we start. "I mean, *if* we start." I looked around. No one had objected to my original phrasing. "We're going to do it—aren't we?"

"I think we have to," Mina said slowly. "The Rhyme, the history...I think it's all been leading to this. And what else can we do? Tell the princes to go back to their island and stay prisoners forever, with their entire population?" She was looking down at her hands, and I suspected she was itching for a book to hold. "And we stay prisoners here."

Laina, the only one to perch sitting on top of a footboard, shook her head. "Vira is right, though, going through the Gate every night is risky. And you were right too, Mina—if we keep opening it, Father will have far more options for trying to get through."

Vira reached out and put her hand over Laina's. "Mina is also right that we have to do it. Whether it's meant to be or not, it's clearly our best chance. We've been in a much bigger stalemate with Father for fourteen years. We've grown up, we've never been out of this castle, and we've had no prospect of any future that's different. We also have no guarantee that Father won't try something disastrous for us or the country at any time. We can't go on this way forever."

I looked around the room, and while it wasn't unanimous yet, I was seeing more nods than doubtful expressions. My throat felt tight. I could feel that this was *it*. This was the moment.

"Helping the princes is our chance to change something." My fingers tapped with excitement. "Even if it doesn't look like it's supposed to change something for us, it's still a chance. People who set out to break a curse always end up with their lives changing." And I was so ready for my life to change.

"I'm not sure your stories are any real evidence," Vira said, "but yes. That does seem to be the case."

It's a funny thing. Despite all of the perfectly good reasons and rationalities we gave for choosing to undertake the task, I don't know if we would have been as certain that we wanted to go below and help the princes if Father hadn't tried to prevent us. There's nothing like running the risk of losing something to make you see how much you want it.

Chapter Six

We were not allowed to return to our bedroom in the morning. Serving women arrived at the tower with our clothes. They were all quiet women with downcast eyes, afraid of our father and in awe of us. We had always held aloof from the others in the castle. We didn't dare trust anyone.

We were allowed to go about our normal pursuits during the day, not that any of us cared about them very much just then. Keeping us locked in the tower all the time would have created too much of a stir. As it was, there was tension in the castle. I wasn't present when Father explained the situation to his council. I know he didn't tell them the truth. We managed to gather from whispers and overheard remarks that he had made up some kind of excuse about our well-being, about some problem in our room, all vague and unclear. Not everyone believed it, and the atmosphere was uneasy.

Of course we weren't allowed outside the castle during this time. That was nothing new. I was seventeen and I'd never been outside of our castle, apart from the magic forest. Sometimes it terrified me to think about all that we were missing in life. All the people we weren't meeting, the places we weren't seeing, the experiences we weren't having, that I only knew I was missing because I read about them happening to other people. It terrified me even more to think that this might go on and on forever and we would never have the chance to make our own decisions, to chart our own courses, to just finally be ourselves and shape the lives we wanted to live.

I was thinking that way a little too much, during those days we were locked out of our bedroom. For the first time, we actually had a possibility for escape—and being blocked from that possibility just made me feel even more trapped.

We went on in our stalemate for two weeks, and I don't know if the uneasiness in the castle would have developed into something more, or died away instead. We never found out, because after two weeks Marjoram burst onto the scene.

My sisters and I were in a west-facing sitting room with afternoon light pouring onto our circle of chairs. We were supposed to be sewing, though less than half of us were at all interested. I stabbed with no enthusiasm at a handkerchief I was embroidering, while I mentally plotted out a new story and wondered if there would be raspberry tarts with supper.

As usual for Marjoram, she appeared with no warning at all. One second the room was quiet—the next there was a clucking woman in the middle of our circle, hovering a foot off the ground and shedding pink sparkles everywhere. "Oh, my dear, dear girls," she trilled, "I have been hearing the most *extraordinary* stories!"

Marjoram was our fairy godmother. She had been in the family for generations, and she took the job very seriously.

We all got to our feet and made our most proper curtsies and our most proper "hello, how nice to see you" speeches, because there was just no use getting excited when Marj popped in, however sudden and invasive she might be. She was like a force of nature, and complaining about rain won't make it any less wet. Talya still jumped whenever she appeared. The rest of us were used to Marj's sudden arrivals at irregular intervals.

As far as we knew, Marj couldn't tell us apart. She never remarked upon the fact, but she also never called any of us by name.

We got Marj another chair and she plopped into it with a renewed shower of pink and gold sparkles. "Now then, my dears, I've just spoken to your father, and I want to discuss with you this little quibble going on between you and him."

I kicked Mina's foot next to me, because Marj would see it if I rolled my eyes. Mina kicked me back and we shared a mental eye roll over Marj's description of the situation as a "quibble."

Marj took her job very seriously—but if you considered her job to be helping her goddaughters, she was very bad at it. That's how we saw it, anyway. I'm sure she wouldn't agree.

Vira spoke up to address the topic at hand. "Father found out that we've been able to open the Gate recently, and is…displeased that we won't open it for him."

Marj nodded, blond curls bouncing. "Yes, he mentioned the gate. And I entirely agree, you mustn't let him through it. That's simply not How Things Are Done, and I told him so. Though really it's quite sweet of him to want to spare you the ordeal of confronting a magical trial."

"That's not it at all!" Talya cried out, and I regretted that she was too far away in the circle for me to kick her. It would have been a different kind of kick, this one meaning, don't bother, there's no point.

We had never been able to convince Marj that our father was an obsessive madman. She helped him marry Mother all those years ago, which in her book cast him forever in the role of Brave Adventurer, despite all evidence to the contrary.

"Now, now, my dear, I think I understand quite clearly what's going on here," Marj said with a sweet smile. "Perhaps your father is a bit misguided in his concern, but I'm sure I can get him sorted out. I'm here because I wanted to be sure *you* understand how very important it is that you keep going through the gate."

There was a moment of dead silence, as we all tried to work out what that meant. It seemed wildly improbable that Marj could actually agree with us about something.

"We understand it's important," Mina said carefully, "though perhaps you could tell us a bit more about why…?"

Marj beamed at her, sparkles going a brighter hue. "It's very simple, my dear. This is obviously your *chance*! Every girl who wants to have a really proper happy ending must undergo trials first. It may be a bit scary at times, but don't you worry. You just have to have faith that a handsome young man will come along and rescue you in the end."

"We don't need rescuing actually," I said, because I was so irritated by all that nonsense that it overwhelmed my better judgment. "We have this other idea." I wasn't going to tell her the whole business. I wasn't so irritated as to be that foolhardy. I was probably going to just say that there was this spell we could break and so we didn't need rescuing, thank you very much.

Marj broke in before I could, with, "Of course you need rescuing, dear. This is How Things Are Done." And when you talk to Marj, you simply don't argue with How Things Are Done. She cast her gaze around the circle. "So you all understand it's simply imperative you go on traipsing through your gate? You'll all go ahead with it, once we clear up this little snafu with your father?"

What else could we do besides nod and say we understood? We'd given up seriously trying to convince Marj of anything years earlier.

She gave us a few more utterly unhelpful pieces of advice, made a few air kisses, waggled her fingers and vanished in a burst of pink hearts.

"I swear someday I'm going to hit that woman," Laina growled.

"She'll probably just stare at you blankly and explain that isn't how princesses do things," I said, using my half-embroidered handkerchief to brush stray hearts and sparkles off my lap. The servants always had extra sweeping up to do after Marj came to visit.

"Really this is a good development," Mina said. "Marj may actually stumble into helping us for once, if she convinces Father to let us back into our bedroom."

I raised an eyebrow. "So that we can undergo magical trials and be rescued? That's good?"

"It is," Mina said with a nod. "The goal is to go through the Gate. Even if Marj has different reasons in mind, it doesn't matter as long as she brings about the same result."

Because Father never explained any decisions to us, I have to imagine it was a combination of factors in the end. Marj leaned on him. The castle was tense. And, I like to believe, we wore him down by failing to show any distress or capitulate to his demand. Maybe we would have out-waited him in the end even without other factors, though probably the other factors hastened the situation along.

Whatever the precise details, Marj appeared to us in the afternoon and Father let us back into our bedroom that night. Naturally we went below as soon as we could.

The Gate opened, the princes were waiting, and we explained where we had been for the last two weeks. As Vira had predicted, they had surmised as much.

If the entire situation *wasn't* fated and meant to be, it still unfolded as though it was. We agreed that we would work together to try to break the curse; they agreed to arrange conditions suitable for dancing. That attended to the chief business of the evening, but none of us were in a hurry to leave. Would you be, if you were on an enchanted shore with twelve princes you had the prospect of getting to know much better in the future?

I met several princes more formally that evening, but I may as well admit right here that there was only one that really mattered. It was the same prince who, the first night, had mentioned knowing a lot of rhymes. I'm a storyteller; that's the sort of detail that gets my attention. It required paying attention to details to be sure he was the same one, considering how much they all resembled each other. He was the only one with a lock of hair falling over his forehead that just brushed his right eyebrow.

He was the third prince I spoke to that night, and by then I was used to admitting that I didn't have the faintest idea regarding his name.

He inclined his head slightly and said, "Dastan. Seventh in line. And you're the princess who likes stories, but I didn't get your name committed to memory either."

I was more surprised by what he did remember. "How did you know that? That I'm the one who mentioned stories?" It felt very odd, to have someone other than my sisters know about me and stories.

"I remembered your face," he said, just as though he didn't find me nearly identical to eleven other girls. "And the name to go with the face...?"

"Oh—it's Alyra. Or just Lyra, really."

He bowed slightly. "That is a lovely name. Musical, even. Lyrical."

For just a moment I didn't know how to take that—it was even odder having a friendly conversation with someone I hadn't known closely for years—but then I spotted the grin lurking in his eyes, and grinned back. "Not a very lyrical girl, though. Dalia's the singer in the family.

"Dastan's lyrical," another prince put in, effortlessly joining the conversation as he slung an arm around his brother's shoulders. I had already been introduced to this one as Damek. "Sometimes tryingly lyrical."

Dastan sighed. "What my brother is not clarifying is that I play music. Which, when you pair it with songs, does involve lyrics."

I told him he should meet Dalia in that case. She was busy talking to someone else and somehow Dastan and I both got off into other conversations and that was that. It didn't seem important at the time, and when we went back up the stairs I was thinking about a different conversation entirely.

That's one difference between a story and life. In life, you can't always spot the important parts while they're happening.

Chapter Seven

We all wanted to start on breaking the curse right away, but the princes needed a few days to get musicians and lights and so on set up for a dance. It's complicated, when everyone in your country becomes insubstantial during daylight. It took three days, during which we went down to the enchanted shore every night, and Father stared hard at us every day but otherwise didn't act. That made me nervous, which was slightly ridiculous since it would have made me even more nervous if he had been doing something. Probably. At least, I couldn't think of anything he might have done that would have made me *less* nervous, although since he did nothing, it left me free to imagine every possibility and worry about them all at once.

Finally the big night came, our first night of officially trying to break the curse. The dresses we each selected to wear seemed crucially important at the time; I'll spare you that detail. At the shore, there was no particular method to who got into which boat. I wound up in Dastan's boat, which was entirely unpremeditated on my part. He claims he planned it. I have doubts.

I didn't give it much thought at the time. On that particular crossing, I was more interested in the surroundings than in who was taking me through them. Dastan handed me into the boat, and then took up the oars. After Mina's experience with the acidic water, I made sure to keep my hands in my lap and my skirts tucked around my ankles. I sat on a bench at the stern, just before the back of the boat rose up in a sweeping curve. Dastan sat near the middle, facing backwards and toward me as he rowed.

All the boats pushed away from the beach, and Dastan rowed us out over the lake—or sea, or whatever it was. I wondered how the boat could handle the burning water. The wood shone; maybe it had a coating that resisted the acid? Or maybe it was magic. Maybe I'd ask Mina later if she had an idea. It felt strange, having to remember to ask, instead of being able to turn to her at once. It gave me a sudden pang of loneliness, one that was undoubtedly amplified by the setting.

As we left the shore behind, we left everything else with it. Picture the blackest night you've ever seen, and then if you can, imagine a world even blacker than that. The lantern at the prow of the boat cast a circle of light around us, but it seemed swallowed by the emptiness beyond it. I was wearing my favorite blue dress again, a fact that I mention only to make the point that what had been a perfectly cheerful color in my bedroom looked gloomy here.

The water I could see in the meager light looked somehow even darker than it had by the shore, ebony, deep, infinite. Beyond the circle of light, there was nothing. Blackness overhead. Blackness in every direction. I'd say there was blackness to every horizon except there were no horizons, unless you count the edge of the light.

I shivered and wished I had brought a cloak, even though I knew the issue wasn't really the cold.

We had been silent since leaving shore, a silence I broke abruptly with, "Is it me or is it very sinister out here?"

"No, it's sinister," Dastan said at once. "Definitely sinister."

It should have been reassuring. At least I wasn't imagining the oppressive quality of the surroundings. Instead of feeling better, I found myself looking at the situation from a new angle. I was the one who kept saying curses were difficult to break. When I said it, I had mostly thought about dangers and challenges from the dancing, or my father, or the forests. I hadn't thought much about getting into a boat with a near-stranger to go across a magical lake. What if the princes' story wasn't true? What if there was something menacing going on after all?

I didn't mean for my thoughts to show on my face, but they must have.

"Hey, don't look at me like that," Dastan protested. "*I'm* not sinister. The surroundings, yes. Not me."

I forced a not-very-convincing laugh. "So you and your brothers, you're not actually demons plotting to kidnap us?"

"Not to my knowledge," he said, fitting a shrug in between the strokes of the oars. "And if my eyes appear to be glowing red, let me know."

"Not so far," I said, and twisted nervously at a silky fold of my skirt. It was easy for him to treat it as a joke. I told myself I was being ridiculous, that there was no reason to be alarmed. Only...were demons any less probable than cursed princes? They seemed friendly, but I was all too aware that I had very little experience judging that sort of thing.

He frowned, looking worried. "You're not serious, are you? About the demons, not about my eyes."

I looked away. "Of course not."

The splashing of the oars stopped, cutting off the only background sound. "Lyra, I promise, we're not demons," he said, voice steady against the engulfing silence. "Or any other kind of horrible monster you're going to pull out of some story. We're not dangerous to you or your sisters. I can't promise that trying to break this curse won't be dangerous, but none of us want to harm you."

"Right. I know." I did know. Really. Sort of. I waved a hand at the void around us. "It's...this, the darkness, there's just something about it, getting into my head. I don't even mind the dark usually; it's Talya who's afraid of the dark." The mention of my sister reminded me of what I ought to be seeing—and wasn't. I sat up straighter in renewed alarm, straining to see anything at all beyond the edge of the lantern's reach. "I can't see the other lights. The other boats, they had lights. We should be able to see them!"

"Logically, yes. Little things like natural laws don't seem to apply out here." His voice was quiet as he added, "It makes it lonely."

I looked at Dastan looking at the blackness and although this wasn't logical either, I felt more comforted than I had been by his vowing that he wasn't a monster. I thought about crossing this lake without anyone else at all, and wondered how many times he'd had to do that.

He looked at me again. "Is the lack of lanterns going to bring you back around to the demon idea again?"

"No." Maybe a little loneliness in the dark didn't tell me much about him. Except it made him human.

The darkness lifted eventually, in a way. It was still night, but it looked like *night* again, instead of the unnatural emptiness we had been traveling through. We had come out of the cavern somehow, because I could see the stars overhead, in positions I recognized. I was glad to see them, gladder to see a lit shore ahead, and gladdest of all to see, spread out on either side of us, lanterns bobbing from other boats.

After quickly counting to make sure all eleven lights were there, I turned my attention to the shore. The castle was perched directly on the water, with a cluster of soaring towers at the center and two wings spreading to either side. At several points, winding paths reached down to the water's edge. It was easy to see the shape of it even in the starlight; every window was lit and lanterns marked out the paths to the water.

The castle was a beacon, ablaze with light and life, a sharp contrast to the emptiness we had passed through. It was *just* like something out of a fairy story and I loved it at once, all the more for coming right after that horrid crossing.

"It hasn't been lit up like that for…two hundred years, I guess," Dastan said, looking over his shoulder towards the castle. We had discussed Mina's history book discoveries with the princes; they all agreed that it didn't feel as if they had been cursed for that long, and also that they couldn't prove they hadn't been. "Haven't had a reason before."

"It's *beautiful*."

"You don't think it resembles the pits of Hell?" he asked, face far too innocent to be genuine.

I put on my primmest expression and tone. "I wouldn't know, never having been there. They do say evil is seductive. Demons are probably very handsome."

He laughed, and within moments we were pulling up to a long wooden dock stretching out over the water, finding a place among the boats bobbing there. Dastan gave me a hand out of the boat, and I joined the cluster of my sisters already on the dock.

A breeze from across the water teased over my cheek as I watched for the remaining boats, and I closed my eyes, savoring it. Do you know how rarely you feel a wind when you live all the time inside of a castle? I felt the wind ruffle my hair and my skirts and knew for the first time that leaning out a window just isn't the same.

I realized the scent of the breeze seemed vaguely familiar. After a moment I knew why—it reminded me of the smell of the metal forest. That made my stomach clench and hope I was wrong about the similarity. I inhaled deliberately, tasting salt on my tongue, and though it *was* like the forest, there was a difference, a freshness to it. Was it the water?

Dastan was still the nearest prince, so I asked him, "What does the wind smell like? It's sort of salty and…metallic or…something."

He looked puzzled for a moment, took a deep breath, and grinned. "That's the ocean."

I tilted my head, looking speculatively at what little water I could see in the darkness. "I've never seen the ocean."

"The view was better when we weren't cursed."

The nearest boat reached the dock then, and Talya leapt out. As soon as she was off the boat, she flung her arms around me. "Lyra, it was *awful*!"

I forgot all about ocean views. "What was?" I asked, and glared at the prince in her boat. "What did you do?"

"Nothing!" he protested.

"It was *dark*!" Talya moaned.

I really should have expected it. "Is that all?" I said, and shrugged an apology to the prince.

"I told you we aren't dangerous," Dastan remarked.

I ignored him and patted Talya's hair. "Sweetheart, you got into a boat underground. What did you expect?" I asked, just as though it hadn't alarmed me too. It was never a good idea to tell Talya she was right to be scared about something. It only encouraged her.

She clutched at me. "But it was *really* dark!"

"Well then, you're in luck, because there's a lovely bright castle to go to now."

After the last boat arrived, we all walked up a brief slope, on a winding path paved with stones and lined with torches. We weren't organized enough for a formal procession. I walked next to Talya, and I didn't comment to her about the shadows. The castle was lit—but the shadows around it didn't look right. They were too dark, and there were too many of them. The light didn't seem to spread the way it should.

At the end of the path solemn-faced footmen swung open tall double doors as we approached, releasing the sounds of lilting music and reassuringly human conversation. We all walked through the doors, into the ballroom.

We found ourselves at one of the narrow sides, narrow only by comparison to the way the room stretched back and back as if forever. I was dazzled by all the pillars and arches, decorated with intricate carvings and shining with gold. The left-hand wall had tall windows framed by thick pillars, while the right-hand wall had matching pillars with mirrors between, reflecting and magnifying the already enormous space. I suddenly felt that my hair was not nearly elegant enough for a room like this.

I tried to shake that nervous thought by turning my attention to the masses of brightly clad people standing on the polished floor. There were a few hundred people in the room, conversing with one another, clustering around the long buffet tables before the windows, or listening to the musicians in one corner. To complete the picture of a magical dance in an enchanted castle, everyone was wearing a mask.

Looking at the people might not have been the most calming idea. We were standing on a landing before the doors, wide enough for all twenty-four of us to be there without crowding, and it had very much the feel of a stage. Three steps led down to the dance floor.

The musicians stopped and silence fell as we stood by the doors. Conversations died away, and one by one every figure turned towards us. And then, like a ripple, curtsies and bows spread through the room. If they had all been in unison, it would have been terrifying. Instead they were uneven and uncoordinated, and at least a few distracted people had to be nudged by their neighbors. Like Dastan's gaze across the dark water, it was very human.

We all curtsied in our turn, and then the music started again. I was swept up by the nearest prince—I've forgotten now which one it was—and the dancing began.

We had always been good dancers, though until then we'd had little opportunity to make use of the skill outside of lessons. Father was not given much to putting on parties.

After a few steps reassured me that I could handle the dancing, I spent the first sets with my attention mainly on the surroundings. We danced across an expanse of polished blackness—an elegant blackness not at all like the terrifying darkness outside. The floor spread out to a grand staircase at the opposite end of the room. Marble steps led up to a landing, before splitting into two stairs sweeping off at right angles.

Overhead, the arched ceiling was decorated with paneled murals bordered by gold molding. The murals showed airy dancers, not quite human but not quite fairy either, misty and delicate. Below the murals hung a dozen crystal chandeliers, lit by branches of candles, casting sparkling light on the crowds below.

We twirled and whirled, traded partners and were swept along on a river of music and rustling skirts, and for a little while it didn't seem so hard to believe that maybe, just this one time, it would be pleasant to break a curse.

I was up to my third dance partner of the night by the time I recovered enough from the novelty of it all to remember to ask about the masks.

"Don't you wear masks at your dances?" Daemyn asked.

"Only sometimes, if it's a masquerade."

"Masks are a tradition with us. Dances are intended to equalize everyone, whatever their rank."

"You and your brothers aren't wearing masks," I pointed out.

He shrugged. "We usually do—or did, before the curse. Since the point of the masks are to let us get lost in the crowd, it didn't seem practical now."

We had to keep track of each other now, since we had to dance together to break the curse. It was possible we didn't have to dance with the princes—the Rhyme didn't specify who our partners had to be, only that we had to dance. But it made more sense and seemed safer to assume that we had to dance with them. It could have become very confusing if we were all hiding behind masks, although I envied some of the prettier ones going by. "So you really have masquerades all the time?"

"More often than not. Half the fun of dances is hiding who you are. A kind of hiding. I read somewhere that you can be most yourself when you're wearing a mask."

Maybe so, maybe sometimes. I could have used a mask that would let me be *more* me. All my life I'd been behind a metaphorical mask that did just the opposite. "Do you remember who wrote that?" I asked, more because I had to say something than because I really wanted to know, and because it didn't seem diplomatic to tell him what I was actually thinking.

He frowned thoughtfully. "Some philosopher, I think; I forget which one."

"Ask Mina," I suggested. "Maybe she's read it too."

"I will," he said, just before the dance whirled us apart and off to new partners.

Somewhere later in the evening I noticed that he had ended up dancing with Mina, and wondered if they were discussing philosophers.

I think I danced with all twelve princes that night. It takes hours of dancing to wear holes into slippers. That was the only interpretation we had been able to make on that line of the Rhyme: *"They'll dance until they wear their shoes away."* So we danced until our slippers had holes.

It's not impossible. Our dancing slippers were flimsy things that tore easily. Of course, we'd go through a lot of slippers quickly that way. We didn't have enough slippers to last 366 nights, but there were cobblers in Marilleigh, and even if they weren't solid by day, they could work at night.

My feet hurt by the time I had rips in both soles, but it was a survivable pain. I tried not to think about whether it would become much more painful, next week or next month, if we danced this much every night for a year and a day.

It might have been easier if Mina hadn't analyzed the sentence structure of the Rhyme and raised the idea that dancing until our shoes wore out meant *continuous* dancing for each ripped pair of shoes. Even if we couldn't know if that was true, we couldn't know that it wasn't, and didn't like to take the chance. And after all, if we took breaks it would just make the process stretch even longer each night.

It was still late enough by the time a hole had been worn in the last slipper that we were ready to return home. Most of us.

Talya got as far as the docks and balked. "I'm not going out there again; it's horrible."

"You can't stay here," Vira said, with tired frustration.

Talya crossed her arms mutinously. "Why not? We're coming back tomorrow. Why can't I just stay instead of crossing through that awful darkness?"

"Because we could never explain it to Father," Vira pointed out.

"So why can't *all* of us stay?" Talya persisted, and I can't say it wasn't a tempting notion.

"Because it doesn't fit with the Rhyme," Mina said, worn slippers dangling from one hand. "We have to walk through the forest and cross the water. I don't think it meant just once. Not to mention, we don't know how the curse would affect us in the morning, when everyone turns insubstantial."

"You don't understand," Talya protested. "It's frightening."

"As *I* understand it," Dathan commented, effortlessly detaching from the crowd clustered around and joining the conversation, "it's not really the dark that's frightening. It's the prospect of what might be in the dark."

"Yes! And I get out in all that black, and I start thinking and—"

"But this should be particularly undisturbing darkness," Dathan continued. "Its peculiar quality is that there's nothing in it at all. And nothing can't hurt you."

Talya hesitated, which was progress in itself. He took her by the elbow and guided her towards the boat. "I promise we can talk about sunshine and blue jays and sunflowers, and whatever other bright things you want."

And so Talya went after all, and all the rest of us did too. I think I was in Darshan's boat on the way back; I don't recall our conversation, except that it probably wasn't about blue jays.

We arrived safely on the far shore, where I made a point of noticing the smell again. Definitely ocean, like the scent was somehow wafting through all the way across the lake from Marileigh, most of a continent away. We went back through the forest (which dwelt tonight on jewel-encrusted masks), and made our way up the long stairs. We were all grateful to reach our beds, but we also felt that there were certainly worse ways to break a curse. So far, this was fun and not too hard at all.

That pleasant illusion lasted for exactly three nights.

~ ◆ ~ Part Two ~ ◆ ~

They all slept together in one chamber, in which their beds stood side by side, and every night when they were in them the King locked the door, and bolted it. But in the morning when he unlocked the door, he saw that their shoes were worn out with dancing.

Jacob and Wilhelm Grimm

Chapter Eight

We thoroughly enjoyed the first three nights of trying to break the curse. If we weren't getting as much sleep as we used to, we also had more fun than we used to. Sasia had an herb paste for blisters, a tea for sore muscles, and we always sat down most of the day anyway.

Father stared at us with particular intensity, but he'd been ominous for as long as I could remember. Fresh with the thrill of finally *doing* something, I didn't care about Father's stares.

And then the morning after the third night of dancing we went to breakfast, only to be confronted by piles of worn slippers spread across the table at the head of the room. We came into the hall from the opposite end, and we all stopped within a few paces, staring at those shoes.

My spine prickled and the seventy or so slippers felt as though they covered the table from end to end. Father stood behind the table, behind the piles of shoes.

The members of the court, from aristocracy and officials down to courtiers and travelers, were in their usual ranks sitting at the long tables on either side, with the servants standing against the walls behind them. Dozens of people, and everyone was silent. Everyone turned toward us as we stood there.

I was used to being invisible most of the time, and to standing blank-faced before the court whenever anyone did look. Today I felt as worn and ragged as the slippers, with just as many holes in my armor.

Worn slippers weren't a crime, and they weren't proof of anything in particular. Except they showed that *something* was happening, and it was a something we didn't want anyone, especially not Father, to know about. Perhaps we should have left the slippers on the other side of the Gate, or hidden them some other way, but then we'd have disappearing slippers to explain instead.

I took a deep breath past the tightening of my throat, then reached to my left for Mina's hand, to take strength from her. I reached to my right for Talya's hand, to give strength to her. With a few glances exchanged, we resumed our walk down the long length of the room. I kept my eyes forward and pretended not to feel the gaze of the court tracking us as we passed between them. We halted before the head table, forming into a line, side-by-side, to await the reckoning that was plainly at hand. I tightened my fingers on my sisters' hands, so that my own hands wouldn't shake. They both squeezed back.

Father's gaze lifted from us and swept around the room. "I have brought you all here this morning as witnesses." His voice was solemn, cold. "You all can see my daughters' dancing slippers. These were whole only a few days ago. Perfect, like new. And yet, every night for the last three nights, each of my daughters has somehow contrived to wear holes into a new pair of shoes." His gaze returned to us, piercing in its intensity. "I await your explanation."

"We don't have one," Vira said, voice quiet. What else was there to say? My head spun with wild stories, none of them believable or worth anything. Father knew something was happening and that it had to do with the Gate. Nothing we said would convince him otherwise.

The court rustled and shifted, a blur of color out of the corner of my eye, and I could feel the unease in the room. No one spoke up and Father continued. "Every night you have been locked in your bedroom. No unusual sounds have been heard from inside. And yet every morning, your slippers are worn to pieces. *Can you explain it?*"

He knew perfectly well that whatever was going on, it wasn't happening in our bedroom. But of course he'd continue to guard the secret of the magic forest.

Vira didn't respond this time. None of us did.

I don't think Father's intent was ever to get an answer. He had to know that he wouldn't. But he had a distinct touch of the theatrical. Much as I dislike to admit it, I probably get that from him.

Father looked out over the rest of the room again. "You witness here a second strange thing. My daughters offer no explanation for their behavior. This is not like the obedient girls I know they are." His eyes glinted. "I believe they are under a curse."

I had read far too many stories about girls accused of being under curses. What now? An accusation of witchcraft, or that we'd been consorting with demons? An attempt to 'cure' us? Talya was pinching my fingers and I didn't try to wriggle them away. I was thinking of the supposed cures for witchcraft. Burning at the stake came immediately to mind.

"I want a message to be sent out," Father announced. "I seek a solution to the curse afflicting my daughters. I seek a champion who will find the answer to this mystery, who will stand before this court and provide an explanation for my daughters' tattered shoes. Any volunteer will be granted three nights spent in a room adjoining my daughters' bedchamber. At the end of three nights, he will have the opportunity to offer an answer. The man who takes up the challenge and succeeds may choose a princess for his bride. Any man who takes up the challenge and fails will forfeit his life, according to ancient custom and tradition."

After that, breakfast was a silent affair. Even more so than usual. We escaped afterwards back to our bedroom, piled onto a few of the beds nearest the fireplace, and the delayed storm of reaction broke.

"Maybe no one will volunteer," Rayna said. "*I* wouldn't risk my head for something ridiculous like this."

"Someone will volunteer," I said, certain and hating it. "Someone always volunteers for this sort of stunt." I had also read far too many stories about so-called champions, eager for the hand of a princess.

"Never underestimate man's stupidity, or his greed," Mina said, sitting cross-legged at the end of one bed. "I've read entire books on both. Father will have plenty of volunteers."

There were so many distressing aspects of Father's proposal that we hardly knew where to begin. We had never given much attention to the closet adjoining our room—one doesn't, to a closet. It was barely large enough for a bed. Having a strange man sleeping there under normal circumstances would have been awkward and unsettling—not to mention completely inappropriate. Under these circumstances, it could be disastrous.

"Maybe he's bluffing about killing champions," Talya ventured, hugging a pillow against her chest.

"Do you really think so?" Rayna asked.

"No...I was just hoping."

"It's all simple enough," Laina said, her furious pacing a contradiction to the confident words. "We just have to find some way to keep the champions from learning anything."

"Do you have a plan for that?" Mina asked, voice dry, plainly knowing the answer. Laina just glared in response.

"We could stop going below," Talya said, barely above a whisper. "Maybe this would all go away if we don't wear out more slippers."

"But that means giving up on our princes," I said. We were already beginning to think of them that way—as *our* princes. At the least we felt an attachment, a sense of the rightness of what we were doing, a sense of the tragedy of that island and all of its inhabitants remaining imprisoned forever. "And giving up any chance of escaping by breaking the curse."

"So what's our other option?" Rayna demanded. "Keep going below until a champion finds out, and then one of us gets sacrificed like a piece of cattle?"

Mina was apparently trying to be the voice of reason. "You know princesses often end up in arranged marriages—"

Rayna pitched a pillow at her. "It's not the same and you know it!"

I shivered, and wished I could hug a pillow like Talya was, without looking silly. It did feel different. To be offered as a prize to a stranger, to end up locked into a marriage with whatever man got lucky, no matter how horrid or unsuitable he might be... I almost felt I'd rather burn at the stake.

"That's not the biggest risk," Vira said quietly. "If a champion actually finds a way to get through the Gate, and tells Father..."

There was no need to finish that sentence. If Father finally got through the Gate, then the disaster we'd been trying all our lives to prevent would be upon us.

Chapter Nine

We hadn't come up with any answers by the time we went below that night. At least Father didn't have a champion ready and waiting to go, which was the smallest of consolations. We found our princes on the shore, and delayed setting off across the water to crowd up in a loose circle by the boats and tell them about this new…complication.

There was a comforting amount of outrage in response.

"He's going to just let some stranger lay claim on one of you?" Daemyn said. "That's disgraceful."

"It comes up in heroic ballads often," was Dastan's comment, as he leaned back against the prow of his boat. "Not that I'm advocating the idea—just saying that it didn't require much creativity to come up with it."

"It happens in stories too," I agreed. It was nice to hear someone else cite something as fanciful as a ballad for information. My sisters had been known to roll their eyes if I referenced stories too often. I felt they were immensely relevant to our present situation. "The idea never seemed as horrid in stories."

"Funny how songs are like that too," Dastan said. "Maybe not being real is what lets them comment on things that would otherwise be too horrible to discuss."

"Speaking of horrible," Rayna interrupted, hands on her hips, "hadn't we better discuss what we're going to do?"

"This doesn't quite make sense," Daemyn said. "What does your father gain if someone *does* learn about the Gate and the forests? He already knows about them."

We had discussed that amongst ourselves already. "That's probably not what he really wants," I said. "We think he's just trying to throw more people at this on the chance that one of them will find a way past the Gate."

"We also think our fairy godmother may have had a hand in the idea," Mina added. "It's her style. So terribly traditional."

I nodded, lacing my hands behind my back. "It's convenient for Father too. He doesn't have to reveal the secret to anyone at the court; he looks like the good father trying to help his daughters; and presenting it this way brings in a different class of champion than if he revealed the entire truth. They'll probably be smarter and more honorable." Which didn't mean they wouldn't be horrible. Even if they were coming from the most altruistic motives possible—and I doubted that hugely—you still have to wonder about someone who gambles his head in order to marry a stranger, by prying into said-stranger's business.

Dathan picked up the thread again. "So we can't let the champions learn the secret, in case they actually find an answer to opening the Gate. They're in an adjoining room; can you keep them there?"

Vira shook her head. "The door doesn't lock, and it swings into their room, so we can't barricade it."

"Could you incapacitate the champions themselves?" Damek asked, hands shoved into fists in his pockets. "Hit them over the head or something?"

Laina nodded with what seemed like unreasonable enthusiasm. "We could do that. We'd just have to get behind them—"

"We don't want to hurt them," Mina protested.

"I do," Laina countered. "Presumptuous, meddling bastards."

I didn't want to hurt them *badly*. But I wouldn't have felt too guilty about inflicting a little damage.

Still, it was just as well that Sasia had a better idea. "I know about herbs; I could mix something that would render them unconscious if they drank it. We could put it in wine maybe."

"That could solve the first problem," Mina said, "which then causes the second problem. Three nights go by, we drug them so they don't learn anything…and then they can't tell Father anything. So he'll chop their heads off."

"They signed up for it," Laina said.

"But it's murder!" Talya protested, face pink.

Laina frowned and shrugged broadly. "I don't *like* it. But we have to consider priorities. It's like casualties of war. No one wants them, but sometimes bad things happen for a bigger cause."

Laina was probably meant to be a general. It wasn't that she didn't care; just that she could balance outcomes. For me, and most of us, I couldn't stomach the idea of handing a man a glass of drugged wine that I knew would set off a chain of events ending with him dead. It felt like we'd be giving them poison.

While we were arguing aloud about war analogies, our princes were having a silent argument. There were glances flying back and forth, the kind that people who know each other very well can use to replace words. I noticed the glances when I looked to see if Dastan was going to make another ballad comparison; ballads are so often about wars. He didn't make one, and after watching the argument of facial expressions go on for a minute, I asked, "Are you going to tell us about it?"

Half of them jumped.

Daemyn, sounding reluctant, said, "We may have another idea." He looked at Sasia. "Could you mix up something that doesn't actually put them to sleep, just sort of…gets them to the point of sleepwalking? So they'd be groggy and maybe wouldn't remember it later, but they could still walk down stairs?"

Sasia put on her 'reviewing herbs' expression. Mina got the same look when she thought hard about information she'd read. She told me I got it whenever I tried to puzzle out a hole in a story I was making up. "I *think* so," Sasia said after a moment. "They couldn't manage it by themselves, but if we got on either side and sort of directed them…except having them down here is what we're trying to avoid."

"Not necessarily," Daemyn said, paused to shoot a couple more looks at his brothers, and slowly said, "If they could get away from the castle, without learning anything, that would work it out neatly."

Vira sent her gaze scanning around the circle of princes. "It would. I still don't see how bringing them down here will help."

More looks darting about, and I was tempted to shake whichever prince happened to be nearest.

"We were going to tell you," Daemyn said, looking harassed.

"We were waiting for the appropriate moment," Dathan contributed. "We wanted you to have the full picture first."

"And keeping a secret really wasn't a demon plot."

I didn't even have to look to know that was Dastan; in spite of myself, I had to smother a laugh.

Others were more focused. "*What* secret?" Vira asked.

"We've been here several times over the years," Daemyn said. "We've done some exploring and…we found a tunnel. If you don't go straight through the forest—if you come through the Gate and turn left before the first trees, you'll find another tunnel. It's not that far, although you can't see it until you're practically on top of it. There's another gate—much smaller and less impressive, but along the same lines. We couldn't open it so we went through once in daylight—when we stop being solid, you know—and the tunnel leads up to the surface. It lets out into a forest. A normal one."

"It would probably open for us," Mina said, "almost definitely, since we can open the other Gate."

Sasia was nodding. "We could leave the champions on the other side of it, close it behind us—they can't get to the magic forest, but they can escape up to the surface."

"And we could too." I wasn't surprised when Rayna said the words out loud. We were probably all thinking it. I was.

There was a way out. My thought the first night, about a passage with a sign reading 'Leave Everything Behind' wasn't just a fantasy. I doubted there was a sign—but the passage existed.

"We'll think about that," Vira said. "At the moment, we have slippers to dance through."

We already knew by this point that if we wanted to get any sleep at all, we had to make dancing a priority, whatever our other concerns. Slippers don't wear through quickly.

I wound up in Dastan's boat again, for the first time since that initial trip. While I wouldn't say I sought him out this time either...well, I didn't try to avoid him.

"So are you angry with us about the tunnel?" he asked, once we were away from the shore.

I twitched my skirts to better settle them in the boat, and side-stepped the question. "Are you ever going to let go of the demon joke?"

His grin was distinctly unrepentant. "Probably not."

I hoped my cheeks weren't turning red, and wished I'd chosen a different dodge. "You know it was a perfectly valid question at the time!" If they were red, maybe he wouldn't be able to tell in the murky shadows anyway.

"I never said it wasn't." A few more strokes of the oars. "Do you think we made a valid decision not mentioning the tunnel?"

I leaned back and looked at the blackness overhead. It was the least unsettling direction. "I'm not sure yet. It does rather smack of the manipulative, you know. Were you really going to tell us about it?"

"Yes, we really were." The words were even, no hesitation. But what did I know about judging whether someone was lying? Vira didn't hesitate whenever she lied to our father. "As long as we're confessing things," he continued, "there's a third tunnel too."

I looked away from the blackness to stare at him instead, trying to reconcile the nonchalant tone with what sounded to me like important information. "Where does *that* one lead?"

"Nowhere useful. It just links up between your metal forest—"

"It's not *my* forest."

"All right, *the* metal forest, and our castle. Same as the lake. And since the prophecy specifies crossing the lake, the third tunnel falls under the category of useless information."

It was true, I could think of no likely use for a tunnel like that. Perhaps it had been meant as a test for the princes, an easy way to get out of rowing across the lake every night. If the prophecy was right, it would have ruined the whole attempt to break the curse. I dismissed that tunnel in favor of thinking about the more important one. "The second tunnel—that one's not useless information." Not if we were going to give up trying to break the curse. Maybe that's why it was there. Maybe it was a test for *us*.

"We were going to tell you about it," he repeated.

I looked back up at the darkness overhead. "Just not at the beginning."

"Look at it from our perspective. We barely knew you. You barely knew us."

"We hardly know you now," I pointed out.

"At least you seem to be past thinking we might be demons. That's progress. Anyway, we were asking near-strangers to commit to a difficult undertaking. If we told you there was a way to escape…"

"So you didn't want to give us that option." I was so very *tired* of not having any options.

His voice was quiet. "We have an entire country depending on us. On you. We didn't know what you'd do. It's like Dathan said, we were waiting for the right moment."

"After we were committed."

"After you knew us a little. After you saw the castle and saw what it would be like. You might have committed, but you're still not trapped. You can still turn around." There was a pause, during which he evidently considered that statement. "Well, not literally right at this moment. Navigation is completely impossible down here and I have a terrible feeling that if I ever tried to change direction we'd end up lost. Or we'd still end up in Marileigh, it could go either way. In a larger, metaphorical sense, you could still turn around."

I looked down from the empty heavens and he looked up and our gazes met. "What would you do?" I asked. "If we decided to run?"

"I can't speak for my brothers…"

"I didn't ask about them." People always assumed that my sisters and I were of one mind all the time; we encouraged it, but it still frustrated me. "What would *you* do?"

He shrugged one shoulder. "I'd be sorry. And I'd say Godspeed and good luck."

"You wouldn't try to stop us?"

He looked away, across the water. "How do I put this… I love my country. It's a good place, good people. But I've been trapped there my entire life. Since the spell, sure, and before that too. I don't believe in trapping other people."

At least he had an entire island. "Try being trapped in just a castle."

"I'd rather not. How do you stand it?"

Do you know, no one had ever asked before. My sisters had known me forever, and they were all in the same situation besides. No one else at home would have that kind of conversation with us. They wouldn't ask—and even if they did, we wouldn't answer. Our anonymity held us together, and it also kept us separate.

So there was a definite thrill to answering, "I read stories. In one way I've never been out of the castle—until now—but in another way...I've been so many places." Some days, the stories weren't enough. On other days, they helped.

He was nodding. "I like songs from far away. They're like a piece of a distant place."

"Yes, exactly!"

And so we were off, comparing stories and songs and whatever we'd been able to glean about the places they came from, and the places they told about.

We were docking before Dastan said, "You never did tell me if you're angry."

I ran a hand along the edge of the boat. "Well...I can't speak for my sisters, of course."

I could hear a smile in his voice. "I didn't ask about them."

"Well, then. No. I think I understand."

He stood up and I did too, carefully in the rocking boat. He stepped onto the dock, and extended a hand to help me out. "So are you going to use the tunnel to escape?"

"I don't think so," I said as I took his hand. I won't say I wasn't tempted. Of course I was tempted. Only, that parallel about being trapped—I didn't like the idea of leaving them trapped either. I looked up at him. "Are you surprised?"

He shook his head. "I was hoping I knew you well enough to guess right about that."

It wasn't an easy decision for us, about whether to take the tunnel. In the end, though, we elected to stay. We had begun something, something with a purpose, and we weren't ready to walk away from that. We were hoping to accomplish something that would help, both Marileigh and us too. Staying was in some ways the harder choice, but we also hoped it would end up giving us a better chance. After all, trying to escape through a forest in the middle of the night wasn't an easy path either, for twelve girls who had never been out of our castle. We'd never even been in a real forest. The champions, who presumably knew something about the world, had better chances going that way than we did.

We didn't reach the decision that night, but we talked it into enough unproductive circles after we got back to our room that Vira finally said we should put it aside until morning. By all logic, at that point we should have gone to sleep—we were tired enough. After all that discussion, some of it highly emotional, no one felt ready. So I ended up telling a story.

I chose the story about the girl who had to lift a curse on her brothers. I had been thinking about it lately.

It all began once upon a time, with a king who had seven children: six sons and one daughter. This would probably seem like a large family, if I didn't have an unusual perspective on the subject. The children's mother had died, and one day the king decided to remarry. In life, this is often a perfectly good idea; in stories, never. The king's second wife was an enchantress, and though he married her, he didn't trust her. One may wonder why he married her at all. Some versions of the story suggest she used a spell or other trick. However she got him to wed, he nevertheless feared to have her near his children. He took the children away to live in a castle in the woods, separate from the court and hidden from his second wife.

The king went to visit his children frequently—too frequently, perhaps, as his wife noticed his absences and wondered. She bribed the king's servants, and learned the secret. The king had been right to mistrust his wife, for one day when he was out hunting, she sought out the children. She brought with her silken shirts, woven with enchantments.

When she reached the castle, the children came out to meet her. She put the shirts on each of the six brothers, and they were straightaway transformed into swans. They took fright, as you might expect, and flew away. The sister had stayed back when the stepmother first arrived and, seeing what happened to her brothers, she fled away into the forest, still in her own shape. The stepmother, whose information had apparently been quite incomplete, didn't realize there was a daughter to be considered. She left the castle, pleased with herself for having got rid of her stepchildren.

The sister hid in the forest and there she stayed, wandering here and there and surviving as best she could. One day she reached a lake, and saw a flock of swans. Thinking of her brothers, she remained by the water. She was rewarded, for at midnight the swans came to shore, shed their skins, and stood up as the girl's brothers.

They told her they could only assume their human forms for a few minutes each night, and so she asked if there was any way they might be freed of the spell entirely. They told her there was, through a near-impossible task. In order to free them, she must weave six shirts from nettles, one shirt for each brother, and until she completed the task she could not speak a single word.

When their time as men passed, the brothers returned to the lake as swans. The sister elected to undertake the effort to free her brothers. She began at once, gathering the nettles she needed to create thread, weave cloth, and sew the first shirt.

She went about her work in the forest for a long time, until one day a party of huntsmen came upon her. She had wandered far from her castle in the woods, and this was the party of another king, from a neighboring country. The men asked her who she was and what her business was in the forest, but she answered not a word.

The king looked on the girl and was overcome by her beauty. Beauty was apparently his sole criteria in a wife, and so he decided to marry her, despite her strange origins and that he knew absolutely nothing about her. This was a rather questionable decision on another level as well; since she couldn't speak, she certainly didn't say yes, and this doesn't seem like the sort of situation where the absence of a negative is sufficient proof of a positive. But if you'd rather give the king the benefit of the doubt, perhaps she nodded in such a way that her feelings were clear.

And so they were married, and the girl became queen, all the while continuing her work of sewing shirts, never speaking. In due course, a baby boy was born. Tragically, the king had a mother who was at least as wicked as the girl's stepmother, maybe more so. She felt (not entirely without reason, it must be admitted) that her son had made a mistake by marrying this mysterious girl he found in a forest. On the birth of a child, the king's mother saw her opportunity; she took away the child and had him killed, then blamed the young queen.

Still unable to speak, the queen could not defend herself. However, the king was confident that his wife must be as good as she was beautiful, and refused to acknowledge the accusations. His mother was unwilling to give up, and so this happened again with a second child, and then again with a third.

On the death of the third child, the king could no longer hold so surely to his wife's innocence, and so he handed her over to be tried. The verdict was guilty, and the sentence was death by burning at the stake. They took her out to the courtyard and placed her on the pyre. She carried with her the six shirts she had sewn for her brothers—five were complete, and the last was missing only one sleeve.

As they lit the fire and the wood beneath the girl's feet began to burn, six swans swooped down from the sky. The girl threw the shirts over her brothers, and they turned immediately back into men—except for the sixth brother, who still had one swan wing where the last sleeve had been missing. Restored to their own shapes, the brothers rescued their sister from the fire. Now able to speak, she was able to declare the truth of what had become of her children, and the king's mother was duly punished in her turn.

And so the spell was broken and the curse was defeated—and after that? Well, perhaps the girl truly loved her king-husband, and he loved her, and they lived happily ever after together. Or perhaps she had been no less trapped than her brothers and, just as they shed their swan forms, she shed the life she had been leading too, and they went away together to seek a better one. But that I leave to the listener to decide.

Chapter Ten

It took only two days for the first champion to arrive. We learned of his arrival when we came to supper. We entered the hall, and I could feel immediately that something was wrong. It was a certain atmosphere I knew too well, a tension among the people of the court. Usually it meant Father was in a particularly bad mood. Today it was the opposite. Today Father was in a particularly good mood.

Today there was a stranger sitting at the high table, in the seat at Father's right. I studied him carefully as we walked in; I assumed that he was a champion, so in the worst possible of scenarios I could end up married to him. He was broad and dark-haired, not unhandsome, although I didn't like his scraggle of beard. And I didn't like him. I was probably biased by the circumstances, but there was just something…the way he sprawled in his chair, or the set of his shoulders. Or the way his gaze raked over the line of us appraisingly, as boldly as though he already owned us all. It made me wish I was wearing a cloak, a very thick and concealing one.

"Ah, my lovely daughters," Father said as we approached the high table. He was at his most jovial, which I always found terrifying. "We have a guest tonight." He indicated the stranger with a sweep of one hand. "Sir Herbert, noble knight of the realm, and our first champion."

Knight of the realm, fine. Noble? I doubted it.

"Heard about your challenge yesterday, and came straight here," Sir Herbert said, gesturing with the wine goblet in one hand. "Soon as I heard it, I thought, there's an opportunity for an enterprising man. A man like me. Don't you worry, Your Majesty, I'll clear this trouble right up for you. It won't be too hard for me to find out what little secret your daughters are playing about with." He winked at us, an elaborate and suggestive wink.

I exchanged glances with Mina, and saw the same disgust in her eyes that I felt. It was there for just a moment, then she blinked and her face smoothed. We all kept our expressions carefully blank as we dropped shallow curtsies and silently took our places at the table.

It felt like a very long meal. Father stayed jovial. Sir Herbert bragged on and on about his past accomplishments and his confidence about the ease with which he'd solve our mystery. By the second course, I began to think that Laina had had a point about hitting the champions over the head. By the fourth course, I was sure of it. Sasia had mixed her sleeping draught and it was more reliable than a blow to the head, so for practical reasons I knew we'd keep to the plan…but if he refused the wine, or if it didn't work, I wouldn't have qualms about trying an alternative option.

After supper, Father personally escorted Sir Herbert to our bedroom. As he turned to go, he paused—a careful pause—and looked over us all, standing by our beds. "Have a pleasant night." His smile sent a shiver down my spine.

Father left, closing the door behind him, leaving us with Sir Herbert. After the key turned in the lock, we all stood regarding each other.

I was profoundly glad in this moment to have eleven sisters. At least we outnumbered him. I had no idea what a man like this might take it into his head to do.

Father had been posting guards outside the door each night since beginning this nonsense about a curse. If we screamed, the guards would hear us, for all the good that would do. Father had the only key, and they couldn't come in until he returned and unlocked the door. Assuming he would come. Assuming they would even send for him to begin with.

Vira cleared her throat in the silence. "Sir Herbert, my sisters and I need to change clothes in preparation for going to bed."

He leaned against the doorjamb of the adjoining room, and leered. It was nothing so pleasant as a grin. It was a leer. "*I* don't mind."

Maybe the wine really was too kind an option.

Vira drew herself up with all the majesty she could muster—which was plenty. She was good at that. "I suggest you remember exactly who you are speaking to." Her voice was even colder than the cavern below us.

"Oh, I haven't forgotten," he said, strolling farther into our room. "I'm talking to the girls who are going to make me a very wealthy and powerful man. Marrying a princess, that's a fine thing, isn't it? Which one of you should I take? You there are a bit chilly for my taste." He nodded at Vira at that. "I bet some of you others could keep a man warm enough."

"You're remarkably confident for a man who hasn't earned anything yet," I said, which was the mildest of all the things I was thinking.

"Well now, as to that," he drawled, "why don't you just be a good girl and tell me what your little secret is? Ladies like telling me their secrets. And once we've got that cleared up, we can get down to having some fun tonight." He reached out and grasped my chin. "You're a pretty little thing."

Every instinct screamed at me to jump away from him. And to slap him. My judgment prevailed instead. I stepped carefully back, and somehow I contrived to smile. "Before we start discussing confidences, perhaps some wine?"

I put out my hand and immediately Sasia was there with a cup and a jug.

Sir Herbert chortled. "You see, I knew you were a fine group of girls! You know how to take care of a man. Give that drink here."

I poured out a serving of the wine and handed it to him. There was no problem getting him to drink it. He took it in one gulp.

"That was fine—how about another?" he said, and held out the empty cup.

I looked at Sasia. Her eyes were wide, and she shook her head just a fraction. She had mixed the dosage to be one cup. A second cup would, judging by her face, be dangerous to drink.

I drew the jug away. "Oh, surely one is enough for now," I said, trying for a playful tone. "And we were going to talk…"

"After another round of wine," he said.

I backed up a few paces. "I don't think so, Sir Herbert."

The leer came back. "Should we play that game, then?" he said, and started after me.

Mina, God bless her for it, tripped him. He sprawled full-length across the floor with a bellow. "You did that deliberately!" he roared.

"Obviously," Mina agreed.

"Why, you—" He started pushing himself up from the floor, then stopped, swaying, expression uncertain. "You little…" He struggled as far up as his knees, and then slumped down again. His eyes closed.

"You mix a powerful drink, Sasia," I said, and hoped no one could see that my hand was shaking as I handed the jug back to her.

"We're going to do this every night for a year?" Talya said, voice higher-pitched than usual.

"They can't all be this bad," Mina said, and looked down at him doubtfully. "I hope."

"Let's get him into the bed," Vira said. "Sasia, how long will he be out?"

"Eight hours…I think." Sasia sighed. "I haven't been able to actually test this, but it should be at least six. Probably eight."

"Long enough," Vira said, bending down to grab one boot. "Let's get going."

The next morning, Sir Herbert woke up with no apparent ill effects except a headache (Sasia said that might just be from how much wine he drank at dinner), and some confusion about the evening before. When Father came to unlock the door and check the progress of his champion, Sir Herbert put on a grand show of bluster and confidence, with complete vagueness about what he had actually learned. My sisters and I put on our most innocent faces and said nothing.

Sir Herbert's confusion helped us the second evening; if he had remembered the details more clearly, he no doubt would have refused the wine. As it was, it went much the way it had the night before. For all his bluster the next morning, I thought I could see a note of alarm in his eyes that hadn't been there before.

We gave him a different potion the third night. He slumped over and his eyes closed, but if you prodded him enough he'd turn semi-conscious.

When we were all ready to go, Vira shook Sir Herbert's shoulder until his eyes opened halfway to stare blearily at her. "Sir Herbert, can you hear me?"

"Yesh," he said thickly.

"You know that our father will kill you tomorrow if you don't have answers for him."

The panic, though muted by the sleepiness, was clear. "Don't...wanna die, I never..."

"You won't die, because we're going to help you," Vira said. "You haven't earned it and you don't deserve it, but we're doing it anyway. All you have to do is follow directions. We're going to take you somewhere."

We got him up to his feet, Laina supporting him on one side, Rayna on the other. He wasn't so drugged that he failed to notice. "Y'are such...*pretty* girls..." he slurred, swaying towards Laina.

She used her free hand to smack the side of his head. "Don't try anything."

Vira grabbed his chin. "You will conduct yourself like a gentleman towards my sisters, or we will leave you to our father. No doubt you'll be interested to see how he conducts himself towards *you*."

"Yes'm," he mumbled.

I had certainly had pleasanter trips down those stairs. We took turns supporting Sir Herbert as he shuffled down the steps, seeming largely oblivious to the details of what was going on. He did behave, mostly. We finally got him to the bottom, and it was easier hauling him over the flat ground of the tunnel, through the Gate, and off to the left to find the second tunnel.

We had investigated this tunnel a few nights previous. As Mina had predicted, this gate opened for us too. We opened it tonight, and dumped Sir Herbert on the far side.

"Left alone, he'll sleep for a while," Sasia said, looking down at Sir Herbert sprawled across the tunnel floor. "He'll wake up in several hours, and if he has any brains at all he'll find his way to the forest and make a run for it."

It was possible he'd try to come back to the castle, but he had to realize he had nothing of value to tell our father. Sasia said he wasn't likely to remember anything that happened after drinking the potion. The gate he was behind was set too far back in the tunnel for him to even see the magic forest, so he had nothing to tell except a story of mysteriously finding himself in a tunnel that led to the ordinary forest above. Even Sir Herbert wasn't likely to bet his life on that being enough of an answer.

We had a perfectly lovely night of dancing, and in the morning Father came to the door to find out the results—and found no champion.

Father stared at the empty room adjoining our bedchamber for a long, silent moment, and then turned to stare at us. "Where is he?"

Vira shrugged very slightly. "We don't know. Perhaps he fled."

"The door was *locked*." Father's eyes darted to Vira's bed, concealing the trap door. "What did you do?"

"You forget that we're under a curse," Vira said. "Obviously we don't know what we're doing. And we certainly couldn't tell you about it even if we did."

His shoulders were tense, hands closed into fists at his side. He glared around the room at us, breathing heavily. Finally he took a long breath, and his hands relaxed. "This isn't anywhere close to over. There will be more champions. Count on it. And I'm putting a bar on that door."

He was right about the champions. It was truly astonishing how many men were willing to risk their lives for the chance to marry a princess. They lined up for the privilege. I would have been flattered if there had been anything even remotely personal about it. All told, we ended up having 112 champions, give or take one; I've never been able to decide how the last one should be counted.

One advantage of all those champions is that they forced Father to keep up the current circumstances. He wanted people to spy on us, so he had to let us stay in our bedroom and continue going below.

It neatly solved the problem of getting more dancing slippers too. Father had pinned his whole story on those tattered slippers, so he had to keep providing us with new ones, to keep it all going for the next champion. Once or twice we considered leaving our slippers down below each night, to see if the lack of tattered slippers would disrupt his plans any. There didn't seem much point, though; he'd just make something out of vanishing slippers instead.

At the beginning, we tried not to think about how many champions there might eventually be. You can't think about dealing with 112 champions, or about dancing for 366 days—it's too much. Take it a day at a time, and each day can be dealt with.

The champions arrived daily. We gave each his allotted three days, and on the third night we'd leave him in the tunnel to make his own way from there. We could have got rid of each one faster, but that would just have given Father time to bring in more. We were still afraid that one of them might actually succeed, so fewer champions was safer.

We still had so many of them. Some were as bad as Sir Herbert or even worse, convinced that they had a right to the prize before finishing the task. Some were well-meaning, genuinely eager to save us from what they believed to be a horrible fate. A few were nervous and shy, and I wondered why they had ever got mixed up in this to begin with. And then the last one—but that would be jumping far ahead.

Chapter Eleven

We went along, day by day and night by night, drugging champions and dancing with princes and trying not to encourage our father to do anything that would prevent us from carrying on as we were, for the rest of a year and a day. Our feet hurt, and we needed Sasia's blister cream, but you can get used to anything. It may not be ladylike to mention it, but our feet toughened up, and our leg muscles did too, with all that dancing and stair-climbing. The first or second week was probably the worst from that aspect, until we'd adjusted.

Once our feet stopped occupying our total attention, we could focus more easily on the more complicated problems of our father and his string of champions. I tend to date my memories of that time by what number champion we were up to.

During the fourth champion's try (so about two weeks after we started), I realized something was going on with Mina. It was after the dancing, and most of us were back on the nearer shore, only waiting for Mina in the last boat. She was with Daemyn, which, though I hadn't given it much thought previously, didn't surprise me now that I was thinking of it. She'd been riding in his boat frequently. They kept getting into lengthy discussions about philosophical minutiae, so it had been perfectly natural that they continued the discussions as we came back. They had read many of the same books; Daemyn hadn't read anything written in the last two hundred years, of course, but our library was not the most up-to-date, and Mina liked older writers. They had been trading books the last few weeks too.

Philosophy is all right in its way, but if I'm reading a book, someone had better get killed or married. Or if it makes me laugh, that's good too.

Tonight we all stood around on the shore, talking and waiting for Mina and Daemyn. And waiting. Until enough time passed that I got worried.

I stared out into the darkness, watching for the light of their boat. From this direction the lights appeared as specks in the darkness and gradually grew larger, the way you would expect lights in the dark to behave. From the castle, the lights always appeared suddenly a few hundred yards from shore.

Right now, there was no light of any sort. I bit my lip. "They should be back by now," I said, to no one in particular. "What if something happened?"

"I'm sure they're fine," Dathan said from next to me. "And I wouldn't mention those worries too loudly."

We both looked for Talya then. She was talking to Rayna at the far end of our circle, and apparently oblivious. Talya had been handling the dark surprisingly well; the last thing we needed was to set off her fears again.

Actually, the *last* thing we needed was something horrible happening to Mina. I tried to fight down the nervous flutters in my stomach. "So if they're fine, where are they?"

"They're probably just delayed," Dathan said.

"What could delay them?" I demanded, of Dathan and anyone else nearby. "It's an empty stretch of water! It's not like a road. There's no traffic, there's no weather—"

"Maybe Daemyn's demonic side is coming out."

"Dastan, that's really not funny," I said through gritted teeth.

"Sorry," he said, cheerfully ignoring the glares from both me and Dathan. "I'm sure they're fine. Like you said, it's empty. What could happen to them?"

"I don't know! Is it possible to get lost out there?"

Dastan tugged on a lock of his hair thoughtfully. "We don't really know. No one ever has."

"If it was possible," Dathan said, "someone would have before now."

"That doesn't prove anything," I said, nervous flutters rearing up again. "Mina would know if it's possible. Which doesn't help *at all*. But she's the one who understands this sort of—is that a light?"

Dastan and Dathan both looked. "Yes," Dastan decided. "That's a light."

I practically pounced on Mina when she and Daemyn came ashore. "Where were you?" I demanded.

She looked at me with an expression both quizzical and innocent. "On the water. Where else could we have been?"

"Yes, but...it took you a long time. Are you all right?"

She seemed all right. A little flushed, perhaps, which could have just been the strange light. I could see already that I had probably overreacted, but keep in mind that we were in strange magical surroundings. And I wasn't at all used to having my sisters out of my sight.

"I'm sorry if we worried you," Mina said. "Everything's...fine."

I didn't miss it that her gaze went to Daemyn on that last word. And I could tell that that was not the word she was actually thinking of. The smile playing around the edges of her mouth reflected a word much stronger than 'fine.'

I studied her and I studied him and they both looked just a little too carefully casual and nonchalant.

But this wasn't the time or the place to chase down my suspicion, at the end of a long night and with Dastan standing nearby. Dathan too, of course. Everyone, actually.

We all made our way back home. Mina seemed unusually... well, if it wasn't Mina, I would have said dreamy. Because it was Mina, I had to settle for *thoughtful* because it was the only word that seemed possible for my practical, analytical sister.

I kept a good grip on my curiosity and waited until everyone was changed and in bed and the lights had just gone out. I slid out of my own bed and padded over to Mina's, next to mine. I poked Mina's shoulder through the blankets. "Are you still awake?" I whispered.

"The light went out ten seconds ago; how could I possibly be asleep?"

"Good. Move over."

I suppose girls everywhere whisper in the night when they want to share secrets. Mina and I had for years. It was the easiest way to have something resembling a private conversation, considering how our lives were ordered.

Mina sighed, scooted over and lifted the edge of the blanket for me to climb in. If she really didn't want to talk, she wouldn't have. We pulled the blanket up over our heads, leaving a small opening so that we could breathe. A little moonlight filtered in too, enough that I could see her face a bit, once my eyes got used to the darkness.

"What's going on with you?" I asked, voice too low to reach beyond the enveloping blankets.

"Why should anything be going on with me?"

"Because you were very late tonight, and because you've had a funny look ever since. What happened out there?"

There was just enough light for me to see what looked distinctly like a sly smile. "You read lots of stories, Lyra. Surely you can guess."

Surely I could. "Mina! You mean, you and Daemyn...no! Yes?"

"Yes!"

Blankets are good for muffling exclamations and giggles too.

"I never thought—I mean, why not, right?" I said, in something that almost resembled coherence. "I just never expected—though you've been talking to him lately."

"He's so smart! And, you know...nice."

"They're all nice," I said, thinking that, aside from the demon joke, Dastan had been rather nice about my getting upset over not much. And Dathan too. Of course.

"We've been talking and talking and...he made me think about Aristotle in a whole different way." And there followed what could only be described as a dreamy sigh.

So that probably wouldn't make *me* fall in love with someone. But as I'm always reminding myself, I am not my sisters and my sisters are not me. I pulled her back from the Aristotle discussion, then let her wax on about Daemyn for a while. Eventually the conversation turned to a different though very much related subject.

"Do you think anyone else will pair off?" I asked.

"Do you think there's any chance people won't?"

"I suppose it is natural," I agreed. "I mean, we see them every night, and talk to them, and dance with them. And they're *beautiful*."

"Yes!" More giggles.

"So who do you think might end up with who?" I asked.

"Mmm...I think Damek likes Mara. At first I thought there might be something between him and Rayna—but then I decided they really *are* just arguing, and it doesn't mean they're secretly falling in love."

"They're both just argumentative." I tried to think who else might have something in common. Near the beginning I had thought that maybe Daemyn and Vira, as the two oldest...obviously that wasn't something to say to Mina now. What else? "Dastan and Dalia both like singing." There wasn't much opportunity for singing, with all that dancing that had to be done, but Dastan had joined the musicians to sing a ballad or two a few times, and he and Dalia had tried a duet a couple of nights before, after her slippers had holes. It seemed as likely a potential match as any.

There was a moment's silence after I spoke, and then Mina said, "You're kidding, right?"

I was genuinely baffled. "No, they both do. That's a perfectly good basis for something."

"I, ah, don't think she's his type."

You see it already, don't you? I was still oblivious. In my defense, I'm making it easy for you, by only telling you the parts that matter. When the important parts and the inconsequential parts are all mixed up together, it's much harder to see a pattern. I've been telling it to you as though I spent all my time talking to Dastan, when in fact it was just…more time than any other prince.

So certain developments were not obvious to me yet. Mina and Daemyn, however, became quickly obvious to everyone. All my sisters knew by breakfast. That evening, it was evident that word had gotten out among the princes too.

There was excitement of course, but we also had to go on with our plans. There was dancing to be done—Mina and Daemyn still occasionally traded partners, if less often—and champions to be handled.

Chapter Twelve

During the seventh champion, we were invaded. It might have been worse, considering it wasn't by Father, Marjoram, or a neighboring army, but it was still bad enough. Father's head steward, Foster, a fussy little man with a long nose that he stuck into everything, decided to stick himself into the arrangement of our bedroom.

We found him there when we came to dress for supper—Foster, five assistants, and an alarming amount of chaos. They had rearranged half the furniture in the room. My gaze went at once to Vira's bed, still in place hiding the trapdoor, then guiltily darted away, hoping that look hadn't revealed anything.

Fortunately, the steward was occupied by Vira at that moment, who had drawn herself up to her full height to level her most disdainful glare at him. "What," she said, "do you imagine that you are doing?"

Foster lifted his head and straightened his back up to his full height too—roughly five and a half feet, in boots. "I *imagine* nothing. I *know* that I am attending to my duties managing the efficient running of this castle."

I was quite sure that he had never imagined anything in his entire life.

"And how does the efficient running of this castle give you any cause to interfere in our personal chamber?" Vira countered, glare diminishing not one iota.

The five attendants were looking awkwardly at the floor, feet shuffling and beginning to lean away from their still defiant leader. "This ridiculous matter of champions is causing great inconvenience on many fronts," Foster continued. "It is my duty to see that it is handled with maximum delicacy—"

"There is nothing delicate about having a strange man in our bedroom every night," Laina burst in. "Nothing you do is going to solve *that*."

He sent her one dismissive glance, and continued. "With maximum delicacy, and with an effort towards resolving this situation as quickly as possible. The arrangement of this furniture is very poor for surveillance purposes. Half the beds can't be seen from the adjoining room. And surely we *all* want a champion to succeed and break this curse, yes?"

He sent a sharp look around at us, and at least half of us looked away. No one answered, until Vira finally murmured, "Of course."

"Excellent," he said, and pointed at Vira's bed. "We'll move that bed next, right over to—"

"You will not move any more beds," Vira said quickly. The words may have been distracting enough to hide other reactions. Talya squeaked and Mina's hands tightened around her book. My heartbeat leaped up to a faster pace while I struggled not to twist my hands together the way Sasia was doing. "There is a limit to the inconvenience we will accept. Any champion deserving of success will surely be resourceful enough to handle any situation. The only beds you will move will be to put all of these—" Vira waved at the disordered ones. "—back precisely where they were."

The attendants looked even more bashful, while Foster's frown was mutinous. "I must object to—"

"My word is final," Vira cut in. "You will leave now, while my sisters and I dress for supper. After we go to eat, you will return to fix this mess. Or would you like to take this matter up with our father?"

Then the steward finally hesitated. With the exception of Marjoram, Foster was Father's most loyal supporter—but he wasn't stupid, and one of the ways he had maintained his position was by never crossing Father. I was relieved to see him finally show signs of backing down, even while I hated that we had to invoke Father to make it happen.

"Oh, very well," he muttered finally. "I really think you ought to appreciate efforts to resolve this situation, but if you *insist*, we'll return the beds to their former inefficient positions."

"Good," Vira said, and pointed to the door. "You may go."

They went. I sank down on the nearest bed, hearing relieved exhalations around me.

Talya spoke first, in the high pitch of alarm. "If they had moved Vira's bed—"

"They didn't," Vira said.

"But if they had!"

"They would have found a trapdoor, which would tell them very little," Vira said, tone brisk and calm.

Unless they had opened the trapdoor, and gone down the steps, and reached the Gate—and that would have stopped them, of course. I knew that, yet once I had taken the chain of thought that far, it was impossible not to imagine what would happen if the secret of the metal forest ever got out, if the whole court became infected by mad desires for riches. It was a hideous idea.

"Nothing has changed, and the secret is still secure," Vira said. "That's what counts."

Repeating that to myself did help calm the fear stirring up my stomach. It didn't help with the rebellious feelings complicating the mix. "I'm so *tired* of hiding," I muttered.

We dressed identically for supper, spent the meal with our eyes lowered and said nothing more meaningful than "please pass the salt." All that was normal, and all the while my thoughts circled around the subject of *hiding*, like a bird battering again and again at a cage.

It was sheer relief to go below, to cross to the princes' castle, to dance for hours. I was full of frustrated energy and ready to put it into dancing. I wore through my slippers first that night.

By then I had dissipated a good deal of tension and was ready for a breath of quiet. No one seemed to be paying attention, so I slipped out the doors to the pathway down to the dock. The closed doors reduced the music to just a faint murmur, no louder than the waves lapping against the shore. I sat on one of the large rocks beside the path, and inhaled the ocean-scented air.

I was looking at constellations when I heard footsteps on the path behind me, and a moment later a voice saying, "I thought I saw you hiding out here."

"I'm not *hiding*," I snapped without thinking.

I looked over my shoulder and saw Dastan hold up both hands in a gesture of innocence. "I just meant—"

"I know," I said with a wince. "Sorry. Just…kind of a sensitive word."

"Noted." He sat down on another rock across the path, somehow making it look as natural as a chair. "Want to tell me why?"

I knew I could have said no, and that he would have dropped it. That was one of the things making me inclined to answer. "Because most of the time I *am* hiding. We all are." I smoothed my skirt over my lap, visions of our days passing through my mind, every day the same, all twelve of us always acting the same. "We all hide amongst each other all the time…except down here. We don't have to hide when we're here. That's the best part of coming down here."

"And I thought it was the wonderful conversations," Dastan said, tone mock-mournful.

"It *is*. We get to talk to people without having to pretend we're all exactly the same. It's so different, up there. We dress alike and we talk alike and we try to make everyone think we *are* alike, until sometimes I start to think so too." I shook my head a fraction; I hadn't really meant to say that. Dastan was just so good at…well, looking like he understood everything. It made me want to tell him things.

"We don't try to be alike," he was saying, "but with twelve of us it's still not easy to stand out. Especially when we were younger."

"Is that why you ended up interested in music?"

"Not exclusively, but sure, in part. It was something that was different."

I looked out at the waves, tried to ignore the wall of blackness beyond them. "That's the question, isn't it? When we're surrounded by people we're similar to, what makes us different?" When does the hiding stop being merely an act?

"So—what makes you different?"

I had my automatic answer. "I tell stories."

He vetoed it. "Too easy. Important, but too easy, and I already knew it. What else?"

I blinked, taken aback. That was my *way*. That was my defining quality. That was the thing that said who I was and that I wasn't someone else. Or so I had always looked at it. "I don't know."

"I don't believe you." He crossed his arms and looked at me thoughtfully. "You tell stories and you have eleven sisters and there has to be more to you than that. I'll make you a deal. I'll come up with one way each evening that I'm different from my brothers, if you tell me one way each evening that you're different from your sisters."

No one had ever asked. The implication that it would be hard for me to come up with ways bothered me; it bothered me even more that it really did seem hard. And the idea sounded like fun. All of which led me to say, "Raspberry tarts." By which I meant I was agreeing.

He was insightful, but he didn't put that one together. "Sorry, what?"

"Raspberry tarts. They're my favorite food. Our cook makes them; they're all warm and gooey in the middle and crispy on the edges. Most of my sisters prefer cake for dessert. I like raspberry tarts. Your turn."

Dastan, it turned out, was the only one of his brothers who liked blueberries.

Hardly defining details, but he had ruled out storytelling as an option. And I suppose we were no more (or less) absurd than Mina, Daemyn, and their Aristotle discussions.

It wasn't as though we never talked about stories. Three nights later, when I was in Dastan's boat en route to the castle, all ready with a detail about a favorite constellation (Orion), he asked a different question. He wanted to know my favorite story.

I gaped at him in genuine horror. "I can't *choose* one! That's like…like asking me to choose my favorite sister!"

"You mean it's not Mina?"

"No! Well…yes, most of the time, sort of, and don't tell anyone I said that, but…but *no*! And stop laughing, can *you* choose a favorite song?" I could have asked him if he had a favorite brother, but no, I went back to the songs and stories.

It worked, anyway. Dastan stopped laughing and looked almost somber. "No. I can't. Once in a while I think I can but…"

"But there are so many others," I said triumphantly. "Picking one would be like betraying the rest." I frowned. "I mean…not that they have feelings, of course." Really, there was just something about him. I kept saying ideas I usually only thought.

"Right, but it would be," he mused, very calmly considering he was validating something I had never dared try to articulate to anyone before. "I take back the question about your favorite story; what's *one of* your favorite stories?"

That was easier, still hard. Finally, I selected "The Enchantress and the Lazy Girl." I didn't tell him that I had made it up myself; it sounded arrogant, and also, what if I told it to him and he didn't like it? I didn't tell it to him that night—there wasn't time. But you're not in a boat about to reach shore. I can tell it to you.

Once upon a time, there was a shopkeeper's daughter who was very beautiful. It was a sad fact that because she was beautiful, people's automatic inclination was to do things for her, and she loved to take advantage of that.

When her mother asked her to clean the house or to help with the laundry, she'd make endless excuses to get out of it, preferring to spend the time combing her hair or trying on dresses. When her mother did insist on her working, she was so slow about it that the good woman would eventually give up in exasperation and do the job herself.

When her father asked her to mind the shop, she would avoid helping customers if ever possible. Customers frequently ended up waiting around, though the men rarely complained. The women were far less pleased.

One day the prince of that country passed through the town and his party stopped at the shop to buy fresh supplies for their journey. It happened to be a day when the girl was (in theory) helping her father. The prince saw her, and was sure that he had never seen anyone so beautiful. He had been reading too many stories, and become convinced that such a beautiful face could only indicate a kind nature, a worthy spirit, and a personality that would match his own—in other words, that her beauty proved she was his soul mate.

He proposed to her at once. She was lazy but she wasn't stupid, and she was quite sure that the wife of a handsome prince would have all the dresses she could ever want, and no work to do at all. She accepted, and off they went to the royal castle.

Now, the queen was not so naïve as her son, nor was she in a position to be so swept away by the girl's beauty. When they arrived at the castle, the queen took a good look at the girl and decided that it was time to slow matters down a bit. She announced that it was grand and wonderful that her son had fallen in love, and of course if they were going to be married, there was a tradition to be tended to first. The bride must pass three tests in order to marry the prince.

The girl was not at all pleased by the idea, but she could hardly refuse. So she smiled sweetly and said she would be only too willing, and the queen smiled sweetly back and said that she had just known that was what she would say, and that the tests surely would be no trouble at all. Then the queen told the girl a riddle, and sent her off to a guest bedroom to think about an answer, to be given in the morning.

There was someone else at the castle who was intensely interested in the prince's new bride—many someones, in fact, but only one we need be concerned with, and that was the castle enchantress. She was not the venerable and otherworldly sort you might imagine. She was quite new to the job, though not to the castle. She had lived there all her life, had shown a talent for magic, and at the appropriate age had been apprenticed to the previous enchantress. She was very fond of the prince, and very interested in the girl he had chosen, and very curious about the riddle the queen had given…and all those verys led to her dropping by the guest bedroom. Just to see how the girl was getting on, you understand.

The girl let the enchantress in readily enough, but the enchantress was dismayed to find that she wasn't getting on with the riddle at all. The girl announced that the riddle was just so much nonsense, and she wasn't going to bother her head about nonsense.

The enchantress had known the queen all her life, and she doubted that the queen would have set a nonsensical riddle. She asked the girl to tell it to her; the girl didn't remember it exactly, but the queen had thoughtfully had it written down. The enchantress read it through, and found that it wasn't nonsense at all. It was based on references to several well-known pieces of that country's classic literature, with special emphasis on two of the prince's particular favorites.

At first the enchantress thought that she'd just give the girl a couple of pushes in the right direction, to be friendly. She pushed and pushed and finally realized that pushing would do no good whatsoever because the girl really didn't recognize the references. Reading classic literature was something she had certainly never seen the point in. Now the enchantress thought that it would be a terrible shame if the prince couldn't marry the girl he had fallen in love with, just because she hadn't read a few books (or, apparently, paid much attention to any discussions on the subject). So finally she just gave her the answer. The enchantress had read all of the books; she and the prince had been debating for years about the ambiguous ending of one of his favorites.

The girl gave the answer in the morning, and the queen said that was all very well and now there was the second task to be thought of. The girl pouted prettily and said she was dreadfully tired on account of not sleeping well for thinking about the riddle, and surely there wasn't any need for a second task, *really*? The queen said they could wait a bit, and then on the morning of the third day sent her back to her bedroom to tend to the second task.

The enchantress was still very curious, and also she felt rather a vested interest now. She told herself she ought to just leave matters to resolve themselves, waited an hour, and then went to see how it was going anyway. She found the girl sitting on the floor next to an enormous barrel and two large bowls. When the enchantress peered over the edge of the barrel, she saw a mixture of lentils and dried peas, reaching right up to the top.

The task, the girl explained, was to separate the lentils and the peas. She also explained that she thought it was quite impossible and entirely pointless and she was most certainly not going to bother. Queens didn't need to be able to separate lentils and peas.

The enchantress had to agree that it was a very strange request, and she wouldn't have thought it like the queen to ask for such a thing. And since it was so silly…and since she did want the prince to be happy…and since he apparently was in love with this girl who no doubt had all sorts of lovely qualities… The enchantress sighed and waved her hands and cast a spell. The peas and the lentils began jumping out of the barrel on their own, skipping across the ground in a neat line, and hopping into the two bowls, peas on the right, lentils on the left.

This went on for only a few minutes, and the level in the barrel had only dropped a few inches, when the enchantress noticed that the lentils had stopped. The peas were still coming out, but there were no lentils in the line. She looked into the barrel, and saw that, after the very top, it was all dried peas. What had seemed like an impossible task might have been done easily enough after all, with perhaps half an hour of concentrated effort. She made this observation to the girl, who said that it was easy for her to say, as she had magic, which the enchantress thought was missing the point.

The next morning the girl presented the separated peas and lentils, and asked if they were done with all this silliness now. The queen looked very thoughtful, asked her a question about one of the books referenced in the riddle, asked her how long it had taken to separate the lentils and the peas, and then suggested she take a nice walk out in the garden before the third task. The girl did not feel at all inclined to go hiking about over pathways, but supposed she could find a bench somewhere.

The enchantress happened to be out in the garden as well; she usually took a walk this time of the morning. The two bumped into each other and the enchantress told the girl she really had to see the rose gardens, because they were the prince's favorites. The girl said she would if she must, although surely she could look at them after they were cut and put into vases inside. But they went to the rose gardens, and there they encountered a little boy who was crying. The girl asked if he really had to make so much noise, and the enchantress asked him what was the matter.

The boy said that he had hurt his hand on a rosebush's thorns, and though the enchantress couldn't see anything wrong with his hand she supposed that small children often made a big deal out of very little. So she wrapped up his hand in a handkerchief and then used her magic to make big purple bubbles that weren't ordinary round bubbles but formed interesting shapes. The girl said they were pretty enough if rather tedious, and the little boy laughed and asked for different shapes and said he'd have to tell the queen about the hippo especially.

That was when the enchantress realized that this must have been the third task and, quite unintentionally this time, she had interfered again. She looked at the girl and for a moment thought that maybe it was just as well because after all, what did the prince see in her anyway? But apparently he did see something because he was in love with her, although suddenly the thought made the enchantress rather sad. It still wasn't fair that he shouldn't be able to marry the girl he loved when the girl hadn't really had any chance at the third task and perhaps would have done perfectly well given the opportunity. Perhaps.

So the enchantress told the boy that he must tell the queen it was the other girl who had helped him, because that would make everyone much happier. Even as she said it, though, she knew that this was a lie—it wouldn't make *her* happier.

The boy scampered off back into the castle, and the enchantress and the girl followed more slowly. In the throne room, they found the queen and the prince waiting for them, report already received from the little boy. The enchantress bit her lip and then agreed with the little boy's story that it was the girl who had helped him. The girl herself was ready enough to agree as well, once she saw the significance of the question.

And then the queen asked rather pointedly how a girl with no ability at magic had produced purple bubbles shaped like a hippopotamus, and then the game, as they say, was up. The enchantress steeled herself for disaster and heartbreak, and was entirely taken aback to find that the prince was more relieved than not. By now he'd had enough time to actually talk to this girl he'd so impulsively proposed to, and while he may have been impulsive, he wasn't stupid.

He was rethinking that beauty-equates-perfection assumption he had made.

The girl was politely ushered back home, on the grounds of the tasks having been left unmet, and given some nice jewelry as a consolation. She eventually married a wealthy merchant, but spent the rest of her life complaining that she had been robbed of her chance to be queen.

The prince, meanwhile, confronted with the actual facts of the three tasks, found that he was looking at the enchantress in an entirely new way, while the enchantress found that she had to think a bit about why exactly it was so important to her that the prince be happy. And so, not immediately but soon enough, there was a wedding after all. The queen said the tasks could be waived this time.

Chapter Thirteen

We had a good stretch between the seventh and the fifteenth champion. None of them were *too* unbearably horrible, while below ground we were getting ever better at dancing—and Mina's and my speculations regarding romance were bearing out. Dalia paired off with Danton, Rayna paired off with Darius, and, as Mina had predicted, Mara paired off with Damek. The group of us who were still trading dances regularly was dwindling.

All in all, it was just about as pleasant a time as you could hope to have trying to break a curse. Until the sixteenth champion, when Father reminded us that we were playing a risky game.

This champion's turn started out as the previous fifteen had. Number Sixteen arrived during the late afternoon; we heard about him, but the first we saw him was at supper. I looked at him briefly, decided he was a Well-Meaning Meddler (my favorite kind of champion) and turned to the seemingly more important matter of wondering what would be for supper (although now that I look back, I can't remember—possibly lamb).

It was during Father's speech about what was expected of the champion that things changed. At first it was the usual routine he gave to every champion: my daughters are wearing out their slippers, we need someone's help, etc., etc. Then he got to the part about what would happen at the end of the three nights.

Tonight, Father said, "After three chances to observe, you will be invited to give an answer. Explain what is happening to my daughters and give me tangible proof of what you say, and you may choose any of my daughters for your bride. Fail, and you will forfeit your life."

Did you see it? It wasn't the part about dying; Father had been making that part of the speech all along, even though by now he had to expect that this champion, like the others, would disappear on the third night. I think he liked frightening everyone with the idea; I'd heard that, with all the men disappearing, the rumor was that they really had been beheaded. I tried not to think too much about whether Father liked frightening people because the forest had twisted his mind, or whether that had been part of who he was all along.

Anyway, the threat wasn't the part that alarmed us and made us exchange worried glances over our plates. It was the demand for tangible proof. He had never asked for proof before; why would he need it, when he already knew so much about what was going on? We had assumed that what he wanted was for a champion to find a way through the Gate; now it suddenly appeared that he wanted something from below.

It was a small change. But this was a delicately balanced game, and a small change could be enough to upset it completely.

I tried to tell myself it wasn't significant, or that all he was hoping for was that a champion would bring back some gold or diamonds. I couldn't really believe, though, that all he wanted was a branch or two; I knew he was after far more wealth than what one man could carry. I studied Father's face, caught a new gleam in his eye, and couldn't believe either that this wasn't significant.

Of course my sisters and I talked as soon as we could. We drugged Champion Sixteen and then talked all through changing clothes and fixing hair, and all the way down the stairs. We told the princes about it when we met them, and half of them thought we were overreacting; but they had never met Father.

"He must be planning something," Dastan said, brow furrowing in thought.

Though we were all on the same topic, half a dozen conversations were going on as we clustered on shore. I answered Dastan. "So you don't think we're getting alarmed about nothing?"

"No, I've seen you get alarmed about nothing."

I thought of when Daemyn and Mina had been delayed crossing the lake, and shot him a withering look. "Thanks." I still thought my worry then had been reasonable.

"This is different, though," Dastan resumed. "This is getting alarmed about something."

I forgave him. At least he believed us that it mattered. "Thanks." This time I meant it.

I don't suppose it will surprise you that, when we finally left the shore, I ended up in Dastan's boat, conversation continuing apace. "So why would your father suddenly ask for proof now?" he asked. "Why not from the beginning? What's changed?"

"Mina thinks he learned something new, only we can't figure out what. Or how."

"Could one of the champions have told him something?"

That had been discussed, at length. I shook my head. "There isn't any way. We've drugged them all, so the most any of them could remember is that we gave them wine, and then they found themselves in a tunnel. Even if one of them told him that, it's no reason for him to bring up proof. It's not like he's insisted on taking away any wine in our room." It probably helped that he didn't realize Sasia knew something about herbs. So far, no one had looked at us strangely when we requested a few bottles of wine from the kitchens every week or so; since people assumed we were dividing it twelve ways, we were only asking for what seemed like very modest amounts.

"Ruling out the idea that he learned something from a champion," Dastan continued, "he must have learned something somewhere else. So where could it have been?"

I didn't know whether to be hopeful or terrified by the prospect of more information somewhere else. If we could find more information, wonderful—if Father found something, disaster. Never mind where for now, the immediate question was *what*. "What could he learn that would make him ask for proof?"

Dastan's half-frown deepened. "Maybe…he learned that there's something that can do exactly what he wants done. That would explain it, wouldn't it?"

I blinked. "You know that didn't make sense, right?"

"He's always been after a way to open the Gate. Maybe he wants a champion to bring him something from down here that will let him do that."

I stared at him. "That makes sense. But that's…" I had been fighting a sense of rising catastrophe all evening, and now it was engulfing me. I tried to swim above it. "It doesn't really—I mean, it doesn't *really* make a difference, right? Some champion is still going to have to find a way past the Gate in order to get anything, and if a champion actually finds a way in then it doesn't really matter what he brings out because the mere fact that he can get in is enough of a problem so anything else—"

"Breathe," Dastan ordered.

I did. I inhaled deeply, let it out again, and, feeling no calmer, at least managed to be more coherent. "What I mean is, if a champion can open the Gate, what difference does it make if he gives Father some way to open the Gate? It doesn't add anything."

"Except that it means he won't need the champion. And a champion won't have to find his own way to open the Gate. He could just sneak through when you open it."

"No one could; we're careful!" I twisted my hands in my skirt, tried to look at this calmly. "So we just have to make sure we keep the champions asleep. Same as usual. Don't you think so?" I wanted him to think so. I wanted him to say yes, it was no different, everything was fine. Or at least, as fine as it had been before.

What he said was, "I think you'd better find out whatever it is your father found out."

Mina and I were back in the library the next morning. If Father didn't learn something from the champions, there weren't many other sources of information—except possibly the library. Others of my sisters hoped to find out if someone else at the castle could have learned something and told Father, although since we didn't trust anyone the best we could do was eavesdrop. Asking questions was, well, out of the question. While they listened wherever they could, Mina and I dug through books.

"How likely do you think it is that we'll find anything?" I asked, paging through a family history.

"Not likely, but we have to try something." Mina dragged two more history books off the shelves.

We barely knew where to start. Our best guess was to look at anything about our mother's family, or our history books, or even anything about the castle. That focus on family history led us to a rather disturbing trend.

"I never thought about it before," Mina said, running a finger down a family tree in one book, "did you ever notice that we must have a good half-dozen ancestors who just sort of...drop out of the history books? They're listed in the family tree, there might be one or two details early on, then nothing about their later lives. No marriages, no descendents, no accomplishments later in life despite a late death date. Sometimes no death date at all."

"So the record is incomplete. So what?"

"So maybe they didn't *have* later lives. Maybe they went into the forest and—never came out again. Or did come out, went mad, and had to be shut away. We *do* know we have two ancestors who went insane. I've noticed them before."

So had I, though it had required some puzzling. History books don't like to say it directly when members of the royal family lose their minds. I rather wished that Mina hadn't said this, directly or otherwise. It was making my spine prickle. "All right, so maybe Father isn't the first to be, um, badly affected. Let's be thankful we didn't know that before we all went in ourselves, and focus on the proof question, all right?" If we were going to think about disturbing things, better to at least think about the relevant one.

We kept shuffling papers and hunting through book stacks, and it was tedious and unprofitable.

"The trouble is, we've been through all of this," Mina said, leaning back from another pile of dusty volumes. "If there's something in here, we should have found it a long time ago. Missing ancestors aside, I've never seen anything in any of these books that touches on the Gate or the magic forest. Not even in hints."

I considered that. "Does that seem funny to you?"

"What do you mean?"

I flipped through pages without looking at them. "It's been a family secret for two hundred years. You'd think someone would have written something down. A reference, a note, something."

"That's the point, it's a secret. Mother heard it from her parents, who heard it from hers, and so on. They told each other; they didn't write anything...why are you looking strange?"

I suppose I did look strange. I had just had a thought, and it was a thought that made my stomach drop out and my hands badly want to shake. I very carefully shut the book in front of me. "I think I know how he learned something. And I don't think it's anything here."

She was staring at me. "All right, then where? And why are you looking like that?"

"Because you're not going to like where I think the information is. No one's going to like it."

"Lyra, just tell me."

"It's what you said—that Mother learned it from her parents and they were all passing it down. And we don't know that they weren't writing anything. We just know that they were keeping it a secret. So they didn't put any writing *here*." I swallowed. "Mina, I think he must have found something in Mother's room."

Chapter Fourteen

There were many locked doors in our castle. We slept behind a locked door every night. Any doors leading outside were locked. There were all sorts of spare rooms that were kept under a key.

But the most incontrovertibly locked room, the room that was kept the most inviolate, the most untouched and unvisited, was our mother's. It had been locked the day she died and, as far as we knew, it had never been opened.

Mother and Father had always had separate bedrooms; it's common enough among royalty, although I suppose they must have, you know, visited. There are twelve of us, after all. Vira remembered Mother's room. I didn't.

It had always felt as much like a legend as a place to me. It's hard to explain the horror I, and all of my sisters when we spoke about it, felt over the idea that Father might have gone there to look for information. I don't think we could have felt much worse if he had dug up her grave. It was her room, her place, not to be touched, and to violate it for this purpose only made the idea more horrible.

Mina and I kept looking in the library for the rest of the morning, and when we rejoined our sisters in our bedroom, we did spend time talking about other theories and other ideas. But in the end we kept coming back to the same place—Mother's room.

"Maybe we should be more surprised that he hasn't been in there sooner," Rayna said, chin in her hands. "If he thought he could find something, I can't imagine that he'd have any qualms about looking."

"He did look, years ago," Vira said quietly. "Before Mother even got sick. I remember they had a fight about it. He must have been convinced there was nothing to find. At least, until now, when he got desperate enough to try again."

"And he found something." I tipped backwards from a sitting position to sprawl on Vira's bed. Our bedroom was the best place for all of us talk privately, although even that was complicated now by champions. Fortunately, today's champion—we were still on #16—was elsewhere in the early afternoon. "We have to learn what he found. So we're going to have to go in there too. Right?"

I honestly don't know if I hoped someone would contradict me. Part of me had wanted to get into that room for years. I don't remember my mother. Visiting her room—it might tell me something. Not that Vira hadn't told us plenty, over the years, but it would be different, actually seeing *her* room, her belongings. At the same time...it was a frightening idea too. I had thought about my mother so much, and built up my own idea of who she was. I had told myself stories about her—more when I was very small, sometimes later too, more than I ever admitted to anyone. I didn't know what I could possibly find in her room that would alter anything I had hoped or imagined, but somehow...somehow the idea of actually visiting frightened me too.

No one contradicted me.

"How will we get in?" Laina asked, ever the practical one. "The door is still locked." We didn't really know that, but it was a fair assumption.

"Damek knows how to pick locks," Mara volunteered.

"Which would be helpful if Damek was here," Laina said. "Except that if he was, we'd have much bigger problems to deal with."

"He can tell us about it," Mara persisted. "And he has, you know, tools."

It was a flimsy plan, but still the best we had. We delayed for a few days and one more champion (#17 got the same speech about proof), in order to talk to Damek about picking locks, and for him to bring a skeleton key that he swore could open anything, if you jiggled it right. This would have been more encouraging if he hadn't also brought a handful of picks and prods, "just in case."

We couldn't all twelve of us try to get into Mother's room. A group of twelve girls is just too noticeable. In the end, it was Vira, Mina and me. Vira because she was the oldest and remembered the room best; Mina because she was the best at remembering Damek's directions; and me, because I had thought of it to begin with.

We waited until Father was in a council meeting. We weren't too worried about being observed by anyone else. The door was at the end of a corridor and no one else had reasons to go that way.

Vira and I stood in front of the door while Mina tried the skeleton key. Vira contrived to look as calm and undisturbed as though she stood around in front of her mother's locked bedroom every day—but I've almost never seen Vira get visibly ruffled about anything. I should have such a talent.

I couldn't stop myself from fidgeting, or from hissing, "Do you have it yet?" at Mina.

"If I had it, I'd open the door," Mina whispered back. "It doesn't quite…" She trailed off, and I could barely hear the scraping noises as she fiddled with the key.

Of course it felt like forever. In actual fact, Damek wasn't entirely making it up about his miracle key. It wasn't long before a click cut off the scraping. Mina straightened up and carefully pushed the door open.

For not having been opened in fourteen years (maybe), it opened easily. We slipped within, and closed the door behind us. Inside it was dark, and all I could see were vague impressions of shapes.

"There are windows…" Vira murmured, and I could just make out her silhouette moving across the room. A moment later, light flooded in as she yanked draperies back from the windows on the far side. Along with letting in light, they sent an enormous amount of dust into the air.

Once I stopped sneezing, I looked around. The room was airy, spacious without feeling empty, cozy without feeling crowded. There was a four-poster bed with a canopy against the wall to my left. The right side was set off by a small couch arranged like a divider in the middle of the room, and beyond it a table with all the drawers and cubbies you could want in a desk, combined with the delicate moldings and lines of a dressing table, and a mirror against the wall above it.

I took a step into the room, then a second, and found my feet sinking into a throw rug. There were several of them scattered over the wood floor. I couldn't see the toes of my shoes, they were so deep in the plush of the rug. If we had to dance our slippers to pieces on these, it would be an impossible task.

Other than Vira's comment about the windows, we hadn't spoken since we entered. There was a palpable silence, a hush that filled the air. My analogy to a grave seemed even more appropriate. Everything in the room was covered in dust. Everything was dead.

Vira fingered the hangings of the bed. "These were pale blue," she said, voice just above a whisper. They had turned gray now.

I walked to the couch, and sat just on the edge of it. I inhaled, smelling mostly dust but also just a hint of something flowery, maybe a long ago perfume. I closed my eyes for a moment, and tried to imagine. Pale blue hangings. All the wood polished and gleaming. Perhaps flowers in a vase on the table. Myself, a little girl, who must have sat on this couch frequently. There must have been a time when I knew this room, when I thought nothing of running in and out of it, of clambering onto the couch or the bed or my mother's lap, to tell her what no doubt felt like weighty matters at the time, and to beg for stories.

I had hoped that maybe, if I ever came in here, I'd remember something. *Really* remember it, not the half-memories, half-imaginings that were made up much more of Vira's stories than of my own remembrances.

But I didn't. Three years old was just too young. I could imagine the room as it must have been. I could give a setting now to my stories about my mother. But I couldn't really remember it.

I got up from the couch. "Should we each search different places?"

I saw Mina shake herself, and Vira looked away from the draperies only slowly. They had plainly been as far lost in thought— and as far off our purpose—as I had been.

"Yes," Vira said at length. "I suppose. We should see if anything looks disturbed. The dust might help us."

The trouble with that idea was that the dust looked smudged in all the obvious places—on top of the desk, on the bed tables, the handles of the wardrobe. It told us that someone else had been in here, presumably Father, but it didn't tell us much else.

We couldn't be so lucky that the dust would all be lying in a neat carpet except in one spot, indicating that something was missing. And how else do you find something that's absent? Unless we were very, *very* lucky, Father had taken whatever he found with him. The disturbed dust didn't even tell us for sure if he had found anything.

Vira searched the table by the bed. Mina opened the wardrobe, and looked over the expanse of dresses within.

I tried the desk. It was beautiful, all slender legs and carvings. There was a jewelry box sitting on top of it, carved wood inlaid with tiles on the lid. The dust was moved around it. I reached for the clasp holding the box shut, and hesitated.

"Vira?"

She didn't look up from the table. "Hmm?"

"Do you think she…I mean…she wouldn't mind, would she? Us being here?" Reaching for the jewelry box, I had suddenly felt that I was reaching for something private, as though I was poking through one of my sister's belongings. It didn't matter that the owner of the jewelry had been dead for fourteen years. I still felt funny.

Vira did look up then. "No," she said. "I don't think she'd mind. She never did, when we were small."

And of course she'd approve of what we were doing. Helping our princes. Stopping Father from getting into the magical forest. But in that moment it mattered more to me that Mother hadn't minded a dozen little girls running about, a long time ago.

I opened the jewelry box. Inside, I found layered trays of necklaces, bracelets, rings. They were lovely—although a traitorous thought passed through my mind that they weren't as lovely as the magical forests, or worth as much. I pushed that idea away, and reminded myself that they also weren't cursed, and wouldn't manipulate my thoughts.

I lifted out two trays, and was looking at what I thought was the bottom one, when I noticed something. The bottom tray seemed just slightly crooked. Mouth dry, I leaned forward to look closer. There were barely visible lines of black at opposite corners, as though the tray wasn't sitting quite snug within the box. I rubbed my hands together, then lifted the jewelry out to get it out of the way, and fit my fingernails into one of those threads of black. Easing it back and forth, I managed to tickle the tray out, revealing a hollow space beneath.

I swallowed, not sure whether to be excited or not. "I think I found something," I said, and Vira and Mina came to look.

It was a hidden space, and it was empty—or nearly. There was no dust, the space locked up tight enough to keep it out. But there were crumbled tan flakes, and a few thicker wisps in a lavender color.

"What is that?" Vira asked, stirring a few flakes with one fingertip.

Mina and I looked at each other, and I could see she knew too. It wasn't hard to figure out, really, when you spent as much time around books as we did—especially old and crumbling books.

"Flakes of paper," I said. "Old books begin to fall apart around the edges. Those purple bits are probably from the cover. It's dyed leather, and it's peeling. There was a book in here, a small and very old one. And he must have taken it."

We looked around a little more after that, though without much expectation. We didn't find anything relating to the magic forests, or to Father's new demands, but I did find something else. It was a thick book sitting in a bottom drawer in the desk. I drew it out, and blew the worst of the dust off the cover. I used the edge of my sleeve to wipe away more, revealing tarnished gold lettering set into the leather cover. I ran my fingers over the words—*Twenty Stories from Distant Lands*.

"I've never read this," I said, turning to the contents page. "I don't recognize the titles." I fingered a broad ribbon hanging out of the book. "Vira, do you remember this?"

Vira was sitting on the couch, leaning her head on one hand. "Mmm...maybe. She kept books she was in the middle of reading by the bed. If that one was in the desk, not the library, it must be one she liked to read often."

I ran my fingers over the titles in the contents page. "Do you know which story was her favorite?"

"No. I'm sorry I don't remember more."

I looked up at her again, from where I crouched near the desk, and saw her gazing off around the room. She looked tired—and sad. I had always envied Vira her calm and her strength. And her memories. For the first time, it occurred to me that the rest of us had something Vira didn't: an older sister. Of course I had always known that, but suddenly I was really *thinking* about it.

I had always thought Vira was lucky because she remembered the most. It was like she had more of Mother. But the rest of us had *her*. When we were growing up, there had been nurses and governesses and tutors, people who combed hair and buttoned dresses and wiped tears. Vira had always been the only one who mattered, though.

I stood up and walked over to her, putting as much bounce in my step and cheer in my voice as I could in that tomb of a room. "That's all right," I said, plopped onto the couch next to her and hugged her tightly. "You remember plenty."

Mina had been looking at the wardrobe again. She closed it now, and said, "We'd better go. The longer we stay, the more likely we'll be caught."

I stood up, holding Mother's storybook. "We still haven't learned whatever Father found out."

"We need to find the book that was hidden in the jewelry box," Vira said. "And there's really only one place it's likely to be."

Mina looked at her with a horrified expression. "Vira, we *can't*. This was risky enough!"

"If we want to find that book," Vira said, "we have to go into Father's room,"

I had no memory of ever being in Father's room either, which might seem even stranger than that fact did about my mother's room. I mean, with Father alive, it wasn't locked up. But then, having met our father, you might not find it strange after all. The idea of sneaking in there made me feel hollow, and I hugged Mother's book against my stomach.

Vira opened the door of Mother's room a crack to check the hallway; seeing it was clear, we all slipped out, and the door re-locked behind us. I might have felt wistful and philosophical about the symbolism of that, if I hadn't been more focused on Vira and Mina's argument.

"Vira, we can't go in there! He's much more likely to catch us there, and if he does, anything could happen!"

"We don't have a choice. We have to find answers."

"Vira's right," I said, past the cold in the pit of my stomach. "We've already come this far."

Mina crossed her arms and glared at both of us. "And if he catches us?"

The very thought made my palms itch. But I shrugged my most casual and said, "You sound like Talya."

"Sometimes Talya is right to be afraid!"

"Come on, Mina," I said. "Do it for Daemyn."

She opened her mouth, I'm sure to keep arguing, hesitated, and sighed. "Did you have to say that?"

"She did," Vira said. "I think we should go now, while Father's still at that council meeting." She set off down the hall.

"Now?" Mina repeated, but followed. "You're both insane."

Maybe. We were also on our way to Father's room. It wasn't far from Mother's. I suppose that was to make it easier to visit. The hallway was empty when we reached his room, and we went directly in. The door wasn't locked. He knew no one would dare to enter.

It was a heavy room, all dark wood and straight lines. No ornate carvings or pale blues for Father. Like Mother's room, there was a four poster bed at one side, and a desk at the other. There was also a book case, and naturally I was drawn to it. I'm sure I would have been even if we hadn't been looking for a book.

"Lyra, you check the books," Vira said, evidently seeing where I was heading anyway. "I'll try the desk. Mina, check the wardrobe."

There were no small purple books on his shelves. There were no storybooks either, though if I had found one I wouldn't have dared to take it anyway. This time it was Vira who was lucky. She opened a drawer in the desk and found a battered book sitting there. It was old, covered in purple leather, with flowers embossed on the cover. It had to be what we wanted, if only because the flowers didn't match anything else in the room.

"It seems too easy," Mina said, as we all gathered around the open drawer and looked at the book inside. "Could it be a trap?"

"What, like it'll burst into flames if we touch it?" I reached out one finger, tapped the book, and pulled back. Nothing happened. "Why should he bother hiding it? He thinks no one would come in here. And no one would think this was important."

Vira picked it up, carefully opening it to look at a few pages. "It's a journal. And there's enough written that we can't possibly read it here. Let's take it and go."

"Take it?" Mina repeated. "He'll know it's gone!"

"And if he asks us about it, we deny everything," Vira said firmly. "Like we always do when he asks something we don't want to answer. He'll know we're lying, like we always are, and like he always does. Since it serves his ends to keep us alive, healthy and going below, there's not much he can do to us. Now let's get out of here."

As we left, I wondered what it was like to be part of a normal family. I'd have to see if Dastan minded talking about his father.

We survived to make it back to our room, unobserved—and then we ran into more danger from each other, because all twelve of us wanted to see the book. I'll spare you the resulting chaos. In the end, as the storyteller, I got to read it out loud. After three pages, we knew that this was probably the source we needed, and also that it was going to be very dull along the way. I'll condense it for you and just give the interesting details.

Once upon a time, nine generations and almost two hundred years before me, we had a queen who dabbled in magic. Great great great great great great great Grandmother Eleanora did not, as far as I can tell, have any impressive talent. If she hadn't been royalty, she might have become a minor sort of herbwife. As it was, her magic wasn't much more than a parlor trick. But she was fascinated by it, and there must have been a bit of Mina in her (or maybe it would be more accurate to say, her in Mina), because she studied what little she could do exhaustively. We know the studies were exhaustive because her notes on them were too.

It takes a special sort of mind to be interested in whether one's ability to light a candle magically is affected by the waning and waxing of the moon. Maybe it would be interesting if the candle exploded during the full moon, but she never observed any effects so dramatic.

After pages of writing on that and similar experiments, finally Eleanora wrote, "Lately I've been thinking of the secret I had from my mother," and we all started paying closer attention. She was vague throughout, which was both a relief and a frustration. It limited what Father knew, but there was a good deal she didn't say that we would have liked to know too. Putting together what we knew, what we could guess at, and what she wrote, we thought we had a nearly complete picture.

Eleanora's mother, Juliana, was the first to encounter the Gate and the forest, and to keep the secret. She told her daughter about a vision she had one night, of a shining woman who told her about all this, and also told her a strange rhyme. We felt sure it was *our* Rhyme. Eleanora did not write down any rhyme, so Father still didn't know that. When Juliana went to investigate below the castle, she found everything as it had been in her vision—and as we still saw it.

Juliana also said that there had been secret tunnels, caves, and even an underground lake below our castle since long before her vision. It was the Gate, the forests, and the acid water that were new. Eleanora's theory, described after a great deal of repetition and divergences, was that everything would revert to the way it had been once the promise of the Rhyme was fulfilled. In other words, the tunnels and cavern would remain, empty of the Gate, and empty of the metal forests.

In a way it was good to know that the horrible, mind-twisting forest would vanish with the curse holding our princes. Except it also gave Father all the more reason to stop us.

That detail didn't give us an answer to his sudden demand for proof. That came at another point in the journal, after a long and dull passage about the effect of diet on magic (eggs apparently help, but stay away from goat cheese). Finally she turned to the subject of the Gate. Only someone like Eleanora would have bothered trying to find ways to open the Gate, considering that she could open it herself just by touching it; apparently that ability really does run in the family. Eleanora wanted to find out if there were any other ways, and launched a series of experiments trying different spells and keys and devices. Nothing worked. Except one experiment.

She collected water from the lake, the strange black acidic water, and boiled it over a fire near the Gate. When the steam struck the Gate, the bars shimmered. From this and other experiments I won't detail (she did), she was convinced that if lake water was poured directly over the Gate, it would melt the bars away. She hadn't tried it, but she was convinced by the theories, and believe me, anyone who reads Eleanora's journal and her details on her experiments will be convinced about anything she finds convincing.

So it seemed that Father wanted a champion to bring back water from the lake, because then he'd be able to create his own opening in the Gate, and reach the magic forest. It was like wanting a key that was held behind the door it could unlock, and I tried to shrug it away as a similar dilemma and nothing to worry about. Unfortunately, Dastan was right—this meant that all a champion had to do was get through once when we opened the Gate, and then he'd be able to find his own way through again. It's easier to get at that key behind the locked door when the door opens every night.

We talked all afternoon, until we had to stop for supper. It seemed to me that Father stared at us particularly hard that night. If he had discovered the theft of the book, he didn't say anything. It would be a long time before he ever did say anything about it. Maybe he saw no purpose in confronting us, or maybe he was unwilling to admit that we had won a victory by successfully stealing it.

We were still intent on deciphering the book's contents, and once we were out of Father's sight we talked again until Champion #17 came in. We drugged him and kept talking while we changed clothes and went below. We brought the journal with us, on the theory that the other side of the lake would be the safest place to hide it.

You might think all that talking would have got us somewhere useful, but it didn't. We went through it all again with the princes, and by the time I sat down in the stern of Dastan's boat I was sick to death of the entire subject. There was nothing we could do but carry on as we were. End of discussion.

I leaned back against the carved stern and closed my eyes. "I've had enough about magic water and gates and Father and Great great great great great great grandmother Eleanora. Talk to me about something else."

"You missed a 'great.' "

I groaned. "That's not another topic."

"Sorry." There was a moment of silence interrupted only by the splash of oars. Then Dastan asked, "What are you going to do when this is all over?"

"Depends how it ends."

"If it ends, as it will, with the curse lifted and everyone free and you can do anything at all."

"Cut my hair." I said it because it was the first thing that came to mind, and I had been developing a possibly dangerous habit of telling Dastan whatever I was thinking.

"Evil is vanquished and everyone's dreams come true and you're going to…cut your hair?"

"I hate my hair."

"Why?"

I opened my eyes to see that his expression was as adorably baffled as his voice. "It's a nuisance." I held up the curls hanging over one shoulder. "You know how long it takes to comb every morning? And I can never get it to stay up; I always wear it down when I'm here because I can't get it to do anything else. Mina's goes up practically on its own but not mine, even though it all looks the same. Nila is the best at hair and she's the only one who can get mine so it will stay up when we're wearing it that way, up above. I've always hated it and I've never been able to do anything about it because I have to look like everyone else, and half of them would rather die than cut their hair. So when this is over, I'm chopping it all off. And you can't possibly be all that interested in the trials of my hair."

"Well…not exactly. But it is beautiful hair."

All right, so my stomach fluttered. I told myself that was silly, all my sisters and I have the same hair, which should have reduced the compliment a little—it wasn't like mine was anything special—only I was the one he was saying it to and I fluttered.

Internally, I did. Externally I shrugged and said, "I'll keep some. Most of it goes. What are you going to do when this is all over?"

"I always wanted to be a minstrel. You know, the wandering kind."

"Can princes do that?"

"Why not? Father wasn't exactly thrilled by the idea—he wanted us to all be knights or diplomats, but I was talking him around. I would've, eventually." He was silent a moment, then shook his head and continued in a more cheerful tone. "So after the curse is lifted, I find a ship, and I find somewhere that's better than an island for wandering. Then I find new songs. There must have been all kinds of things written in the last two hundred years."

"Isn't it funny," I said, "if there hadn't been a curse, you could have gone wandering over the continent two hundred years ago.

Maybe you would have ended up at our castle. You could have met Great great etcetera grandmother Eleanora."

"It's not funny, it's strange." He twitched his shoulders in something this side of a shudder. "It makes me feel like a ghost."

"Oh well, I think Grandmother Eleanora was probably very dull to talk to anyway."

"Not nearly as interesting as your treatise on your hair," he said, perfectly deadpan.

I made a face. "If that was normal water down there, I'd splash you. Anyway…aside from the hair, I don't know what I'll do when it's all over. It's hard to imagine an *after* to a situation I've been in my entire life. I'll come up with something. Something far away and separate from all my sisters."

"Sounds lonely."

I shook my head in an emphatic negative. "It would be amazing. To not be Vira's and Mina's sister, or my father's daughter…to just be *me*, by myself, not number nine of twelve."

"I admit there are days when I would like to drop at least half of my brothers into the ocean, but they're also part of who I am."

I flapped a hand at that. "Yes, all right, my sisters are part of me. And I've spent seventeen years being part of them. Maybe I'll finally get a chance to see what the *rest* of me is like. Maybe I'll become a wandering storyteller and go looking for new stories."

"Maybe." And I think he was going to say something else then…but just then I saw the castle come into view and before I realized he was going to keep talking I remarked about the castle, and then we were pulling up to the dock and the former conversation had already ended.

I hopped out of the boat myself while he was tying up. We were all getting very good at negotiating boats. "You know, you still owe me a fact tonight," I said, as I smoothed out my skirt.

"Wanting to be a minstrel doesn't qualify?"

"Not since you rejected my storytelling as a fact. It's too obvious—unlike my hatred of my hair. So come up with something good." I flashed him a grin, and started off down the dock.

I looked back after just a few steps, and caught him in the most charming of smiles.

Maybe that was the moment. Or maybe it was during one of the hundreds of times we danced, that night or some other evening. Maybe it was much earlier, as far back as when we each understood the magic of a story or a song from somewhere far away, or much later, when Dalia paired off with Danton and I realized I was glad my singing sister was no longer available. Or the day I admitted to myself that it wasn't random chance that was putting me in Dastan's boat more often than not.

I don't know exactly when I fell in love with him. I don't even know when I first knew about it. By the time I could have put it into words, it felt as though it had been true for a long time—and as if I must have known, long before I named it for what it was.

Chapter Fifteen

I do know the day the situation became a good deal clearer between Dastan and me—or the night, rather, because of course it was at night. It was during the twenty-fifth champion, and was the night I ripped my shoe.

I wore my shoes out every night, but this was different. This was a fairly spectacular trip involving some skidding. In a proper story Dastan would have caught me. In actual fact, he missed. At least he was prompt about giving me a hand up and asking if I was all right.

"I'm fine," I said, pushing hair out of my eyes with my free hand. He hadn't let go of the one he'd used to help me up. I wish I could say I had tripped over something, but no—it was just a trip on a smooth floor. Dance for hours on end night after night and it's bound to happen eventually. You just step wrong.

Or right, as the case may be, because when I inspected my shoe, I saw that the bottom had split, presumably during the skidding. It was my left shoe, which was good news, because I always wore the right one out first. I've no idea why; it had to be something to do with the way I danced, and was the kind of thing you'd never notice if you weren't dancing holes into your shoes every night. This night, I already had a small hole in the heel of my right slipper.

"Do you think that counts?" I asked, looking dubiously at my split slipper.

"You did it dancing, didn't you?" Dastan said. "Of course it counts. You know, if you could do that deliberately—"

"I couldn't." I wasn't at all sure that he wouldn't want me to try, and I'd rather dance for hours than sacrifice the dignity involved in *trying* to trip and rip a shoe.

"Oh well," he said, and brightened immediately. "At least it makes things easy tonight."

It was significantly earlier than I usually finished. "My feet are grateful."

"So am I. There's something I've been wanting to do and there's never been any time." He still had hold of my hand, and I was beginning to wonder if he planned to ever let it go. Now he gave it a tug, towards the back end of the ballroom. "I want to show you something."

I hesitated. I wanted to go. But... I looked at the still-dancing couples. "You could spell someone else..."

Dastan barely gave them a glance. "No one's hurting for a partner. Come on."

Of course I went.

I had been coming to the castle for three months by then, and had never been beyond the ballroom. Most of the night was spent dancing, and even when I finished and was waiting for whichever sisters were slower about wearing out their shoes, there was rarely much time to spare. Besides, by then it was late and I was tired.

The farther reaches of the castle were deserted; I suppose everyone else was in the ballroom, or tucked away behind the scenes doing things like making the food for the banquet tables. Every hallway was brightly lit despite its lack of inhabitants, and for the first time I wondered if the beautiful, blazing vision of the lighted castle was not because of some practical need for light, and actually the point in itself. If maybe the castle's inhabitants were trying to do their part to call their princes—and now us—back out of the dark fog they had gone into.

Perhaps the empty halls should have been ominous. Only, they weren't like the empty halls of the ghost stories I tell, all covered in cobwebs and full of strange noises and shadows. These were hallways with gleaming wood and bright colored wallpaper, smiling portraits and the occasional statue, couch or end-table. The nature of the curse seemed to be to freeze everything as it was for two hundred years, so why should the castle crumble? It was also hard to be spooked walking along with Dastan—yes, still holding my hand. Even if there had been cobwebs, he probably would have started some conversation about demon spiders and it would have made me laugh and I still wouldn't have been spooked. Besides, I'm not Talya.

So I wasn't feeling any actual worry when I remarked, "You know, if you were a demon, this would definitely be the moment when you'd be dragging me off to your lair."

He sighed theatrically. "You caught on. I've just been biding my time until I could get you alone."

"You're a very patient demon, then."

"You have no idea," he said, and it sounded less like play-acting this time.

Before I could pursue that line of thought, he stopped at a large, ornately-carved door. He pushed it open to reveal a few steps leading out into a garden.

"This is better in the daylight, but at least there's a full moon tonight," he said, stepping out. "We do seem to still have phases of the moon."

He was right about the moon, and my eyes adjusted quickly to the darkness, after the bright hallway. I could see a garden with neat hedges, flower beds, and carefully laid-out paths. It was pretty enough, and I said so.

"Yeah, it's nice. Kind of artificial, though, and not really the point. Come on, this way."

We struck off through the garden, and out through a gate at the opposite end. The ground was cool beneath my split slipper, not uncomfortably so. As I passed through the gate, I said, "If I really did think you might be a demon, I'd be getting very suspicious—oh…"

The "oh" was not about the garden or the gate or the possibility of demonic plots. It was about the trees up ahead.

"This was the point," Dastan said, sounding smug and tightening his fingers around my hand.

There was an orchard beyond the gate, stretching out in long rows. I couldn't see the end of them in the shadows. Branches arched overhead, moonlight turning the leaves a silvery green.

I hesitated. "It looks a bit like…"

"No, it doesn't," he said instantly. "It's not at all like. They're not metal and they're not cursed, not more than anything else around here, and yes, they're laid out in rows, but they're normal trees, not magical ones."

Behind his voice I could hear wind rustling through tree branches, the leaves swaying and brushing against one another. The metal forest never rustled. It was a reassuring sound, an earthy sound. I let him pull me on towards the trees.

"See, I was thinking," he went on, "you said you never got out of that castle. Even if you got into a few gardens now and then, I was thinking you'd probably never been into an orchard."

"No. Never." I looked down at the dappled pattern on the ground, made by the moonlight shining through the leaves. Then I looked up at the moon through the lace of branches overhead.

"It was always…a good place. I mean…" Dastan, who was never at a loss for words, seemed to be fumbling for a sentence. "I mean, there aren't that many places to get off by yourself when you have eleven brothers, but I could always find an empty tree. And the birds didn't seem to mind having another musician with them."

Without really thinking about it, I squeezed his hand. "It's like my library," I said, even though on a surface level there were few places less like a room full of books. "It's quiet and private, and a good place to think, and…" I paused, inhaling. "…and it smells good."

He laughed. "That's the apples. They seem to be permanently ripe over the last few months. I think the island's confused about the season."

"Of course it would be, the poor place is under a curse. Are the apples any good?"

"Delicious. The curse doesn't affect their taste."

I finally twitched my hand out of his so that I could reach up to a branch overhead. I could see an apple hanging from it, just at the edge of my reach if I stood on my toes. I got my hand around the apple and pulled. It didn't come off on the first or second tug, and then on the third it snapped so abruptly that I lost my balance for the second time that night. This time he caught me.

We had danced together so many nights; we had spent enormous amounts of time with our arms around one another. It shouldn't have made my pulse speed up or my skin tingle. But it did. Maybe it was the moonlight. Or not having hundreds of other people in close proximity.

I turned so that I was facing him, his arms still around me. I looked up at him and he looked down at me and I think I raised my chin just a little. And he kissed me.

"Are you sure there's no magic around?" I asked at length, with what little breath I had left.

"Well, I said the trees aren't magical. Although there is something in moonlight—"

But I didn't really want to talk just then, so I kissed him again. It's still the most effective way for me to make Das stop talking—and the nicest.

Eventually we sat down under a comfortable looking tree, him leaning back against the trunk and me leaning back against him.

"I dropped the apple," I said, the thought of it occurring to me for the first time in many minutes.

"Do you actually care about the apple?"

"No, not really." I didn't care about anything at that moment, because he was running his fingers through my hair in a wonderful and distracting way.

"Are you sure about cutting your hair?" he asked, with a sigh that tickled across my temple.

"Yes. But I'll keep it long enough for you to play with." That seemed like a definite necessity of a sudden. "I was never planning to cut it short enough to look like a boy anyway."

"You wouldn't look like a boy no matter what you did to your hair. Trust me."

That set me off blushing.

Even though my ripped shoe let us steal a couple of hours, we couldn't sit out in the orchard forever. We *did* care about a few other things, and my sisters were going to be wearing through their slippers. Eventually we had to get up to go back. He took my hands to help me to my feet. I didn't need the help but let him do it anyway. This led quite naturally into another interval of kissing, until Dastan kissed my neck and the curve of my cheek and whispered, "I love you," into my ear.

It wasn't exactly surprising, after the last two hours—or the last three months. But I was *so* glad. It almost scared me how glad. Which may be why I leaned back and smiled and said, "Is that your fact tonight?"

He laughed, put his hands around my waist and swung me around. "Yes. That is my unique, very important fact tonight." He set me down again. "Is it too obvious?"

"A little. I'll let it by though." I leaned in again, tightening my arms around his shoulders. "Know why?"

"Tell me."

"Because I love you too."

On that night, I swear I didn't even notice the magical forest.

~ ◆ ~ Part Three ~ ◆ ~

On the opposite side of the lake stood a splendid, brightly-lit castle, from whence resounded the joyous music...They rowed over there, entered, and each prince danced with the girl he loved.

Jacob and Wilhelm Grimm

~ ◆ ~

On some days, I could almost forget that we weren't just dancing for fun. Almost—because inevitably something would remind me of the higher stakes of the game we were playing. Maybe my feet would be particularly sore; though that happened less and less as the year went on and we all got used to the endless dancing. Or some nights the enchanted forest would be unusually persuasive, tempting in the ease and freedom and escape it promised, and I'd be left shaken from trying to ignore its siren call. Most often, Father would stare at us especially hard and my stomach would twist in fear, and defying him wouldn't seem like fun at all.

Then during the thirty-eighth champion, we were reminded that we had another potential enemy to consider.

The thirty-eighth champion lingered in the dining hall on his second night, long after my sisters and I were all back in our bedroom in the evening. Though it was easier to drug drunken champions, it was irritating to have to wait for him. We combed our hair and chose dresses and tried to start getting ready without looking like we were doing it.

Marj appeared in the middle of our bedroom in her usual cloud of pink sparkles and gold hearts, and suddenly the room smelled like an herb garden. There was a universal sigh. We were already impatient to get below, none of us ever wanted to deal with Marj, and it was going to take forever to get the sparkles out of our blankets. She shot them all over the room.

Fortunately, Marj spoke over our sighs and probably didn't hear them. "My dear girls, don't you think you're taking matters a bit far?" It was so like her to start mid-conversation.

Vira curtsied and said, "Good evening, Godmother." We all dipped down into curtsies as well, as Vira asked, "To what do we owe the honor?"

"It's this business of champions," Marj said, plopping heavily down on Laina's bed; I saw Laina grimace. "I understand you've been getting rid of them."

"I'm afraid we can't discuss that," Vira said.

"Oh no, of course not, I quite understand," Marj said, nodding as vigorously as her wings were fluttering. "One simply can't discuss the *details* of magical compulsion. To look at it in a general way—well, my dears, you do know one of you has to marry a champion eventually."

I knew no such thing. I denied that idea wholeheartedly.

"There's no need to prolong this *too* long, you know," Marj continued. "Eventually one of the champions must break the spell and marry one of you. You understand that?"

We should have all just said yes immediately. Half of us *did* say yes, but everyone hesitated first and no one was enthusiastic, and Marj saw through it with an unusual degree of perception.

She looked around at us with widening eyes. "You *don't* understand, do you? Just what do *you* think you're doing when you go through the gate?"

Vira tried to halt that line of thought. "As I said, we can't discuss—"

"That's only valid if you're heading the right direction! If you're straying down the wrong path—oh, my dears, you simply must let me know what's going on so that I can guide you down the right way! I don't *want* to interfere, though if I must to avert disaster…"

The possibilities of just what Marj might do if she decided to really interfere were appalling. Good Fairies look immensely silly with their sparkles and their fluttering, but they're immensely powerful too. They can bring down empires.

Vira and Mina were exchanging glances, and I could see when a decision was reached, even if I wasn't entirely sure what the decision was. Vira nodded slightly, and immediately after, Mina approached Marj.

She sat down on the edge of the bed next to the Good Fairy and took her hand. "We *do* have a secret, Godmother. And if we were to tell it to you...you wouldn't tell Father? Would you?"

Several of my sisters stirred, clearly on the verge of protest. Vira shot them a sharp look and shook her head.

"Oh, no, no, my dear!" Marj said, pressing her free hand against her large chest. "I never tell maiden secrets. It wouldn't be proper. Consider me bound by the secrecy of the confessional."

"You promise?" Mina persisted. "You swear on the Fairy Queen?"

Marj's eyes widened. "Now where did you ever—"

"You *do* swear?" Mina said quickly. "We can trust you absolutely?"

"Yes, of course, dear, I swear on the Fairy Queen that I won't breathe a word of your little secret. Not a *word*."

Mina exhaled, apparently relieved. "Well then. When we went through the Gate, we met twelve princes. And you remember of course how you always wanted us to marry princes?"

I twitched. Yes, I was pretty far gone on Das, no doubt of that, but marriage was a whole other idea...I kept my mouth shut. Of course Mina was just talking for Marj's benefit. Of course.

Marj looked troubled too. "Yes, dear, under certain circumstances..."

"So we met these twelve princes, and it turns out they're enchanted," Mina continued. "All we have to do is keep dancing with them, and that will lift their curse—"

"Oh no, *no!*" Marj yanked her hand away and rose a foot off the bed, wings flapping madly. "My poor girls, you're so obviously confused!"

"We are not," Talya protested.

Marj clasped her hands together. "Let me explain. It's *men* who rescue *girls*. Not the other way around. That's the—"

Way Things Are Done, I thought, a beat before Marj said it aloud. Out of the corner of my eye I saw Laina make a sudden movement, only to have her arm caught by Vira. Laina glared at her and subsided.

Mina wasn't standing next to me anymore, so there was no one to grab my arm before I said, "Why is it so important to follow the Way Things Are Done anyway? Why can't anyone do anything new?"

Marj's eyes widened and her mouth dropped open in horror. She fluttered away from the bed and over to me, putting one plump hand on my forehead. "Oh my dear, do you feel feverish? Do you have any pain? You look tired."

"Of course I'm tired," I said, pulling away. "I dance every night."

"Yes, that's true," Marj said, biting her lip. "I think you should get a *great deal* of rest during the day. You're obviously not thinking clearly. To ask me why you should do Things the Way—why, you may as well ask me why one can't wear white in December!"

I so wanted to. But I was afraid she'd collapse from the shock and insist on staying with us for a month until she recovered.

"Don't worry, Godmother, I'm sure she's just tired," Vira said. "And we all understand the situation *perfectly* now." She looked around the room at the rest of us, expression pointed. "Don't we?"

The responses were quicker this time, everyone on cue. Even I grumbled an affirmative.

"Well..." Marj subsided somewhat, sinking back onto the bed. "If you're quite sure..."

"Yes, Godmother, clearly we'll have to marry one of the champions," Vira continued. "Of course, you also always taught us that a princess should be very particular."

Mina nodded with enthusiasm. "So there's really no need to rush, after all."

"And curses in stories go on for months," I ventured. "Sometimes years."

"That is true," Marj said, though she sounded doubtful. "It wouldn't look right to have a champion succeed *too* quickly."

We all fervently agreed aloud that it wouldn't look right at all.

"Though if it takes too long, I may have to give a bit of a helpful nudge to the best candidate…"

"Oh, but not for a long time," Mina said quickly. "We wouldn't want to inconvenience you, and of course, there's no hurry."

Marj floated over to Mina and patted her cheek. "My dear, it is *never* an inconvenience for me to help my dear goddaughters. All the same, I am glad it occurred to me that a properly long curse will greatly increase the prestige of the eventual success, if you see what I mean."

I sort of did. I had no intention of asking for clarification.

"And I'm so *very* glad that we had this little chat. My mind is quite relieved." Marj clasped her hands together, sparkles taking on a positively blinding brightness. "You just go on being good girls, and I'm sure a happy ending is waiting!" With that, she vanished, leaving a pile of sparkles and hearts on the rug below where she'd been hovering.

All over the room, girls slumped onto beds and into chairs. Dealing with Marj was exhausting.

Laina stepped up to the rug with its pile of sparkles and hearts, picked it up by the corners with an expression of disgust, and shook the mess into the nearby fireplace.

"Wait, I'm not sure that's—" Mina began, already too late. A burst of greasy smoke shot out of the fireplace. "A good idea," she finished.

It smelled like some particularly nasty herb, and made us all cough.

"Sorry," Laina muttered.

Much perfume was worn that night.

Even with our above-ground worries, we were still having a wonderful time below-ground. No one agreed with Marj's opinion about the unsuitably of our princes as romantic possibilities. Between the twenty-fifth and the forty-second champion, Sasia paired off with Darnell, Laina with Dacien, and Nila with Dagan. I don't expect you to remember half of this; sometimes I had to stop and think about it. Vira fell in love with Daylin, and I was thrilled for her. I was thrilled for all of them. I was immensely in favor of love. Love, romance, it was all splendid.

At least, until Talya fell in love with Dathan.

I held my tongue and kept all my alarmed thoughts just thoughts, because if I had learned anything from stories it was that forbidden love inevitably wins out—or at least that people will go to great lengths trying to make it win out. I kept my mouth shut until I was alone in a boat with Das and then all my worries spilled over.

He waited patiently through a lot of semi-incoherent and definitely repetitive worry, and finally on the third, "And she's just too young!" he pointed out, "She did turn sixteen last month."

"That's still too young," I said obstinately. Sixteen might be a magic threshold for some people. Not for my baby sister.

"How many stories have you told about girls who are cursed on their sixteenth birthday, and find their true love in the process?"

"That's what Talya keeps saying. It's different. Those are stories." Never mind that our lives had been proceeding like a story. *This* was different.

"All right, but it happens to plenty of girls in the real world too." He frowned. "Well, not the curses, those are more unusual, but getting married at sixteen happens more often. Not that anyone mentioned marriage. Er, not that anyone is suggesting *not* getting married..."

I could have gone along with what was probably half-manufactured awkwardness and confusion, and he would have eventually made me laugh and we would have ended up by kissing, likely more than once. It was tempting. It was also distracting from the main point. "I still say she's too young. And why did she have to fall in love with *Dathan*?"

Das straightened up at that. "Hey, wait a minute, he doesn't deserve that tone of voice."

"No, I didn't mean—he's lovely, he's wonderful, except he's eight years older than she is! Why couldn't she have fallen for Damek? He's only eighteen." Not counting time spent cursed, anyway.

"First, be glad she didn't because he's gone and fallen in love with Mara so that plan wouldn't have worked. Second, because he's the sort who would think it's funny to say 'boo' to a girl in the dark. Dathan, on the other hand, is very good at talking Talya down when she gets upset about something."

I knew that. I knew all of that, and I knew that Damek, apart from his convenient age, was wrong in every other way for my timid sister. I felt no better. "It's just that...she's my little sister."

"She's the youngest; she's *everyone's* little sister."

"I know, but...she's *mine*. She's always been the one I watch out for." She was the only one who had ever needed me that way. My only other younger sisters were Rayna and Mara, and as twins they had always banded together. "I practically got started telling stories by telling them to Talya."

That's when he stopped rowing and came to join me on my seat.

"We have to get to the castle," I protested.

"We'll get there," he said, putting his arm around me. "But if you're making emotional storytelling references, this must be serious."

I let my head drop onto his shoulder. "I just—I *worry*."

"Yes. I've noticed."

I gave his chest a shove for that—a light one. You don't push too hard when you're sitting in a boat over magical, acidic water. "If Vira feels this way about all of us, she's been incredibly restrained."

"Well, she is, isn't she? Listen, it's going to be all right. Really. Watch Talya and Dathan together for a while. They really do…fit. And you don't have to worry about her with him. I'd vouch for all my brothers that they wouldn't set out to break a girl's heart, but if there was any of us I'd say it was especially unlikely for—aside from me— it's Dathan."

"Very reassuring," I said, with a sigh.

I didn't want to admit it, but it actually was. We got to the castle, not too late (although we may have been delayed just a smidge more by a kiss or three), and I watched Talya and Dathan. Not just that night, others too, and I did eventually end up reassured. They fit, somehow. The more I watched them together, the better I felt about it. Of course, I think that's how people became reconciled to my mother marrying my father, and we saw how that turned out; still, the parallel wasn't really there, and it wasn't fair to Dathan to try to force a comparison. And my reasons for worrying to begin with were very different too.

I had always been the one who looked after Talya, but circumstances had changed that dynamic as we went below. You can't look after someone in a separate boat, or while you're off dancing with different partners. Or, if I'm being honest, when you're very distracted by your own partner. Dathan had already been stepping into the breach. And Talya, much as it gave me a peculiar pang to admit it, was not as young as I usually thought of her as being.

I got reconciled to it all in the end, but honestly, I've no idea how mothers handle this sort of thing. It made me wonder what our mother would have done.

Chapter Seventeen

Our fifty-third champion turned out to be one of my favorites. Possibly my absolute favorite, depending on how I choose to qualify the last one. Champion #53 caused one of the very few times I ever laughed during supper with my father.

Like most of our champions, I saw him for the first time when we came in for supper. He was already sitting at the table by Father. I promptly classified him as one of the Well-Meaners. They were the ones who smiled at us when we came in. The Greed-ers didn't pay much attention to us, and the Cattle-Buyers leered.

This champion smiled, and when the court politely rose to their feet, he tried to do the same. Instead, there was a spectacular tripping that made my trip and ripped shoe look graceful. I have no idea how a person trips over a chair he's trying to stand up from, but he managed it. Then he picked himself up without a trace of embarrassment or any indication that he felt this was out of the ordinary, which was even funnier.

My sisters and I got to our seats with tightly clamped lips and a lot of pink cheeks. Father, whose mouth may have twitched a little, introduced #53 as Sir Richard of Ryvideau, and then went through his usual speech about the slippers and proof and so on.

Richard got back into his seat without incident, and food was served. There were five courses. He knocked over his drink three times (which let me see he was drinking water, so it wasn't *that* kind of clumsiness), dropped a chicken leg, and misplaced four napkins, in succession. He stayed amiable and unperturbed through it all, which made me wonder, first, if this was normal for him, and second, if so, how he could possibly have ever become a knight. By the time the fourth napkin disappeared, my jaw hurt from my efforts not to laugh— and I'd already lost the fight more than once.

There were many explosions of laughter and exclamations along the lines of "If he'd lost another napkin I would have just *died*" when we got back to our room.

We had got ourselves back into our 'solemn, unassailable and anonymous' mode by the time Richard came to the room. Maintaining our composure was a challenge when he tripped coming in the door. Our doorway did not have a raised lintel. He caught himself before he actually fell, and the rest of us caught ourselves before we lost all control—though I did hear a giggle from Talya's direction.

Father came directly after Richard, made a routine speech wishing this new champion luck (though even Father seemed doubtful this time), and locked the door. Then we all stood around looking at each other. There was a certain type of champion who got very nervous when all twelve of us stared at him. Richard was definitely that type, and we took whatever advantage we could.

After a long silence, he scratched behind one ear and asked, "So…what happens now?"

"Now is when you try to find out what our secret is," I said, as though perhaps he just needed reminding.

"Ah. Right. Of course." He nodded vigorously. "Um…any advice?"

"We can't help you; we're on the opposite side, remember?" Mina pointed out.

"Yeah. Right…"

I think he looked the most woebegone of any of our champions (and we had had some woeful ones). The amiable clumsiness and the utter confusion was surprisingly endearing. I don't mean he was any competition for Das—just that it made me want to pat his head and straighten his shirt collar for him.

I gave up the inscrutable part of my appearance and plopped down on the edge of my bed. "Why are you here anyway?" I asked, deciding to give him amiability back in return for his. "You don't seem like the type to have much to do with evil curses."

"Yeah, well." He scratched behind the opposite ear. "It just seemed, you know, awfully sad, nice girls caught under a curse. I thought it was a chance to do something really good. Important."

Definitely a Well-Meaner. "You must rescue girls in distress all the time," I said. "Isn't that part of the job description for knights?"

"Oh, sure. Rescuing distressed girls. All the time." The vigorous nod was in play again.

"That must be a relief to distressed girls everywhere," Laina said in her driest tones.

I shot her an *oh, leave him alone* look, realizing only as I did it that apparently I'd adopted Richard. Well, what was the harm?

Richard, meanwhile, was rambling on. "See, I thought, it can't be that impossible to find out a secret, right? No one mentioned fighting monsters or anything. And people seem to like telling me things." He looked around hopefully.

I remembered our first champion, who had said something rather similar in substance about girls telling him secrets. It had been entirely different in tone, and the tone really did change everything.

"We're not going to tell you anything," Vira said, not unkindly but definitively.

"Oh." Richard's face fell. He picked up his spirits and his chin with a visible effort, and said, "You know, you don't *seem* like you're under a curse and forced to go off dancing with demons. You don't seem upset enough."

"You have a great deal of experience with cursed people?" Laina said, crossing her arms and ignoring my looks in her direction.

"No, it's just that I…spend time at an inn. You meet lots of people that way. You sort of get a, you know, feeling." Richard waved a hand expressively at that, and knocked a vase off of Mina's dressing table. "Oops." He looked down at the shattered pottery by his feet. "Sorry."

"Don't mention it," Mina said, the corner of her mouth quirking. She bent down to sweep it up. "Sasia, why don't you get our guest something to drink?"

It *was* time we got going below. Not to mention, rendering him unconscious would protect the rest of our belongings. Sasia quickly got her jug of drugged wine and a cup.

"Here, it's very good," Sasia said, pouring the wine.

That's when amiable Richard showed the first signs of causing actual trouble. "Oh no, I don't drink wine," he said, shaking his head. "It makes me clumsy."

More than one giggle escaped us at that comment.

"Um, clumsier," he amended, with a sheepish grin.

Sasia stared at him, clutching the full cup. "...are you sure?"

Giggles or not, we all saw the problem. We had been relying on the wine to keep the champions unaware. If one actually refused it... None had so far, and we didn't have a reliable back-up plan. There were some champions that I wouldn't have minded hitting over the head, but it didn't seem right with this one.

Richard seemed unaware of our perturbation. "No, no wine for me."

"I really think you ought to," Sasia persisted, trying to hand it to him.

With anyone else, he would have just refused to take it and she would have gone on holding it. With Richard, it ended up fumbled between them, and inevitably spilled across the floor.

"Sorry," he said again.

"Don't mention it," Sasia said, voice grimmer than Mina's, and knelt to mop up the spill.

"So…I suppose there must be something I ought to be doing, as a champion," Richard said, glancing around the room. "Investigating, like."

He began walking down the center aisle between our two rows of beds. None of us was surprised when he tripped before he got to the far wall. He stumbled over a small rug and took a more dramatic spill, plummeting towards the nearest bed. He grabbed onto one of the bedposts to steady himself. Unfortunately, the bedpost slid out in front of him, causing him to pitch forward with a yelp.

You see, he had fallen into Vira's bed. The bed had rolled back, as it did so easily, and revealed the trapdoor beneath.

We all converged, in a tangle of exclamations along the lines of, "that bed has always slid easily," and "oh dear, are you all right?" and "don't worry, we'll slide it back." Maybe we thought we could distract him.

It didn't work. At the center of our flurried cluster, he was staring down at the trapdoor under his feet. "It's a *door*. There's another way out of here!" He looked up at us, with a slightly wild look in his eyes. "The king locks the door—and this must be how you—that means—are there demons down there?"

"No," I said, "there aren't any demons."

"There might be demons," Vira said. "Why don't you *have a drink*? It'll calm you down, and then we'll talk."

Vira looked meaningfully at Sasia, who hurriedly ran off to the other side of the room; she came back with the cup, and a new jug. He still looked confused, but this time he drank the wine.

"So you 'ave a trapdoor…" Richard said, slurring the words already. "But your father…and tha' must mean…"

We didn't find out what he thought it meant, because his head drooped and his eyes closed. There was a universal exhalation of relief. Immediate crisis averted.

It's very possible that hapless, well-meaning Richard had come closer to our secret than any of the fifty-two champions who came before him. We didn't really know. All the others had drunk the wine and fallen asleep before we started getting ready to go below; none of them had ever seen us using the trapdoor. We didn't know if any of them had found it at other times. Some of them had had the sense to search our room during the day (though a surprising number didn't bother), and the trapdoor wasn't so well hidden that some of them couldn't have found it. If any had, they'd never mentioned it to us. Secrets within secrets.

Vira brushed her hands off on her skirt, a symbolic gesture since they weren't dirty. "So much for the immediate problem, although if he refuses the wine tomorrow—"

"We have a problem tonight too," Sasia said, sounding unhappy. "That was the wrong wine."

"What do you mean it was the wrong wine?" Laina demanded, turning to stare at Sasia. "He's unconscious."

Sasia hefted the jug she was carrying. "This is the Third Night wine. He spilled all the First Night wine; I was almost out and I was going to mix more tomorrow, so I didn't have anything to give him except Third Night wine."

"So he's not actually asleep, he's just very groggy." I snapped my fingers in front of his face. "Sir Richard? *Sir Richard.*"

He stirred, and half-opened his eyes. "Sam. Mostly go by Sam."

I thought about the phrase "Sir Sam" and just had to ask, "You're not really a knight, are you?"

I had to lean in to hear his mumbled response. "Nah, I work in an inn…th'Nightingale in Ryvideau…can't tell a king that."

"Of course you can," I said. "Perfectly respectable work." Every bit as good as being, say, a wandering minstrel.

Over our heads, a debate was on. "Can't we just leave him here anyway?" Laina asked. "He's still not in any condition to follow us."

"He isn't now, but this isn't as strong as the First Night wine. If he starts to come out of it in a few hours, he could try to follow us." Sasia had set down the jug, and was twisting her hands together. "You know he'll fall and kill himself on those stairs; there isn't even a railing."

"We'll have to take him down to the tunnel tonight," I said. There were champions I had been tempted to push down those stairs. Richard—Sam wasn't one of them.

"I don't know if we can do that either," Laina countered. "Can you imagine trying to walk this man down stairs? He'll still fall, and take us with him."

In a way it sounded silly, but it was a genuine concern. Those stairs were high and steep, open on one side with a long drop down to stone.

Mina had her most thoughtful expression on. "What we really need is to take him out of the equation. I don't want to rely on his balance on those stairs at all. We'd need to be able to just carry him straight out."

Laina rolled her eyes. "Oh sure, that's a plan. That would work fine if we had that kind of arm strength, which we don't."

Sam wasn't very big, but any adult man would have been beyond our ability to carry down stairs. By now we were good at hauling unconscious champions over to the bed in the adjoining room, but that was with several of us working together. The stairs were not wide enough for more than two of us to wrangle a third person, and there were no two of us who could handle it.

"We don't have that kind of strength," Mina said, "but we know people who do."

There was a moment of thoughtful silence.

"Can we *do* that?" Talya asked, wide-eyed.

Mina nodded decisively. "I can't think of any reason why not, if we open the Gate for them. We know other people can go through it. Father did."

Our princes had never gone farther than the shore with us. We had never taken them through the Gate because it had always seemed best to keep the two worlds as far apart as possible. We didn't know what would happen if one evening Father came to the bedroom and found twelve men there; it wouldn't be anything good. He must have guessed that we were dancing with someone, but that still would give him far more information than we wanted him to have.

Under the circumstances, it seemed like time to take a risk. It was that or leave poor clumsy Sam to fall down the steps or stay and be killed by Father. None of us could figure out another way to get a man who tripped on flat ground down steep stairs.

For modesty's sake, we dragged Sam to the other side of Vira's bed, where he couldn't see the rest of the room. Then we changed into our evening clothes and went through the trapdoor, the Gate and the forest. At the shore, we explained the situation to our princes.

"So...you don't think he can manage a flight of stairs?" Damek said dubiously.

Laina snorted. "We've seen him trip three times so far, in much less trip-worthy circumstances."

"He's very nice," I put in, "just...balance-challenged."

The plan unfortunately required two extra trips through the forest, and an extra trip up 366 steps.

"You climb these every night?" Das said when we were two-thirds of the way up. "*After* dancing?"

"You get used to it," I said. "The forest is worse."

Up in our bedroom, Sam was still sprawled where we had left him. Das grasped his wrists while Daemyn took his ankles.

Sam groggily opened his eyes as he was hoisted into the air. "Are you demons?"

Das looked at me, eyebrows raised. "What have you been telling him?"

I shook my head. "I swear he came up with that one on his own."

"Sure, we're demons," Das said, "so don't move."

This turned out to be the wrong thing to say. Sam started struggling. "I don't *want* to be carried off by demons!"

"I take it back, we're not demons!" Das protested, as he and Daemyn tried to keep their hold on Sam. "Look, no horns!"

"I don't want to be carried off to be beheaded either!" Sam wailed.

"We're even less likely to be working for *him* than we are to be demons," Daemyn said, hanging onto a flailing foot.

Sam may have been balance-challenged and drugged, but it still took six princes to hold him down.

"Are we sure we don't want to just let him fall down the stairs?" Damek asked, out of breath as he hung onto Sam's arm.

I knelt down next to the still-twitching champion. "We're trying to help you, Sam. My name's Lyra; I'm the ninth princess, and I *promise* you, no one is going to behead you, and no one around here is a demon. Just trust us. We're going to help you get back to your inn."

He stared at me out of very wide eyes. Terror seemed to be mitigating the effect of the drug. "The Nightingale."

"Right." I nodded. "The Nightingale. Go back to your inn and don't get mixed up in curses again."

There was a little more flailing and a definite amount of cursing, but somehow we got Sam down the stairs and dropped on the far side of the secondary gate. And then we finally got down to the business of the night—dancing.

It was a long and particularly exhausting night. Even if that was Sam's fault (somewhat indirectly), he was still my favorite champion.

Chapter Eighteen

Daemyn proposed to Mina during the 56th champion's tenure. To no one's surprise, she accepted. Vira and Daylin followed with an engagement swiftly after, during the 58th. Maybe there was something in the air, because Drina and Dallon paired off while the 62nd champion was having his try, and the final romantic hold-outs, Cacia and Darshan, became a couple a week later, during the 65th champion. Two days after that, I was the first one to wear my shoes out; it wasn't as early as the night I had ripped my shoe, but it did mean Das and I got to sit on the sidelines for a while and watch everyone else dance.

"It's kind of funny, isn't it?" I watched the couples twirl by, tucked my feet up under my skirt on the bench, and leaned my head on Das' shoulder. "Everyone pairing off so neatly."

"Much better than having everyone pair off messily." He reached around my shoulders to tuck a stray strand of hair back behind my ear, then kept his arm there.

"Doesn't it seem convenient? Twelve sisters just happen to be the perfect matches with twelve brothers; what's the likelihood of that? You'd think at least some of us would have turned out not to suit each other."

"Should I be taking this personally?"

"What? Oh—no, of course not. I didn't mean *us*."

"Reassuring," he said, and kissed the top of my head.

He was reassured, while I was trying not to be unsettled by another *us*. Don't misunderstand me; this was an *us* I loved being part of. It was a completely different us than the us that eleven sisters made. But still, another us—another we. Some day, I just wanted to be *me*.

I pushed that unsettling thought down for the moment, and returned to my original unsettling thought. "Anyway, it just seems too convenient, that everyone matched up."

"If everyone's happy, why question it?"

I wasn't sure why I *was* questioning it. "It just feels...arranged. Like it must have been planned. And isn't it a little disturbing to think that something like that could be arranged? It makes me feel like we're all pawns."

This time he kissed my temple. "Seems to me that there are always other forces going on around us; maybe we know about them, and maybe we don't. But in chess, even pawns can move on their own." He tugged lightly on a strand of hair hanging across my shoulder. "And if a pawn tries hard enough, it can become a queen. In a metaphorical sense."

"If I have to marry an oldest son to make it literal, metaphorical will be just fine."

"Also reassuring."

We stole a few kisses then, and I gave up my philosophical, metaphysical, metaphorical musings for the moment.

"You know," I said at length, "we haven't done facts yet tonight."

"Mmm, true. You first. You always make me go first."

"I do not," I protested. "Although it was your idea to begin with. But fine, I'll go first tonight." I was really only protesting for form's sake. I already had my fact ready to go. "I decided I want to work at an inn someday."

I felt his shoulder shift. "Point to you, I didn't expect that one. Why an inn?"

"Remember Sam, the clumsy champion?"

Das laughed. "Not an easy one to forget."

"Right, and he worked at an inn. Which made me think about it, and it seems like a perfect way to meet lots of people, who would know *lots* of stories."

"That's one way to go about finding stories," he agreed. "Or you could travel and visit inns. You'd hear even more stories that way."

I had thought of that too. I had also thought of problems. "In theory, but there aren't many good ways for a young woman to travel alone." It happened in stories all the time, of course. It just wasn't practical in the real world.

He tugged my hair again. "I didn't say alone."

"True. Plenty of time to think about that, though. So what's your fact tonight?" I asked, which was a complete and deliberate attempt to change the subject. He hadn't said alone; I had. It was that *us* and *me* business again.

The subject change worked, getting him off on something about fencing. I listened and made the appropriate comments, and meanwhile continued worrying over the distinction between *I* and *we*.

It wasn't a worry for just the one night. In between thinking about Father and champions and curses and mind-twisting forests, I somehow found time to worry about *this* too, about something that should have been making me happy (and it was) but had complications too.

Mina always said that she could read my mood from the stories I told. Most of the time I thought she was imagining it, because Mina liked to find information in everything. Sometimes I wondered.

Let me tell you a story I told one evening during this time—it was the second night of the 73rd champion—and you can decide if it means anything.

It was a story about once upon a time in a mountain village, a small place where there lived simple people. They knew their mountains, they knew their business of goatherding and farming, and they knew each other. They knew very little else of the wide world. In this village there lived a girl who all her life had known what the rest of her life was likely to be. Her parents raised goats and a few crops like everyone else, and she did her part to help. Someday she would marry the boy who lived next door, and they would have their own cottage and their own goats and plot of farmland, and so would their children after them. It wasn't that she had to marry the boy next door, but they had lived and played and grown together all their lives; she had always expected she would marry him one day, in a theoretical sort of way. One spring morning when they were both sixteen, he offered her a cluster of blue mountain flowers and she looked into his blue eyes and the theory became the very real and she knew that she didn't only expect to marry him, she very much wanted to—someday.

It was a fall day when her sweetheart asked her to marry him, and he would have described it as a perfect and beautiful day. It was also a day when the birds were in the village.

The village had as many birds as any other place, in the normal way, but once a year a great flock of brilliant-hued blue birds would settle into the village. They flew in from the north, settled for a few days, and then flew away again to the south. They were never seen any other part of the year, and if they made the opposite journey in the spring, they didn't pass this particular mountain village on the way.

The girl's sweetheart felt that it was a magical time, a time of change, and so the perfect time to suggest a marriage. He was wrong. Though he knew the girl very well—better than anyone else, perhaps— this was one thing he did not understand. For the girl, the days the birds were in the village were more than a time of magic and change. They were a time of longing. They were a time of wondering what else there might be in the world beyond her little village, of wondering what the birds had seen, and what they would go on to see, what strange sights and strange places and strange people.

If he had asked any other week in the long calendar of the year, she would have said yes at once and been glad. But he asked while the birds were in the village, and she thought of all that she had never seen. She looked ahead at what her future would be if she said yes, knew all that she would never see, and looked into her sweetheart's blue eyes and said no. And she resolved that this year, as she had longed every year for all the years she could remember, she was going to follow the birds.

Her sweetheart asked what she hoped to find, but she couldn't answer. If she had known the answer, she wouldn't have needed to go.

He tried to understand. For his own part, he knew his place was in his mountains, and had no desire to go beyond them. He also knew that there was no one else in the village he could ever love as he loved her, and so he offered to wait for her. He asked her if she could at least promise to return, and to marry him then, when she had seen whatever she had gone to seek.

It hurt her to say it, but she refused even to promise that. She tried to explain, that she wasn't only going to see the world; she was going to find out who she was too. Though she loved him with all of her that she was, she had to go find out what else of her there could be. It might be that he wouldn't love whatever else of her she found.

Her sweetheart may have been a simple goatherd, but he wasn't stupid. He asked if perhaps, also, the part of her she found might not love him as she now did.

The girl hadn't wanted to say this, but yes, this too was true.

He knew he couldn't force her to stay, and that he wouldn't want to if he could. When the birds flew out of the village that year, the girl went too. She had no destination in mind, so she simply followed the birds, taking the road south because they had taken it before her. She took a few supplies and a little money, and set out to see what might be seen.

The girl came out of the mountains and into the plains below, and she saw flowers and animals and places such as she had never heard of or imagined. Because it was all new to her, it seemed wondrous indeed. The people were strange to her too; though they spoke the same language, some of the words they used were new, some of their customs were different, and many of their belongings, to a girl from a small and remote village, seemed luxury. They, of course, felt that their flowers and animals and they themselves could not be more ordinary, and could not understand how she found them wonderful.

The girl did odd work here and there, watching cattle for a few days or helping a housewife with laundry or baking. Though it wasn't always easy, she managed to make her way. She didn't seek a particular route and she had no destination, yet very often when she stopped for the night, whether in a town or in a wood, she would see at least one blue bird, the same kind of bird she had followed from her village. When she saw the birds, she felt that perhaps she was traveling as she was meant to go.

After weeks or months of wandering, the girl found herself in a deep wood; had she known how wide and dark it was when she entered, she never would have gone in. She had to lie down for the night still beneath the trees, and even the sight of a blue bird on a branch near her was scant comfort among the whispering leaves of the dark forest.

On her second day in the forest she came to a fork in the path she was following. One road was clear and smooth; the other small and overgrown. A blue bird was sitting on the overgrown path, and after a long moment of hesitating, she turned her steps towards the small trail. The trail grew more and more narrow, the forest more and more dense, until she regretted entirely the foolish notion that had sent her this way. By then, she was not even sure she was still on a trail, and she couldn't turn back because she doubted she could find the way.

She pressed on as best she could, until at last she found herself blocked by a crumbling stone wall. Even crumbling, it rose far above her head, covered in ivy. She turned to the right to follow the edge of the wall, thinking to go around. Instead, she found a wrought iron gate, and when she brushed her hand against it, it swung silently open at her touch.

Even a simple girl from a small mountain village heard stories. She knew an enchantment when she saw it, and being a simple village girl, she felt she had no business getting mixed up in something like this. But she was a village girl who had been possessed with curiosity about the world, and so she couldn't resist at least looking though the gate. She saw a castle, in the same state as the wall, overgrown with greenery. The forest was doing its best to take the castle back to itself, and it appeared that the castle's efforts to survive against it were failing.

The place prickled with magic. Even more than that, it gave off a sense of sadness, until the girl wept as she looked at the castle, without knowing why. The sadness seemed the most centered on a single tower that rose up above the rest, and as the girl looked at that tower through tear-filled eyes, she walked through the gate and began picking her way across the overgrown lawn. She didn't know what she was going to do, but the sadness of the castle cried out for someone to do something, and there was no one else there to do anything.

The front door of the castle opened to her touch as the gate had, and she made her way inside. The forest had grown up inside the castle too, entire trees stretching up towards the sky in rooms that had lost their roofs, ivy covering the walls and flowers blooming in the cracks. She found a staircase leading up to the highest tower, and carefully made her way up it, hoping that the stone had fought off the forest enough to survive under her weight.

She climbed through leaves and over ivy tendrils to the very top of the tower, where there was a single round room. The ivy stretched across the floor and up over a bed in the center of the room, half-covering a beautiful young man lying on the bed. She could see the leaves rise and fall as he breathed and knew that he must be enchanted. She saw the gold crown on his head and knew that he must be a prince.

She leaned over his face and knew what must be done to free him and his castle of their spell. She had heard those stories too, and perhaps she would have known even if she hadn't.

She had never kissed anyone except her mountain sweetheart, but now she leaned down and kissed the sleeping prince.

There was a great flash of light and the world thundered and shook. The girl fell across the prince and felt his arms close around her. She caught a brief glimpse of ivy snaking away from him and closed her eyes as the world went on shaking.

When the world was still and she opened her eyes, all the greenery was gone and the stones of the room gleamed. She could hear sounds from below suggesting the bustle of a great deal of human life, and she didn't need to look to know that the forest had been banished and the castle come awake again. The prince, too, was awake, and thanked her for delivering him from his long curse. He took her hands in his and asked her if, as his deliverer, she would also consent to be his wife and his queen.

She looked at the prince, and then looked longer at the blue bird sitting on the windowsill. She thought that surely this must be as it was meant to be, that surely this must be the sort of adventure she had been seeking to find, and so she said yes.

The girl from the mountain village found herself swept up in the life of the castle. Everyone was kind to her and hailed her as their rescuer. The prince showered her with gifts—a sapphire necklace, dozens of dresses in cobalt, azure and indigo. As she waited for her wedding day, she told herself again and again that plainly this was meant to be.

Then one day she asked the prince if he had ever tasted the morning air on a mountaintop on a winter day, and he could only look quizzical and guess that it must be very cold. Another day she asked him if he knew of a small blue flower that grew wild to the north, and the next day he flooded her room with blue lilacs, which were beautiful and elegant and not the right flower at all.

And finally one day, the day before she was to be married, she stood on a balcony in the castle, looked at the blue bird sitting on the railing, and thought of the soft blue sky arching over the mountain peaks, of the deep blue water of a mountain spring, and of the lovely blue of her sweetheart's eyes. She felt a sadness surpassing even what she had felt looking at the ruined tower, and knew she could do only one thing.

She left the prince and the castle and its people behind, and made her way north again. She retraced her steps through the towns she had seen before, and followed the road into the mountains. On a fine spring day, she walked back into the village she had left behind. She went to her sweetheart, to tell him that the part of herself she had found loved him just as fiercely as the part she had already known.

The girl and her sweetheart were married, and they had their own cottage and their own goats and plot of farmland, and so did their children after them. For the rest of her life the girl told wonderful stories of the strange sights beyond their own tiny village, and how she had come to learn that sometimes it's not the wanting of something that matters most, but the knowing that you want it.

I always liked to think that the girl lived happily ever after, because she had done what she needed to do to make peace with her longing.

This was not a story I told to Das during this time. I don't know if he would have found it alarming or reassuring. Or maybe he would have found it to be neither. If he believed it was just a story—as I did, most of the time—there would be no reason to take it any particular way.

In a similar vein, Das still joined the musicians for a song or two some evenings, and I hadn't failed to notice that he was leaning much more to love songs in recent months. I could read into that clearly enough.

As to reading into my own stories...sometimes I began to feel that, in all the stories I told, I was really only telling my own story. When I felt like that, I wondered—about many things.

Chapter Nineteen

As the year went on and champions passed one by one, we fell into habits and routine. Increasingly the part of our lives that mattered was after sundown. After sundown, we'd defeat another champion, enter into a magical world, and go dancing with the men we loved. After we returned, often I would tell a story, to help us all relax after the music and the whirl and the excitement, until we were ready to sleep. Morning always came too soon, and we would sleepily make our way through our day, hardly waking up properly until it was evening again. The world above grew less and less important to us.

I wanted to believe that this gave our father less power over us. Surely if we lived less in his world, there was less he could do to us. He had less ability to hold us. Less ability to frighten us. It was only later, after mistakes had been made, that I realized we were giving him a different power. Or at least, a different opportunity. The less we lived in the world above, the less we paid attention to that world, and the more likely we were to somehow slip.

That realization came later. At the time, I was the happiest I had ever been. I had Das, and my sisters, and the prospect of freedom. I didn't have freedom yet, but with each day it seemed closer and closer, as though all I had to do was stretch my arm just a little farther and I'd be able to reach it—like the apple I had reached for one moonlit night, which had sent me tumbling back into Das' arms.

I still kept having moments, though. Moments that worried me, that warned me, that lurked underneath my happiness and told me trouble was coming. It wasn't trouble above, the obvious place for it; this was trouble below, which threatened just as surely to destroy everything that was making me so happy.

It was during the 81st champion that all those little glimmers of worry and hints of trouble finally came together—and the storm finally broke. It began harmlessly, even pleasantly. It was a normal enough evening, and Das and I were taking a long boat ride back—which meant that we had stopped somewhere in the middle of all the darkness to kiss. A strange place for it, maybe, but it wasn't as though we had many options for private moments. And you get used to it, after a few times.

At length, I shifted reluctantly away and said, "We probably should be getting back."

"Probably," he agreed. "Before we do, there's something I wanted to give you." He reached into a pocket of his coat and brought out a wooden box, dwarfed as it sat on his palm.

"What is that?" I asked, even though I already knew, or at least I suspected. Stomach clenching, I looked at the box with more wariness than delight.

Das didn't seem to see the wariness. He flipped open the box to reveal a gold ring, set with diamonds, and smiled at me. "Lyra, will you marry me?"

I looked away from the smile. I stared instead at the diamonds, which somehow sparkled even in the face of all that darkness. "I…don't know what to say."

"'Yes' would be fine. Direct, to the point, conveys the idea nicely."

"No."

A pause. "Well, I admit it isn't eloquent, but it would still do the job well enough and—"

"*No.*" I squeezed my eyes shut for a moment, and when I opened them again I finally looked at his face. I felt like the hope and the love in his eyes, tinged by just the first hint of uncertainty, were going to tear me in half. I struggled not to choke on the words. "I'm not saying yes because I'm saying…no. I can't marry you."

The hope was still trying to prevail. "I didn't mean *now*, of course, but after the curse ..."

I shook my head. "Not then either—I don't understand, we've *talked* about this."

"We've never talked about marriage." He put the ring away in his coat again, and most of the hope in his expression went with it.

"No, but..." I rubbed my palms on my knees, tried to figure out how to explain what I had thought he already knew. "I never meant to make you think—I thought you understood. I've told you, my whole life, I've just been one of my sisters. When this is finally all over, if it goes the way we want it to, I'll finally have a chance to just be *me*."

He drew in a breath, let it out again. "I'm not trying to stop you from being you."

"But I need to be me alone. Just me, by myself. Not Mina's sister, not my father's daughter..."

"Not my wife." His shoulders had risen defensively and his voice sounded bleak, with not a hint of the playfulness that was almost always there.

That scared me. I wanted to somehow fix it, to not hurt him, to make it all right again. If I could just make him understand... "Please believe me, it's not because of something about you, or about us. It's just me—I've never had a chance to be alone. I don't know who I am alone. And I want—I *need* a chance to find out who I am."

He dragged a hand though his hair. My fingers itched to straighten out the resulting rumple, but I couldn't reach through the uneasy tension between us. "I don't understand that; you know who you are."

"No, I don't, I only know who I am with my sisters, and most of my life I've spent pretending to be exactly like them. Sometimes I think I don't even know who I am when I'm not pretending."

"And yet you've told me dozens of ways you aren't your sisters." A frown deepened the corners of his mouth. "We haven't done tonight's exchange yet, by the way. I suppose we could just count 'not wanting to get married.'"

I was talking about self-discovery, and he was talking about a game. "Fine, so I know I like raspberry tarts. That's not what I mean—"

"It wasn't all raspberry tarts," he interrupted. "What do you think you need to find out that you don't already know?"

"I don't *know*, that's the whole point." I realized my fingers were tapping, and laced them together in my lap. If I couldn't be calm, I could at least be still. "You only see me down here. Up there, it's different. Our whole lives we've looked the same and acted the same—our own father can't tell us apart. *You* wouldn't be able to tell us apart."

"Maybe I wouldn't be able to tell Laina from Mina," he said quietly, looking at me through lowered eyes, "but I would always know you."

There was a long silence then. I stared at the darkness and tried to ignore the increasing blurriness of my vision. I knew what I was doing. I knew what I had to do.

"What if..." Das said, "what if you took whatever time you needed, to be by yourself, and then afterwards..."

I closed my wet eyes, throat aching. "No. I mean, maybe. And I do promise I won't just disappear. I'll tell you when I'm leaving and I'll tell you later what I find out. But I can't promise more than that. The whole point is that I don't know who I'm going to end up being. You might not want to marry whoever I become."

His voice was flat. "Or that girl you think you're going to turn into might not want to marry me."

I'd never heard him sound like that, and it terrified me to think what feelings had to be behind it. If I could just tell him he was wrong about that—but that wouldn't be *true*. "I don't know."

I wished this was only a story. Nothing hurts as much, when it's just a story.

"Are you thinking…that you might find someone else?"

My eyes snapped open to stare at him. "*No!* No, that's not it at all!" Finally, something I could answer the way he wanted me to.

His shoulders relaxed slightly then, and just a little of the hope came back into his dark eyes. "You know, I've been surrounded by eleven brothers my whole life. Why can't we go find out who we are together?"

My own momentary hope flickered out. If he could ask that, it was obvious I hadn't managed to explain anything, hadn't made this better for him at all. "Because then I wouldn't be finding out who I am alone," I whispered past the choking in my throat.

"Well." He looked away, nodded slowly. "That seems definitive. In that case, I don't suppose there's much else to say." He picked up the oars and we began moving again.

I watched him for a minute, while he steadily didn't look at me. It used to be Das who watched me, for weeks back while I was still imagining to myself that we were just friends. He had always been more sure of us, quicker than me to see how well we fit together. And didn't that prove I was right? That there was still more I needed to know before I could make a life decision?

Although I had figured some things out. "I do love you," I said softly. "So much."

"Just not enough, apparently," Das said, shoulders tight as he stroked the oars in choppy motions.

And then I got angry. I was *trying*. Maybe I wasn't succeeding very well, but I was trying to explain, to not hurt him, to make this as all right as a horribly wrong situation could be. Was he even trying to understand? "That's not fair. I keep telling you, it's *not about you*."

"It's me you're not marrying," he snapped, "that makes it about me."

I shook my head, wisps of blond hair flying. "That's not what I meant. Yes, of course, the situation is about you, but the reasons aren't and I can't help it and I'm *sorry* but I just can't!"

"You can do whatever you want to do and you obviously don't want—"

"Why did you have to do *this*?" I glared at him. "What possessed you to go and propose anyway? Everything was good, we were happy, there was no reason we had to even talk about this."

"Right, my fault, guess I just wanted some commitment. Some kind of future. What could I have been thinking?"

He had given up rowing again, but the boat was swaying from our movements. I grasped the sides of the boat, knuckles white. "I have no idea what you were thinking when you knew—I've told you, you *knew* that I wanted a chance to be free."

"I'm not trying to trap you!"

"It feels like a trap!"

His lips pressed together. "In that case," he said through a clenched jaw, "I am sorry for suggesting such a distasteful idea."

I already knew I shouldn't have said it. "That's not what I— you're just not going to like anything I say tonight." I was too frustrated to take it back. Besides, if trap was a strong word, it still wasn't an entirely inaccurate one.

"Should I remind you that you started out by not liking what I said?"

I crossed my arms and glowered at the darkness. "I just—I have nothing else to say, there's no point."

"Fine."

He resumed rowing, and we passed the rest of the mercifully short remaining trip in cold silence.

We were the last ones to arrive that night. I apparently hadn't kept anything off my face because I had barely stepped ashore—

without Das' help—before Mina came over to me, brow creased in worry.

"What is it?" she asked. "Something's wrong."

"*Nothing's* wrong," I said, too savagely.

Mina looked at Das. "What did you do?"

He spread his hands in denial. "Why assume it's my fault?"

"Because my sister is obviously upset."

"For that matter, so am I," Das retorted. "Can I get some sympathy? I'm the one whose heart got stepped on."

If it had been a normal lake, I would have pushed him into it. "You say that like I *wanted* to do it!" I wasn't quite angry enough to push him into the acid lake. "I keep telling you, it's not about how I feel about you. And you did start all of this."

"I proposed marriage, I don't see how that makes me the villain here!"

Mina frowned, a puzzled frown. "Didn't you know she didn't want to get married?"

I could have kissed her. "Thank you," I said to Mina, and to Das I said, "You see?"

He took a long breath. "No. Obviously I didn't know that. It has now been made abundantly clear. So, fine, just do whatever you want to do, it's obviously none of my business."

"Good. It isn't. And I will." I put my chin in the air, turned, and pushed past the crowd of my sisters to stride toward the trees.

Let the forest do its worst tonight. Whatever thoughts it gave me couldn't be more upsetting than the ones already spinning in my mind.

I had to wait for my sisters to catch up when I got to the Gate, but I led the way all through the tunnel and up the stairs. There was very little talking. Back in our bedroom, we all set about to change clothes, and I tried to ignore Vira, Talya and Mina gathered in whispered conference. It was harder to ignore Talya and Mina when they sidled up and sat on the foot of my bed, just as I was about to slide in beneath the quilt.

"Do you want to talk about it?" Mina asked.

"No." That seemed to be all I was saying tonight. No, no, no.

"Would you maybe feel better if you told a story?" Talya ventured.

"No." And then I abruptly reversed direction. "On second thought, yes."

I had thought of just the story. "The Maiden Without Hands," it was called. It was a strange little tale, and it had always had some rather troubling aspects to it. Usually I was willing to tell it essentially as the book I read it in had told it. Tonight, I was in a very special sort of mood.

The story began with a miller, who once upon a time lost all of his money and so made a deal with a wizard for riches. It's a funny thing about riches; wave them in front of some people and they lose their minds entirely. The miller met the wizard one day when he was out in the woods. The wizard promised him great wealth in exchange for that which was behind his house.

The miller had probably lost his money on account of being a great fool. The cryptic phrasing of the agreement should have been a warning to even a minor fool. If there is anything that stories have taught me, it's that you never, ever, ever make an agreement without being absolutely sure on what you're agreeing to, and sometimes not even then. And don't say yes to anything at all unless you know, without doubt, without hesitation, without reservation, that it's something you want, and that it's not going to stop you from doing something else you really need to do. But the miller felt blissfully confident that the wizard could only be referring to the apple tree behind his house, making it a perfectly harmless bargain. It apparently didn't occur to him to wonder why a wizard could want his old apple tree, and so he agreed.

Sometimes nice things happen under apple trees but that's a different story and not really relevant and anyway those nice things don't guarantee everything working out in the end.

The wizard told the miller to go home to seek his riches, and that he would come in three years to take what they had agreed upon. Why he felt so patient, I have no idea. Men quite often aren't that patient, and instead have to push for things right away, when matters could just as easily and much more comfortably be left alone.

So the miller made his way home, where he was greeted by his wife. She told him that a strange thing had happened—suddenly all of their cupboards were full of gold. She asked if he knew what could have happened.

The miller explained about his bargain with the wizard, expecting her to congratulate him on his great cleverness at obtaining riches in exchange for an old tree.

Instead, the miller's wife told him that he was a great fool, because their daughter had spent the afternoon behind the house and the wizard must have meant her.

It certainly was more reasonable that the wizard would want a beautiful girl than that he'd want an old apple tree, although why the miller even had the power to give away his daughter is a different question entirely. The daughter didn't really belong to anyone but herself, yet somehow her father's idiotic deal was still binding on her.

They had three years to come up with a solution, yet when the three years were up they had nothing. On the day the wizard was due, the maiden washed herself up beautifully, because apparently the wizard had a terror of cleanliness, drew a circle in chalk, and went to stand in the middle of the circle. Sure enough, the wizard had no power to touch her.

Furious, the wizard went to the miller and ordered him to keep his daughter away from any water. If the girl couldn't wash, the wizard could take her.

It should have been obvious that the maiden had a good thing going here, but the miller nevertheless did as the wizard ordered. And yet the next day it all went as it had before; the maiden's hands were still beautifully clean, because she had spent all night weeping over them. This would take a lot of tears, but I suppose she had reasons to cry.

The wizard was even more enraged, and now he went to the miller and ordered him to chop off his daughter's hands, or be sacrificed himself in her place.

Any halfway decent father would at this point tell the wizard to go ahead and take him. In fact, the only right thing to do would have been to offer himself to begin with, since he was the one who got this whole mess started. Instead, the miller went moaning to his daughter and told her he had to cut off her hands or forfeit his life. The daughter must have been as much a fool as her father, because she put her hands out on the table and let him do it.

This time the wizard was sure he would be able to take the maiden. Instead, she had wept so much over the stumps of her arms that she was still too clean for the wizard to touch her. After that he had to go away, because he couldn't make more than three attempts, because magic has strange rules like that.

The miller at least had the decency to thank his daughter and vow to take care of her forever. Instead of accepting, the maiden insisted that she had to go make her way into the world to search for people to take care of her, even though she had someone right there offering. Although, considering the disaster her father had got her into so far, maybe she knew what she was doing to get out now. The time to get out would have been before the chopping block came out, but better late than never.

It goes to show that sometimes a person just has to get out into the world, by herself. Especially a person who is far better equipped to handle it than a maiden without hands, and who can make plans and arrangements.

The maiden not only had no hands, she had no plans either, and unsurprisingly enough, she found herself lost and lacking food and water. She came eventually to a castle, surrounded by fruit trees. She longed to eat the fruit from the trees beyond the castle's moat.

For the first time in all her distress, she appealed to the heavens for help, and a Good Fairy promptly arrived. There was a vast number of things the Good Fairy could have helped her with, like the hand issue, or the lack of food. Instead the Fairy just parted the water in the moat and let the maiden fend for herself among the fruit trees. Good Fairies tend to be ineffectual that way.

The maiden came to a pear tree and, unable to pick any fruit without hands, she contrived to eat a single pear as it hung on the branches. That must have been a very messy business, which may be why she only ate one before retiring to sleep among some bushes.

The next morning, the king came out to walk in his garden, and noticed that one of his pears was missing. He decided to hide nearby to see if the thief would return. That evening, the maiden ventured out to eat another pear, and the king confronted her.

The maiden told the king her sorrowful tale, and he was so impressed by her beauty and her goodness that he asked her to marry him. She probably should have been wary of marrying a man who actually *kept count* of the pears on his tree, but then, she didn't have many other prospects. Of course, he didn't have to propose to her at all; he could have just offered to be good friends and perhaps a bit more without needing to make it all permanent and binding, but no, he felt he needed to get her into some sort of lasting agreement. So she said yes because she didn't have the courage to say no, and they were married.

The king had a set of silver hands made for her, which sounds pretty, as well as completely useless and uncomfortable. He probably meant well, and that's the worst kind of trouble, when a man means well and then goes striking off in completely the wrong direction without actually knowing what a girl wants.

According to legend, they lived happily ever after, although you do sort of have to wonder about that kind of legend because life is just so much more complicated than happily ever after would lead you to believe.

When I finished my commentary-laden telling of "The Maiden without Hands," Talya cleared her throat awkwardly and said, "So, you're kind of upset about Dastan?"

That, to my great embarrassment, was when I dissolved into tears.

"It's just—that—I really thought he understood," I sobbed into Mina's shoulder. "He's so *good* at understanding."

She put her arms around me while Talya scooted over and hugged me from the other side. "I know, dear," Mina said. "But it's asking a lot to expect him to immediately understand that you don't want to marry him. He's likely to take that personally."

"I *do* want to marry him, that's half the problem! Only I don't want to marry him now, and by the time I will be ready, I don't know if I'll still want to…" And in the meantime, I didn't know if he was going to forgive me for not wanting to marry him right away.

I couldn't tell if I was more afraid that I was going to lose Das entirely by saying no, or that I would let that fear convince me to say yes.

Chapter Twenty

The next evening was not a significant improvement on the previous one. I would have happily ridden in someone else's boat. Unfortunately, everyone seemed to think that throwing Das and me at each other would help, so I couldn't avoid him without making a big issue out of it. We got halfway across the water in total silence before Das finally said, "Are you going to talk to me at all?"

I went on staring at the complete nothing around us. "I don't have anything to say." I had tried to explain yesterday and it hadn't helped at all.

"You always have something to say."

"Not tonight."

I heard him exhale, an exasperated sigh. "I'm sorry, but are you actually *angry* with me for proposing? I just don't see what was so terrible."

"I'm not angry...exactly." I wanted to be angry. I was sure it would be easier if I was *just* angry, instead of my confusing muddle of feelings. I was sad and guilty and feeling horribly bad for him, and horribly afraid that I'd feel so bad that I'd take back my refusal, which would be an awful reason to marry someone and not fair to him since it would probably just make me resent him in six months or a year or ten years, and I was equally afraid that maybe I really should just marry him after all because I loved him and maybe that was enough, but how could it be when I didn't know myself and how could I know marrying him was the right thing and why had he proposed and set all of this off and maybe I could be angry with him for that after all and I kind of was, but I was also sad and guilty and...

"I'm...I don't know what I am," I said finally, and made a snatch towards the anger. "It happens when you have a lack of self-knowledge."

He was still rowing, and the oars hit the water with a particularly vigorous splash. "I also don't see why you don't know who you are. *I* know who you are."

I turned then to look at him, finding the anger suddenly easier to hold onto. "You don't find that statement at all presumptuous?"

"No, not really," he said with a shrug.

I crossed my arms, like Laina at her most off-putting. "If you don't know why I don't feel that I know myself, then you obviously don't know me as well as you think you do."

His mouth set in a hard line. "And suddenly I find that I have nothing to say."

"Fine."

And the rest of the evening featured a great deal of silence. You can dance with someone without talking to him. After a lot of weeks of love songs, Das did not sing anything at all that night at the dance.

We rode back without speaking too. I concentrated on staying angry, even in the face of that depressing darkness, because any other emotion was going to crack my resolve and I couldn't let that happen.

I wished the prophecy didn't specify crossing the lake. For the first time in a long time I was thinking about that third tunnel, the one I'd never actually seen, that Das had told me connected the forest and the castle. Walking through a tunnel couldn't have been as uncomfortable as being stuck with each other in total silence for a boat ride. And maybe it would have been easier to stay angry with someone if I didn't have to look at him.

I don't know how long all that silence might have lasted. It didn't help that half my sisters thought I ought to just marry him, and most of the rest at least didn't understand what I was upset about. Talya welled up with sympathy, was sure that I must be in the right, and remained utterly baffled about what exactly the problem was. I think Mina and Vira were the only ones who really understood. The attitudes of most of my sisters just made me feel contrary and even more inclined to stay upset and un-engaged.

Das, however, had his own ideas.

The next day, the day after our silent evening, I felt like I just had to get away from everyone, however briefly. I couldn't stand the looks of reproach or the looks of sympathy, and with eleven sisters hovering around I received far too many of both. I excused myself from the sewing circle on a vague errand, and fled. I didn't have a destination; I was just wandering around mostly empty corridors and probably would have wound up at the library eventually. Instead, I stopped wandering when someone behind me called my name.

"Lyra!"

I was turning automatically before it occurred to me how impossible this was. The someone's voice had been male, and there was no man above ground who could recognize me, let alone think of dropping the first 'a' from my name. Once I was able to see the speaker, I found that what was already impossible had only become more so.

I gaped at him. "Das, what are you doing here?"

He shrugged, crossing his arms in a nonchalant pose. "I wanted to talk to you. And I thought you might talk to me if I tried something different."

He couldn't have been as calm as he looked. *I* certainly wasn't calm. I forgot about being angry, in favor of being flabbergasted. "You mean if you tried something insane? How did you even get here?" A horrible thought occurred to me. "The Gate's not open, is it?" If it was—and if Father—

"No, of course not. I went through it." He waved a hand, and passed it directly through one of the stone pillars lining the hall. "Noncorporeal during the daytime, remember?"

I stared at his hand. He *looked* solid, which made it even more disconcerting to see his hand go through stone. "That is so strange…"

"Yeah, it took us a while to get used to it." He passed his hand through the pillar again, and shook his head. "And to some extent, you never do."

I tried to focus. "Can anyone see you? If anyone did, this is so dangerous—"

"If anyone did, they wouldn't know who I am anyway, so what's the harm, right?" he said with an easy grin.

He had a point, and yet I felt sure this had to be potentially disastrous somehow. I wanted to shake him, except that I expected my hands would go right through his shoulders, which would be so unnerving that I didn't dare try it. "What are you even trying to accomplish by being here?"

He ran a hand through his hair, proving that apparently he couldn't go through himself. "I don't know, exactly. I just—it was bad, last night, and I thought maybe…I don't want to fight with you, I just…"

Despite all my best intentions, I was starting to melt. Why inarticulateness should have that effect, I don't know. "I don't want to fight either."

"So we agree on something!"

"We agree on plenty of things, only…"

I trailed off, not because I didn't know where I had meant to take that sentence, but because I had heard something. It was the last thing in the world I wanted to hear right then: voices, coming from around the corner behind me. And I recognized at least one of them.

"That's Father!" I hissed. "You have to get out of here!" Without thinking, I put my hands out to push his chest, the kind of gesture you might make when you want to turn someone around and hurry them on their way.

I forgot all about the noncorporeal business. My hands went directly into him. It was like putting my hand into a sunbeam, completely insubstantial. I stared at my wrists coming out of his chest and managed nothing more coherent than a gasped, "Oh!"

Das looked down at his chest and disappeared.

I don't mean he ducked out of sight. I mean he just disappeared. Not even any dramatic smoke, just there and then gone. I jolted back a step, hesitated, and waved my hand through the space he had been in. Since I couldn't touch him even when I could see him, I don't know what good I thought that was going to do. It did none at all.

I was still staring at empty space when behind me I heard footsteps come to a halt, and Father say, "Hello, my dear. How unusual to see one of you girls alone."

I tried to drag my wits together, and turned around to face him. Father was with Foster, the head steward. I curtsied, to give myself an extra three seconds to recover. My skirts hid the shaking in my legs. "Hello, Father." Somehow I steadied my voice, and my chin when I nodded to the steward, who looked at me disapprovingly. That was his usual expression.

"At least, you seem to be alone," Father said, sounding as though he were musing over an interesting puzzle. "And yet, I'm sure I heard voices as we were coming."

The shaking in my knees grew worse. "You must have been mistaken," I said, and waved a hand to encompass the empty hallway. "No one here."

"In fact, I almost thought I heard a man's voice." Father looked at me with his piercing stare, the one that made me feel as though he was reaching into my head and rifling about. "I suppose you wouldn't know anything about that."

I strived to keep my face completely blank. "Nothing at all."

It wasn't as though I expected him to believe me. He knew what he had heard, whatever it had been, and I wasn't going to talk him out of the idea. I was far too rattled to come up with any convincing story about reciting poetry, or practicing a play. My only recourse was to give him a flat enough denial that he'd leave it alone. That's all we ever did with Father. Denied and denied and denied until he gave up, until the next time. Beyond that, I could only hope he hadn't heard anything that mattered. I didn't think we'd been saying anything important; not anything that would be important to anyone else, at least.

That stare of his went on for a long time. Finally he looked away, and it was all I could do not to exhale audibly. All he said was, "Curious," and walked on down the corridor. Foster shot me one more disapproving glance; coming directly after Father's stare, it felt about as threatening as a paper sword. Then he followed Father.

I waited until they were out of sight around a corner, then put out a hand to lean against the wall, not trusting my legs. I waited a while longer to be sure Father was out of earshot, then whispered, "Das?"

It was every bit as effective as waving my hand through empty space.

I couldn't hang around a corridor all afternoon, and I couldn't imagine going to the library after this. I went back to the circle of my sisters, where my arrival promptly broke up the sewing. My face was probably pale, considering Mina took one look and immediately asked me what was wrong.

I sank onto the nearest empty chair. "I don't know. Maybe nothing. Maybe absolutely everything. Das was here."

"What?" Talya squeaked. "How?"

I waved my hand vaguely. "Floated through walls, or something. He wanted to talk to me."

I swear Talya clasped her hands together in a gesture you usually only see in stories. "That's so romantic!"

"It was madness," I contradicted. "Father almost caught him. Only he didn't, because Das disappeared." I clenched my hands together on my lap. "I mean—he just—*disappeared.*"

"Oh, that's all right," Mina said, perfectly calm, as though it was natural for people to vanish into air.

"It is?" I said, desperately wanting her to know what she was talking about, and hoping the desperation wasn't as apparent as it felt.

"Of course. Daemyn and I discussed it. It seems to be another facet of the insubstantiality."

Mina's vocabulary had always been unreasonably large, and spending time with Daemyn had only increased it. "You're saying that disappearing is just normal?" I said, hearing my voice shake.

"For them, yes. During the day when they aren't solid, they can exert willpower to dissolve. It's not as useful as it could be, as it automatically snaps them back to the throne room at the castle. Daemyn thinks that's because the curse was originally cast there and I think that's a reasonable assessment. Of course it doesn't work at all during the night, when they're solid again. Dastan never mentioned any of this?"

I clung to Mina's scholarly-sounding explanation as an antidote to the horrifying sight of Das vanishing into nothingness right in front of me. "We don't talk about the curse much. So...he's all right then?"

She reached out to squeeze my hand. "I'm sure he's fine."

"Good." I let that thought settle for a moment, let the worst of the fear slide away and waited for its replacement. Back to anger. "Because I'm going to kill him."

It was an interminable day. Mina's scholarly reassurances only calmed me so much. You try watching someone you love disappear into thin air and not feel rattled.

Finally we got below, got though the forest, and I found myself on the shore scanning a crowd of dark-haired men for the right face. I did that every night, but usually not with this much anxiety.

Fortunately, he came out of the group to find me. No holes in his chest or any other sign of injury, though he looked anxious too. "What happened with your father? Is everything all right?"

No injuries meant I could yell at him. "You *idiot!*" I shoved his shoulder, and was more relieved than I would have admitted when my hand connected.

"Yes, all right, I know, but what happened?"

He didn't deserve to find out. "How could you possibly think that was a good idea? We've told you what he's like, we're trying to keep everything secret—"

"It seemed like a good idea at the time and I didn't think it through and I meant well." He tried a smile. "Does any of that help, and will you tell me what happened?"

"No!"

He sighed, and looked around at the crowd. "Will anyone else tell me what happened?"

Laina did. "She denied everything, and Father probably suspects something, but we don't think he learned anything important." I glared at her, and she shrugged. "It was that or listen to the two of you go in circles for ages. Maybe now we can just get in the boats and go."

"Fine. Let's." I headed for the boat.

Das came along behind me. "Does this mean we're not talking again?"

He sounded so wistful about it…except if I stopped being angry, I was going to end up weepy. "I haven't decided."

"At least you talked to me up there," he pointed out, as we pushed away from shore.

As if that justified it. "Don't get the idea that means you should try it again."

"I wasn't going to."

Silence again until we were out in the blackness. I blame the usual depressing effect of that dark lake for my anger crumbling away.

I wasn't looking at Das, but I could hear when he stopped rowing and cleared his throat. "Are you—"

"No."

A pause. "Are you sure?"

"Fine, yes, I'm crying," I snapped, and wiped my eyes with the back of my hand. "I was *worried*, all right?"

Now he looked worried too. "Um…about your father…?"

"No, about you! You just—" I gestured wildly. "—vanished, and it was horrible, and then—and Mina said it was fine, but…"

By then he had got over onto the seat next to me and put his arms around me. "It is fine, really, I promise."

I sniffed, and tried not to cry all over his shirt. It had been a far too emotional few days. "All those things you told me about yourself, and you never thought of mentioning that you can disappear during the day?"

I felt him shrug. "I don't like talking about the curse. And it isn't who I am. It's a temporary situation. I hope."

"Of course it's temporary."

"Sure." For the first time in my memory, he didn't sound convinced. "We don't ever talk about—if all this doesn't work."

I raised my head to look at him. "You're always the one who insists on *when*, whenever I put an *if* on anything."

The corner of his mouth twisted. "Because I know it's an if. We're half-guessing about what the Rhyme means, and there are still all kinds of ways this could go wrong." He looked down and reached for my hand, playing with my fingers. "Remember…you said I should have just left things the way they were? Before I proposed?"

"Things were good," I whispered.

He shook his head, one shake. "It wasn't enough, the way it was. We don't know what's going to happen or if there's ever really going to be a time after the curse. I wanted something solid, something to say there's going to be a future. I shouldn't have tried to push you if you don't want to marry me."

"But I do, it's just—"

"You *do*?"

"—complicated," I finished, then frowned, not sure whether to be alarmed by his sudden excitement or not. "Didn't I tell you I do?"

"No, that part you didn't tell me."

"But I can't," I said hastily. "Not before I have some time to figure things out. And that's half the problem, that I do want to but I *can't*. I tried to tell you…I think I want to marry you but I can't *know* if I don't have any chance to find out who I am. And if I don't know that it's right—then it can't be right." Listening to myself, I groaned. "That made more sense in my head."

"It made sense." Das twined his fingers through mine, looking down at our joined hands. "You're just not sure."

"And if I'm not sure, then I know it will never work. I can't do that to us." I swallowed, looking down at our hands too. "To you."

"Does it help if I say I'm willing to risk it?"

"No." I curled my fingers, tightening them around his. "I'm not willing to risk hating you someday."

"Because I didn't give you some time?"

"Because I didn't take some time." I took a deep breath. "But if I *do* take some time, then maybe…afterwards…I just can't make a promise *now* because I don't know what either of us will feel *then*."

"All right," he said, and nodded once. "Then I have an idea." He leaned back a little and took my other hand so that he was holding both of them. "I asked the wrong question before."

Did he really understand? I looked doubtfully at his hands holding mine. "Das…"

"Just let me finish before you say anything. Lyra, will you marry me—at some point in the future, after you've done whatever you feel you need to do to find out who you are, assuming that by then neither of us have changed our minds about wanting to?"

I ran that through my head twice. "Das, it's not much of a promise if it includes the idea that we can break it if we want to."

"It's something, though. I'm not sure what, other than a compromise, but it's something."

"An understanding. Rather than a commitment."

"We could call it that."

I thought about it. It did feel like something, and something that mattered, yet still something that wasn't going to ruin everything else. "All right."

For almost the first time in three days he was looking really hopeful again. "Was that...?"

"Yes." I smiled. "That was yes."

Then he kissed me, and one way and another, we were very late to the dancing that night.

"You know, that trip up into the castle did prove something," Das remarked as he helped me out of the boat at the already-emptied dock.

"The heights of folly that mankind can—"

"No, not that," he said, tugging my hand and pulling me towards him. "I recognized you."

He had, hadn't he? There were more, ahem, delays.

We finally walked into the ballroom holding hands, and Talya immediately announced to everyone in earshot, "See, I told you they were late because they'd made up."

Nearby, Laina shook her head and said, "It was that or they killed each other. Even odds."

Chapter Twenty-One

Over thirty more champions came and went. None of them got as close to our secret as hapless Sam had, and I didn't feel as fond of any of them either. We got all of them down the stairs and out into the second tunnel on their third nights. None of them ever came back. All hundred-odd champions seemed to be keeping their mouths shut once they escaped, and the prevailing belief beyond our castle was that Father had beheaded all the champions. It amazed me that men kept coming under those circumstances.

Laina, Rayna and Sasia all became engaged to their princes, and, with Mina and Vira, were planning a joint wedding for after the curse was lifted. If there was one thing I was very sure about, it was that I never wanted to share a wedding with any of my sisters. They all seemed happy, though.

I was too. Das and I decided we were "conditionally engaged." Sometimes I thought it was all a bit silly…and sometimes I got sentimental about it. Never sentimental enough to take the conditional part off. He didn't bring out the engagement ring again, but I knew he had it, and he knew that I knew…and for something we didn't ever talk about, the knowing still mattered.

Das went back to singing love songs, not every night but sometimes, if my slippers wore out early and there was time for him to join the musicians. I told my sisters stories about freedom and curse-breaking and sometimes love too.

You might remember that I told you, much earlier in this story, that we had a total of 112 champions (give or take one, depending how the last one counts). If you've been keeping track, you know we're getting down near the end now. I had been counting up champions all along, without counting down. It was almost a shock when I realized, during the 109th champion, that there were only two weeks of that year and a day left.

The last month was hard. The beginning had been hard too, until we adjusted to dancing every night, trekking up far too many stairs, and never getting enough sleep. We didn't ever really get used to it, but we learned to cope. Near the end, it was as if eleven months of all that was piling up on us, and it felt more exhausting than it had for months. It may have been *because* it was near the end. When you can't see the end of the tunnel, you accept the darkness. When the light comes into sight, you begrudge the distance still to go. All I know is, we all felt it. We went on anyway. Sore feet were hardly going to stop us at this point.

Something else still could. We had a week left when Father came into our bedroom one morning. It had been the third night for the 111th champion. Father had barely been glancing in recently; he didn't expect the champions to be there on the third morning. Today he came in, and made a show of looking into the adjoining room.

"Another missing champion?" he observed.

"Strange how they do vanish," Vira said, perfectly deadpan.

Father sighed, and sat down in the nearest chair. It was a slender thing in front of Vira's dressing table, and I would have found his too large frame perching in it to be funny, if I was in a mood to laugh. "How long are we going to go on like this?" he asked.

The rest of us remained standing by our beds, and all Vira said was, "I'm afraid I don't know what you mean," in cool tones.

"How long are you going to keep playing this game about wearing out your slippers and refusing to let me into that forest?"

"We're not *playing* at anything," Talya snapped.

He turned his gaze on her. "Then what are you doing?"

She faltered and backed up a step. "Nothing…"

"Why don't we all just stop pretending?" he said. "We've all read Eleanora's journal. No, don't bother claiming you've never heard of it. You're trying to break some spell." He looked around, looking each of us in the eyes as he continued speaking. It wasn't his terrifying stare; this was an open, honest gaze. "Why can't we come to an agreement? You tell me what's really going on. Let me into the magic forest. I won't try to stop you doing whatever it is you're after with all this dancing."

He sounded so reasonable when he said it. It was one of the rare times when I could see the charming man my mother had fallen in love with.

We all knew better, of course. However reasonable he could sound, we all knew what that forest had done to him, knew all the reasons we couldn't let him into it again. We'd had years of experience to teach us. But no matter how little it usually felt like it, he *was* our father—it was tempting to think that maybe we didn't have to be at odds.

I don't think I really believed it. And Mina kept her head about it. "If you've read Eleanora's journal," she said, "then you also know that when we succeed, your forest ceases to exist. I find it doubtful you'd be reconciled to that idea."

His face darkened. "What clever daughters I have," he growled. "Fine. No agreement. No truce. And that means I'll do everything in my power to stop you."

"You can't," Talya said. "And it'll be too late soon."

He pounced, metaphorically. "*How soon?*"

Her face went white. "Oh...um...I didn't mean..."

"Months," I said. "Years. She didn't mean soon, it was wishful thinking."

Unfortunately, Father was clever too. He stood up, paced back and forth down the aisle between our beds. "Oh no, I think little Atalya meant what she said. Whatever you girls are doing, it's over soon.

Now let me see...how long has it been since those slippers started wearing out? I ought to know, I've been paying for endless new ones. It's been almost a year, hasn't it?" He turned to Vira. "Is that it? You need a year for whatever you're trying to do?"

Vira didn't say anything. None of us did.

"No," he said slowly, "not a year. It's never a year in the stories. It's always the same, in the stories. A year and a day."

After Father left, Talya was tearful and we were all worried. We told her it wasn't her fault (even though it sort of was) and that it could have happened to any of us (which it could have). It was all our faults for thinking too much about the world below, and not enough about the world above. We'd stopped paying attention, and we'd all been growing careless.

We knew Father would do something, and had no consensus on what. Give more information to the next champion? Try himself to force us to open the Gate?

We had been hoping for a quiet slide to the end of the curse—to go on as we had been for just a few more days, complete the requirements of the spell and escape without any further confrontation with Father.

I should have known better. I've never yet read a story that didn't feature a final confrontation.

He had been operating through the champions, however ineffectually, and we thought it most likely that he'd continue that tactic. For four days, there was no new champion. It seemed like maybe the men had finally realized what a completely mad idea Father was asking them to sign up for. I started to hope that maybe there simply wouldn't be another champion, and we'd get away with it all after all.

And then, with three nights to go, the last champion arrived.

~ ♦ ~ *Part Four* ~ ♦ ~

They got up, opened wardrobes, presses, cupboards, and brought out pretty dresses; dressed themselves before the mirrors, sprang about, and rejoiced at the prospect of the dance. Only the youngest said, "I know not how it is; you are very happy, but I feel very strange; some misfortune is certainly about to befall us."

Jacob and Wilhelm Grimm

~ ♦ ~

The last champion came on a day when Father held court, and had asked us to attend. I say "asked" as though we had a choice. Once in a while he had us come, sitting in our neat lines, six to his left, six to his right. It was always in the throne room, a long room that was simple but elegant with its rows of pillars and long center aisle. The courtiers and aristocrats gathered around along the sides like a flock of butterflies in their bright colors, while Father and his council met with petitioners and tended to business.

I had given myself free rein years earlier to invent stories while sitting there. I was, after all, the ninth princess; it was improbable in the extreme that I'd ever be called upon to rule anything. Vira and Mina were the only ones who found it interesting.

I took myself out of my daydreams when the herald announced a new champion, my stomach sinking at the news. I had so hoped there wouldn't be another champion. Now I could only hope this one would be no more trouble than the rest.

He didn't look too unusual walking down the center of the throne room. I could tell by his clothes that he wasn't a prince or anyone wealthy. He was tall, young, reasonably good-looking, brown hair—not as dark as Das and his brothers, or as handsome, though I'm biased.

I mentioned the champion first, but the truth is, it wasn't him I was looking at. Because, you see, the last champion was the first champion who didn't come alone. I wouldn't have been shocked by a squire, or some kind of partner. But the last champion brought a girl.

The only women I had ever known well were my sisters. Sometimes visiting nobility or court ladies were thrown together with us, though far fewer had come near us since this curse business started.

Even when they'd been around, we had never really come to know any of them. It was the inevitable result of not trusting anyone. There had never been one who could have picked me out from the rest of my sisters. Maybe because we never got to know them well, whatever women had passed through had all seemed rather the same too; they were either awe-struck girls who deferred too much to our rank, or snobby young ladies who knew exactly what their own rank was and expected everyone else to remember it.

This girl was clearly different, and I was fascinated.

If my sisters and I were moonlight, cool and pale, this girl was fire. Of course it was her hair that made me think of that first, falling in red waves over her shoulders. It wasn't only that. It was the tilt of her chin, the way her gaze darted around the room, examining and assessing. It was her straight back, and the way she strode—really strode—into the throne room. All those court ladies minced.

This was plainly a girl who knew how to stand alone, who wasn't afraid of anyone, and wouldn't be bullied by anyone.

She wasn't literally standing alone, I realized. She was standing with the new champion, of course, and she also had a circle of orange fur around her shoulders. When it moved, I saw it was a tabby cat. I envied her the cat; we had never had pets.

I envied her the confident stance more.

The herald declaimed Father's name and titles, and then went through all of us. He listed off our names, and didn't even try to match the right names to the right faces. Once he was done, he turned expectantly to the new champion.

He bowed, and introduced himself as Jasper. No title, just Jasper. It fit his clothes. I wanted to know *her* name. Apparently Father didn't care because he didn't wait for her introduction, and jumped instead right to his usual speech about our slippers and the curse and all the rest.

Finally Father wound up with, "And of course you are aware of the potential punishment and reward of accepting my challenge."

Jasper cleared his throat. "Yes. About that."

The girl's gaze turned towards him, and she frowned.

"You see," Jasper continued, "I can't marry one of your daughters."

Father's expression darkened. "Why?" He never liked anyone interfering with his plans. Nor was this something that had come up before; 111 champions had all been perfectly happy trying to win an unwilling bride. You'd think it would occur to them that it would mean sleeping with one eye open for the rest of their lives.

Before Jasper could speak again to answer Father's why, the girl stepped closer to him and slipped her arm through his. "Because he's already married. And I would have just one or two objections to my husband marrying one of your daughters."

It shouldn't have shocked us. It certainly explained why she was here. But no one had ever expected a married man to come applying for a challenge that had a bride as a prize.

Jasper glanced briefly at her, then turned back to Father and said, "May I introduce you to my wife? This is Julie."

Perhaps Father should have waited for that introduction earlier after all. It was plain enough, at least to me, that now he felt foolish. That was never good for anyone.

Then Julie flashed a smile—at Father!—and said, "I imagine your daughters would have some objections as well. I'm sure you understand."

No one ever tried to charm Father. He got this *look*, and…but this time it actually seemed to work. Not completely, she wasn't a miracle worker, but his scowl did fade a little. "Yes, well. So why *are* you here, if you don't want to marry a princess?"

It was a fair question. I could usually classify champions by the time they were done introducing themselves. I wasn't sure about this one yet, except he wasn't a Cattle-buyer. Jasper launched off now on a very pretty speech about hearing of our distress and being deeply moved by such a tragic tale and always endeavoring to help those in need. It sounded a lot like what the Well-meaners usually said, only it was all so pretty and so polished that I didn't believe him. I wasn't positive that he was insincere, but I didn't think he was nearly as sincere as he wanted us to think.

Somewhere in that speech he worked in a request for a monetary payment, so I could have classified him as a Greeder—but either he made it sound reasonable or he really wasn't asking for that much. Payment for lifting a curse isn't crazy; it was Father's extravagant offer of a bride and accompanying wealth that had put the whole enterprise into a bizarre place to begin with.

Jasper wound up with the suggestion that if he wasn't getting a bride as a prize, he ought to get a lesser punishment if it all went badly.

Father raised a single eyebrow. "Meaning you want to not die if you fail?"

Jasper shrugged slightly, as though it wasn't really an important question, although I didn't see how it could not be, to him. "It does seem like a logical solution to the situation."

"And *I'd* appreciate it," Julie put in, and flashed another smile.

"Oh, very well," Father said with a dismissive gesture. He could afford to be dismissive. It wasn't his head under discussion. "If you succeed in solving the mystery of my daughters' worn-out dancing slippers, we will pay you in gold. If you fail, we'll cut off your right hand. Lesser reward, lesser punishment. Perfectly logical."

He could have just waived potential punishment entirely. He could have done that 100 champions earlier. Everyone here knew the champions were all disappearing, leaving no good reason for him to offer any threat. But that was Father for you.

There was a little more trivial talk and before I could determine how Jasper or Julie felt about the hand-cutting idea, they were ushered off into the care of Foster, the head steward. He'd take them to our bedroom, as was standard procedure for champions who arrived this early in the day. I supposed they'd have to find a guest bedroom for Julie—unless she was planning to keep watch too. Considering her confident stance, it wouldn't surprise me. We'd need extra wine.

It also wasn't going to surprise me if they searched our bedroom. I had always thought it required a particularly stupid champion to not think of doing that (although you'd think it would need a particularly stupid man to become a champion in the first place). If Jasper was smart enough to talk his way out of a beheading, he was smart enough to do some searching too.

I didn't like it. We were so close to the end. If we had to have another champion at all, I wanted someone simple, easily classified and easily dealt with. Someone different made me nervous, and there was no denying that this pair was going to be different.

I also wondered, very inconsequentially, if I'd get a chance to meet the cat. There are so many interesting cats in stories. I also wondered, perhaps less inconsequentially, if I'd get to meet Julie. I imagined she would be interesting too.

The rest of the court matters, on the other hand, were deadly dull, so I started making up a story about Julie and Jasper. Maybe he had rescued her from something. If any of that speech about helping people in need was true, maybe he'd done something like this before. Perhaps she'd been held captive by a horrible monster, and he had overcome challenges to rescue her. Maybe she had known the secret to defeating the monster, and they had worked together on the challenges because she wanted him to rescue her and then they...

I gave up the story when I realized I was really only retelling my own, from a different angle. And it wasn't wise to start identifying with the people who could ruin the ending of my story.

Chapter Twenty-Three

We didn't get back to our room until shortly before supper. I checked my bedside table; nothing was damaged or too badly in chaos, but belongings had been moved.

I straightened the stack of three books. "They must have searched the room."

"They wouldn't be the first ones," Mina said, lining up bottles of perfume that had got out of order. "It doesn't mean they found anything."

"What if they did?" Talya plopped on her bed and hugged a pillow against her chest. "What if they found everything and they're going to mess it all up somehow, when we're so close?"

Talya had been getting increasingly nervous over the last few days.

"Then we'll deal with it," Laina said firmly. A firm tone was the only one to take with Talya at those moments.

Vira pushed the post on her bed and it slid back to reveal the closed trapdoor. We had never come up with a good way to know if a champion had found the door. Julie and Jasper could even have gone all the way down to the Gate.

"Do you think they found it?" I asked, which just goes to show that Talya wasn't the only one who was getting nervous, since I was asking answer-less questions.

"I don't know," Vira said, then knelt down and ran her hand over the top of the trapdoor. "I think it's likely." She inspected her fingertips. "An orange cat managed to shed under my bed. And if his owner paid any attention to him…"

"Knowing about the trapdoor doesn't mean they can get through the Gate," Mina said. "And as long as they can't do that, they can't do anything to help Father. He already knows about the trapdoor."

True. I still didn't like it.

"Oh, this is interesting," Rayna remarked. She had wandered over to the adjoining room. "The servants have moved a double bed in."

We all crowded into the doorway and looked, as though it would tell us something. All it really told us was that Sasia would need a double batch of wine tonight. Evidently Julie planned to be here too. An extra pair of eyes, double the chance of something going wrong…I didn't like that either, but I couldn't think of anything to do about any of it.

We got to the dining hall before Father that night, and took our places at the head table. From there, I watched Father when he entered and walked the length of the room. I was watching him the way you'd watch any dangerous creature who might turn on you. He seemed smug, yet another thing I didn't like at all. Probably it was because of the new champion.

I hoped it was only the new champion. There was a moment, when Father passed through a block of sunlight from one of the windows, when I thought I saw his black sleeve sparkle momentarily golden. I blinked, looked again too late. By then he was out of the sunlight. I kept watching, but if there *was* something there, the light didn't hit it the right way again for me to see. It could have been my eyes, or it could have been only dust that happened to catch the light oddly.

Or it could have been a remnant of Marj's golden sparkles. If Father had Marj's sparkles on his sleeve, then he must have been talking to her today. I didn't see *any* way that could be good.

I kept one eye on Father, trying to see a more definite clue, and never succeeded. I put the other half of my attention on our new champion and his wife, who were sitting at one of the long tables along the side of the room. They seemed engrossed in conversation, and the cat ate a truly astonishing amount of fish. My sisters and I didn't engage in any meaningful discussion, because we never did when we were in the same room as Father.

Julie and Jasper left the dining hall first, and were already closeted in the adjoining room when we returned. They had the door closed. I had sort of hoped…but this was a terrible time to become acquainted with a cat, or with a fascinatingly-different girl. So it was silly to be disappointed at the lack of opportunity.

"Now what?" Rayna asked, after Father had done his usual ceremonial locking of the door.

"Same plan as usual," Vira said, smoothing her skirts with her palms. "Sasia, get two cups."

Sasia assembled two cups and a bottle of drugged wine on a tray, and Rayna took them to knock on the door. Jasper answered and she offered him the drinks, throwing in a flirtatious, "We *do* try to be nice to our champions." We had all become adept at insincere flirtation, although I'm not sure that was the right tack to take with this one. Maybe—after all, he was married, not dead.

The only response the comment produced was from Julie. I couldn't see her somewhere farther back in the room, but I could hear clearly enough when she said, "It would be much nicer if you'd just tell us about your silly slippers and settle the whole business."

Rayna's voice turned cold. "I do hope you'll have a glass of wine. Maybe two."

"Oh, gladly," Julie said. "After saying evening prayers. A little privacy?"

The wine was taken in and Rayna was ushered out, and we found ourselves with a problem. Every other champion had been willing to drink the wine while we watched. Every other champion had been interested in flirting, or preaching, or asking us how much money our dowries were worth.

"If they're in there, how can we be sure when the wine's taken effect?" Mina asked, putting into words the question on everyone's face. It's much simpler when you can watch them slump over.

"We'll just be careful," Vira said, with a quick shake of her head. "We'll put the lights out as though we're going to bed, and then wait a few minutes until we're sure they're unconscious."

Sasia was twisting her fingers together. "Rayna shouldn't have told her to drink two glasses. A larger dose could be dangerous, especially for her. She's smaller than the champions have been."

That was a possible problem. A bigger one was making my stomach clench with worry. "What if they don't drink it at all?" Could we hit them over the head if we had to? Jasper, maybe. But like Sam, it didn't seem like it would be right to hit Julie. Although if that's what was needed…

"Why wouldn't they drink it?" Rayna asked, tone dismissive. "All the others have."

"There's something different about these two," I muttered. They had thought of searching the room; what else would they think of?

Judging by expressions, I wasn't the only worried one, but one by one we slid into beds. We didn't bother to change clothes, just pulled up blankets and quilts to hide our dresses.

After a few minutes there was a knock at the door from inside the adjoining room, which made Jasper politer than at least three-quarters of our previous champions. Vira opened the door, and collected the two cups and the bottle. He swayed handing them to her, and slurred when he thanked her for the drink. After he had moved away from the doorway—leaving the door open this time—Vira turned the cups so the rest of us could see the beads of liquid within. I lay back against my pillows and told myself to stop fretting.

Vira put out the lights, and crossed the room in the moonlight to climb into her bed above the trapdoor. There were a few whispers from the adjoining room, too faint to understand, and then silence. I lay on my back, stared at the darkness, and wondered why I couldn't shake the feeling that these two knew what they were doing. They hadn't done anything particularly brilliant so far. Maybe it was just how confident Julie had looked. Or maybe I was just getting paranoid because we were so close to succeeding.

After a few minutes, Sasia said, "That wine must have taken effect by now. Let's get going."

There was the sound of feet hitting the floor, and the light flared up again as Vira relit a lamp. We all got dressed; from inside the adjoining room, there was no sound. Finally we were ready to go, or nearly. Nila was last, making a final change to her hair.

"Everyone ready?" Vira asked pointedly.

"Almost," Nila said, jabbing a hairpin through her pile of curls. "Do you always have to be in such a hurry?"

"Do you always have to be so slow?" Vira countered. "There, I've got the trap door open. Are you coming?"

Nila cared the most about her hair and was usually the last one ready, but tonight I resented it. I wanted to *go*, as if starting sooner, walking faster, could somehow bring the whole affair to an end more quickly.

We put out the lights, Nila abandoned her dressing table and we set out below. Talya and I ended up at the back of the group, talking about minor matters to avoid thinking about more important fears. Suddenly she stopped mid-step and asked, "Did you hear something behind us?"

I looked back at the empty stairs. "Like what?"

"Like footsteps."

I sighed. "I haven't told a scary story in weeks, and I thought you were getting over—"

"I *didn't* say I was afraid of anything, I just thought I heard…oh never mind, maybe not."

I looked again and still didn't see anything; with any of my other sisters I would have made a joke about a ghost; with Talya, it just wouldn't pay. Besides, it would take a very shy ghost to not make himself known until now, when we'd been down here so many times.

We went through the Gate and the forest to the shore, where I forgot all about Talya's footsteps as we greeted our princes. We didn't waste time getting on our way; I think we were all eager to get this *done.*

"New champion tonight," I announced as I settled into the stern of Das' boat.

He grimaced, picking up the oars. "Really? That's just bad luck, this close to the end. Is he at least a Well-meaner? Those worry me the least."

I wished I knew. "I can't tell." I smoothed my skirts. "All we really know is that he's married. I don't know if that should worry you more or less."

Das missed a beat with the oars. "He's *married*. Then why would he even…?"

I shrugged, trying to be casual. "Money, maybe, but it's a big risk for a handful of gold. If there's another reason, nobody knows it. And that's what worries me more." I tried to pretend I wasn't as worried as I was, tried to pretend it was mostly idle curiosity and not a prickle of fear in my stomach. It was the strangeness of it. I didn't know what it meant, and that meant anything could happen.

Das was back to steady strokes with his oars, and looked thoughtful. "If the worst should happen, at least I know you won't have to marry him. Something to worry about less."

I smiled and shook my head. "The champions were never likely to pick me anyway."

"Don't see why not," he said with a grin. "*I* picked you. And I have excellent taste."

I poked his leg with the toe of my shoe. "Yes, but anyone who marries Vira would be next in line for the throne. Any champion with brains would pick her."

"Assuming they have brains is a very uncertain assumption."

I forced an almost-natural laugh and the conversation moved on. We reached the shore and went dancing and I tried not to worry.

Most of the evening was normal, but my alarm came back near the end, prompted by, of all things, Rayna's vanity. I had worn through my shoes, and Das and I were sitting by the wall when Rayna came up. "I need an opinion," she announced.

I lifted my head off of Das' shoulder. "About what?"

Rayna put her hands on her hips and half-turned. "Do I look fat?"

I blinked. "No. Of course not." With eleven sisters, this question did come up now and then, usually not apropos of nothing in the middle of the enchanted castle.

"That's a rather intimidating question," Das remarked.

She turned her fiercest expression on him. "Only if you think the answer is yes!"

"No," he said hastily. "No, no, definitely not. You don't look fat."

"Why are you even asking this?" I asked.

"Because Darius said the boat felt heavy tonight!"

Das snickered, and Rayna glowered at him. "It's not funny!"

"No, it's deadly serious. Of course." He would have been more convincing if he hadn't been stifling laughter.

Rayna stormed off in a huff, and I turned ideas over in my head.

"I don't envy Darius trying to keep that one happy," Das said, tightening his arm around me.

Without giving it much thought, I leaned my head on his shoulder again. "She's not fat," I said slowly, "so why was his boat heavy?"

I felt him shrug. "Something to do with the boat, or the oars, or the water, or how Darius happened to feel tonight. Could be anything."

"Those are all reasons it might feel heavy, but what if it actually *was* heavy?"

"I'm confused now." He tugged a strand of my hair, which did not help my concentration. "What are you getting at?"

"Talya thought she heard footsteps behind us tonight."

"Was Talya in the dark at the time?"

"Yes, but what if she wasn't wrong? And what if whatever was making the footsteps got into Darius' boat and—"

"And what if Talya is just afraid of the dark, and Rayna is too sensitive, and you, my love, are very imaginative?" he asked, and kissed the top of my head. "Don't you think that's more likely than that there's an invisible bogeyman stalking around?"

"I didn't say anything about a bogeyman, just someone invisible."

"Was this latest champion, besides being married, invisible?"

"No, of course not, it's only…I know you're probably right, I just…"

But then he kissed me and by the time we had finished I had decided to believe him. It did sound reasonable. The trouble is, I think Das didn't want to believe anything could go wrong now any more than I did.

I checked the adjoining room after we got home that night. I could see two shapes in the bed, where they ought to be. I walked back into the bedroom, and found Talya looking at me with an anxious expression. "They're still here," I said. "Slept through it all." Because of course they would. All the others had.

Chapter Twenty-Four

In the morning, we slept through Father unlocking our door—or at least, none of us got out of bed. We hadn't for the past few weeks. We were all tired, and since Father never tried to wake us up, it also let us avoid an unpleasant and potentially dangerous scene. Julie and Jasper left before we got up in the morning. We saw them again at breakfast, where they had a request. Jasper wanted to go into town, citing only a vague need to run an errand.

"Absolutely not," Father said, thunder in his voice. "Champions never leave the castle after they've begun the challenge. What guarantee do I have that you'll come back?"

Jasper looked personally affronted. "I'll give you my word on it."

Father just smirked. "Not acceptable. Champions don't leave during the challenge. That is not a negotiable matter."

I stirred my porridge, thinking how little of what was said up here really meant what it seemed. When was the last time I'd heard Father say something that wasn't a lie, or concealing something else? Of course, I also couldn't remember the last time I'd said something honest to *him*.

Considering Father had yet to behead anyone, I doubted he really cared whether a champion escaped. They all had eventually. I guessed that he was afraid a champion might find an entrance to the magical forest, take some riches and run. If I wasn't committed to Das and the others, and if I wasn't convinced those metal branches were cursed, it's what I would've done.

While I mused, Jasper tried to negotiate, despite what Father had said. He suggested a time limit or a guard, with no success.

Finally Julie said, "What about me? Can *I* leave the castle?"

And that Father agreed to. She could have run off with riches too, but I expect Father thought Jasper was the one who mattered—the one who would deduce an entrance, and be able to get him into the magic forest. I wondered. And I wondered about the smug expression Father had, after the conversation had ended and as he looked at Jasper. Smug because he had won the argument? Or because he was hopeful about this particular champion?

I wondered, and I worried, and I did so much of both that by mid-afternoon I couldn't have embroidered another stitch without screaming. Instead of giving in to that impulse, I escaped the sewing circle and went to the library. It was the best place, when I was worried. I kept a careful eye out for Father as I went, hoping I could avoid him if I spotted him quickly enough. It turned out to be in the library itself that an unexpected encounter was waiting.

I slipped in, shut the door behind me and only then properly took in the girl sitting at the table. "What are you doing here?"

Julie looked up from an open book with a half-guilty expression. "Well…I could tell you I was trying to find the dining hall and got lost, but you probably wouldn't believe me. The truth is I was snooping around, and then when I found *this*…" She waved one hand, encompassing the shelves of books. "We gave up snooping and stayed."

"We?" I said, my heart suddenly racing. I knew there was nowhere in here for Jasper to hide. Unless he was invisible…

That thought had barely crossed my mind when the orange cat poked his head up over the edge of the table, from his place in Julie's lap, and said a distinct, "Meow."

"Oh. We." I sat down opposite them. "You have a beautiful cat. What's his name?"

"Tom, and don't compliment him. He's already too conceited."

I could swear the cat shot her an aggrieved look, just as if he understood, then sprang up onto the table and walked across to me. He sniffed my fingers, and consented to let me rub his head. I was absurdly pleased by this.

It made me feel friendly. "So you read?" I said, nodding to the book spread on the table in front of Julie. "I didn't think most people could."

"My father taught me, before he died." That was all she said out loud. The wistful tone said so much more about who her father had been.

I wondered what it would be like, to have a father like that. "You're lucky. My father has never taught us anything good. And he's just awful."

Julie hesitated, toying with the edge of one page. "I'm sure I should politely disagree with you, but you're right, he is. Want to tell me what's really going on with him and your slippers?"

I kept my gaze on Tom, whose chin I was scratching. "No."

"I didn't think so," she said pleasantly, "but Jasper would expect me to ask. Anyway, don't feel too badly about your father. My mother's a witch, in every sense of the word."

I was glad of the new topic, and seized on it eagerly. It was much safer than talking about Father. "Is that how you met Jasper? He rescued you?"

"Mmm, in a way. Jasper rescues lots of girls, though." There was something oddly definitive about her tone, as if she was trying to establish something, with an intensity all out of proportion to its apparent importance. Maybe it was important to her. "He's a professional."

I tried to make that last sentence fit with the previous ones, and came up befuddled. "At what? Rescuing people? Like a...wandering hero?"

Julie grinned. "He likes the term 'wandering adventurer' better, but yes, essentially. He travels around fighting monsters. Well, *we* do, now." She idly turned another page, looking thoughtful. "He says it's for the money, but I don't believe him. There are easier ways to earn a living, but that's how he wants to do it."

I had to establish a new category of champion—someone who looked on it as a business. With a sinking in my stomach, I suspected that someone who spent his time dealing with situations like ours would be altogether too good at it. "So he does it for money, maybe; why do *you* do it?" If I could find out more about Julie, maybe I could find out something useful.

She gazed into the distance for a moment. "I spent too much of my life before I met Jasper being very afraid. And now—I get to help other people stop being afraid." Her gaze returned to me, and she leaned forward. "We try to help people. If you and your sisters are in trouble—"

"We're not," I said. "We're fine." We had the situation under control. I didn't care what monsters they had fought, we didn't need them coming in and mucking things up now.

She shrugged and leaned back in her chair, plainly releasing the line of thought. "All right, back to the subject of parents. My mother may be slightly less horrible than your father, but I doubt you have a worse fairy godmother."

I thought of Marj's endless pointless fluttering. "I wouldn't be sure about that. Ours is completely useless."

"Mine always means well, but inevitably makes everything worse."

"Yes, exactly!" It seemed to be the nature of Good Fairies. "Ours never understands anything and—"

I broke off as the cat yawned, strolled away from my hand, and sprang down from the table.

"I'm sorry, were we boring you, Tom?" Julie asked.

He walked over to the door, tail twitching, said another oddly clear, "Meow," and bumped his head against the door.

She got up and opened it for him, telling him, "Stay out of trouble, all right?"

Another "meow" and he trotted off.

"Aren't you afraid he'll get lost?" I asked as she sat down again.

"He'll be fine. Tom can take care of himself."

I had never known any cats well. A few lived in the stables, to catch mice, but they weren't allowed in our part of the castle. It still seemed to me there was something odd about the orange tabby, something I couldn't quite put my finger on. "He meows funny. He sounds just like a person imitating a cat...if that makes any sense." It didn't really, when I said it out loud. How could a cat sound like human sounding like a cat? I was probably just imagining things. Too many magical cats in stories.

"I suppose. Where were we?" she said quickly. "Fairy godmothers—anyway, trust me, Marj is just terrible."

I straightened in my chair. "Marj? You mean Marjoram?"

"You know her?"

"She's our fairy godmother!"

Julie's eyes widened. "Mine too! So you must know how terrible she is!"

"Yes! She's always so sure she's right—"

"—and she's always shedding sparkles everywhere—"

"—and she never listens to anything! Not to mention she's a complete snob..." That thought pulled me up short with a question. "Wait, I thought Marj only dealt with royalty." I had always considered her a plague of the position.

Julie waved a dismissive hand. "I'm distantly related to royalty on my mother's side, and Marj is like a family heirloom. Or curse."

"Us too! She's been no help at all this past year with—" I caught myself. "Never mind."

Julie was looking at me narrowly. "She doesn't support whatever you're trying to do with all this dancing?"

I had my guard back up now, and tried to present my coldest, most aloof expression. "What makes you think we're trying to do anything?"

"Because I've spent evenings dancing. No one dances their slippers to shreds every night for a year unless there's a purpose in it. No one likes dancing *that* much. Either you have a reason for it, or you're being forced to dance."

My palms itched. How dare she come in here at the last moment, start puzzling it all apart, start trying to understand everything when it was *our* business? "So maybe we're being forced," I snapped. "We're under a curse, remember?"

"Maybe," she said, without rising to the irritation in my tone. "But I don't think so. Call it a feeling." She ran a fingertip along the upper edge of the book in front of her. "So does Marj like your father?"

I tried to rein in my feelings. Getting upset wasn't going to help us. I transferred my larger irritation towards a conversation about Marj, and considering how irritating she is, it wasn't hard. "Oh, of course." I forced my tone to be light. "You know how completely oblivious she is. She set my mother and father up years and years ago, and admitting that he's horrible would mean she was *wrong*..."

"And Marj is never, ever wrong," Julie summed up. "The beheading of champions doesn't bother her?"

"She says it's traditional." It wasn't actually happening, of course, but the prospect didn't bother her.

"Of course it is."

"And she just *loves* the idea of one of us marrying a successful champion. Normally she'd have a complete attack about one of us marrying anyone less than a prince, but apparently if some commoner meddles in where he doesn't have any business being, that makes him suitable marriage material."

I had been caught up in my own frustration, but suddenly I realized she was looking very thoughtful again. "So if Marj wants you to marry a champion," Julie murmured, mostly to herself, "and doesn't mind disrupting plans, and of course she thinks that I...that would explain..."

"Explain what?" I asked.

It was her turn to catch herself. "Nothing."

We looked at each other warily for a moment, and finally I sighed. "All right, there's something you don't want to talk about, and I don't want to talk about my slippers, and we're not going to get anywhere at all if we try to discuss those subjects. So. What stories have you read?"

We talked about books and stories and why there was a definite scarcity of stories about women going on quests (it's always the men who get the adventures) and I even told her my story about the girl who followed the birds. It only occurred to me later that this was the first time I had told a story to someone who wasn't my sister or one of our princes. We talked more about our parents (though I was careful on the subject of my father), and eventually she told me about how her witch mother had started selling off her father's books to fund her spells. I reacted with appropriate horror.

"You are the first person who has *really* understood that," Julie said in tones of approval. "Jasper doesn't understand it at all. He doesn't see how books could be more important than, say, furniture."

"Oh no, sell the furniture, keep the books! You can read sitting on the floor."

"Exactly! Jasper, though, would keep the chairs."

"Doesn't he like stories?" I asked, fully ready to condemn him forever for this failing.

She rescued him by shrugging and saying, "Actually, he rather likes stories; he tells good ones, if he can base them off of something he's done. But he can't read."

"Oh." I didn't know how to assess him based on that. "Doesn't that…I mean, don't you find that…sort of a problem?" I was sure there were plenty of perfectly nice, perfectly intelligent people who had never learned to read. I knew most people in the country, and among our neighbors, couldn't read. But for someone who loved books, this seemed like a point of incompatibility in a potential husband that would be insurmountable. Das, if I've never mentioned it, can read.

Julie didn't seem to see it the same way. "I know how to read, but he knows how to do things I can't do. So I can read the map that says 'here be dragons,' and he can fight the dragon. Though I'm pretty good at knife-throwing too. Anyway, it works out."

"I suppose." All this had put me on a new line of thought— although really it was one I had been skirting ever since telling that story about the girl who followed the birds. "Can I ask you a kind of personal question?"

Her eyebrows rose. "If I say yes, can I ask you about your slippers?"

"No." Asking the question wasn't so important that I was going to take stupid risks.

"I didn't think so," she said with evident unconcern. "You might as well ask anyway."

It was, in fact, a *very* personal question. Now that I'd started this, there was nothing for it but to just ask. "How were you sure it was the right thing to do, when you married Jasper?" Julie looked distinctly taken aback, and I hurried on. "And don't tell me it was because you loved him, that's not what I mean—that is, I'm sure you do, but I mean…it's like the girl in the story, she wasn't sure that she wanted that life. How do you *know*?" Obviously none of my sisters were married, and there was no one else I could talk to. No one I could ask about something like this, who had any experience on the subject.

She was silent a moment, and when she did speak, it was a question, not an answer. "Is this something you're personally trying to decide?"

I never should have asked. "I didn't say that." I wanted advice. I didn't want to tell her my secrets.

"No. But you're dancing with someone every night."

If I talked about Das—I might as well just tell her everything. And I couldn't do that. "Maybe he's a demon. And I said I wasn't going to talk about my slippers."

"True." She went back to looking thoughtfully into the distance. I was so relieved that she wasn't pushing the point that I relaxed abruptly, with a sharp exhale. I didn't think she even noticed.

At length, she said, "I think...I knew it was the life that was going to let me be who I wanted to be. And I'm better with Jasper than I am by myself."

"That's the problem," I muttered, "I don't know who I am by myself."

"No, with eleven sisters, I suppose you wouldn't," she said, as though suddenly struck by the idea. "You know, I would have *loved* to have a sister."

"I'm glad I have them, it's just...they're always there."

"Mmm. See, it's different for me. I was alone for five years after my father died. I mean, not technically alone, my mother was there, but in a lot of ways that matter I was alone. I needed someone else to help me see who I am. Sometimes it works that way. There's a reason people come into our lives, and some people can help us become who we're trying to be." She leaned back in her chair. "But that's me. You obviously have already spent lots of time with the people who are going to help you. By all means, go spend some time with yourself. There's something to be said for that too."

"So I should leave the mountains?" To put it symbolically.

Julie smiled. "I think you shouldn't ask anyone else. Decide for yourself. That's the whole point, isn't it?"

Yes. It was.

We got back on the less sensitive topic of books after that, until finally it was getting into the late afternoon and I knew I'd better be getting back to my sisters before we had to go for supper. I had stood up to go when Julie suddenly said, "This is sort of awful, but—I don't even know which princess you are."

She couldn't have realized what a very personal question she was asking. I hesitated, studying her as she sat at the table, books open in front of her, looking up at me. I didn't trust her. Not really. But she loved stories and she understood why I wanted to get out into the world alone, and finally I said, "I'm Lyra. The ninth princess. Alyra, really, but everyone who matters calls me Lyra."

Just the corner of her mouth turned up in a smile. "I'm glad to have met you, Lyra. And good luck with your demon prince."

Chapter Twenty-Five

My sisters were still in their sewing circle when I got back to them, though there was much more talking than sewing going on. Vira and Laina were the only ones who didn't look worried, and I'm sure they were just the best at hiding it. The day was fading, and our second-to-last night below was approaching. 364 nights done. Two left to break the curse.

"Oh good, you're back," Talya said, with a heartfelt sigh. "You can distract us."

"How?" I asked, reclaiming my seat on the couch next to Mina.

"Tell us a story," Talya said. "Anything. Just not about dancing or fathers."

I almost refused. I wasn't sure I could manage a story right then, with so much tension in the air. On the other hand, I could use a distraction too. And I thought I had an idea for a story.

So I told a tale that began once upon a time not too long ago, about a girl whose father taught her to read. That does make this a story about fathers, contrary to Talya's request, though not for very long. The girl's father died when she was still quite young, which left her alone with her mother. This was doubly sad, because her mother, it turns out, was a witch, in every sense of the word. She was far more interested in her magic and her spells than in her daughter, and the girl was mostly left to herself. She explored the crumbly old castle they lived in, and read every one of her father's books.

In due time, the girl grew up into a young woman, one who dreamed of escaping her mother and finding her own path through the world. Since she had never been beyond the castle and knew no one else, she was afraid to run away alone. She was also afraid that her mother would catch her, as a witch has many resources to hand. And if she caught her, there were far too many horrible things she could do.

The girl was smart and patient, and so she watched and waited for an opportunity to escape.

One dark night there was a terrible storm, and out of the midst of the storm came a man on horseback who had lost his way. He came to the castle to ask for shelter. The witch saw that he was young and strong and there were many uses she could find for one such as him. The girl saw that he was handsome, with hazel eyes. The witch invited the young man in, and told him he must stay until the storm was past.

Over supper, the witch asked him who he was and where he had come from. He told them that he was a wandering adventurer, who made his living fighting monsters and breaking curses. He regaled them with tales of his adventures, and the girl longed for a life with such excitement in it. The girl said little over supper, but she watched the adventurer, and it seemed to her that every time she turned her eyes to look at him, she found him looking back at her.

In the morning, the storm had passed and the adventurer announced, with some regret, that he must journey on. The witch laughed in delight and told him he would not be leaving them so soon. In the night she had contrived to steal a lock of his hair and cast powerful spells to bind him. The spells enabled her to cause him pain or even death, and she assured him she would if he thought to leave. She had many uses for a slave.

The girl watched all this sadly, for she knew her mother's cruelty. She also knew that, in time, the witch would feel the adventurer had outlived his usefulness as a servant, and then she could find uses for hair and bone and blood in her spells.

The adventurer knew about spells and curses, and knew that he was well and truly caught. But he was clever, and he also knew that there are ways to break free of binding spells. He proposed a bargain to the witch: let her set him three challenges of her devising, and let him win his freedom.

The witch considered, and thought that this would be as good a way to make use of him as any. She could set challenges which, if passed, would be of benefit to her; and she was confident she could devise at least one task he could not accomplish.

The witch swore to the bargain, and the adventurer and the witch's daughter both breathed easier then. They both knew that the witch could not kill him while he was pursuing the challenges and that, if he was successful, her vow would force her to set him free.

The witch proposed the first challenge that same night. In a castle in the mountains there lived the Queen of the North, a powerful and wealthy sorceress. The adventurer must bring back one piece of the Queen's treasure. The witch would give him three days, starting on the morrow. The binding spell would force him to return, and she had ensured that, even if he died in the attempt, his body would come back to her by magical means.

Late in the night, after the witch had gone to sleep, her daughter knocked at the adventurer's door. She knew that her mother had laid a trap in the challenge, and she wished to help the adventurer succeed.

Among her father's books, the girl had read one which spoke about the Queen of the North. The Queen was famed for her wealth, as well as for her collection of pets, both exotic and ordinary. Anyone who visited her castle would see her great quantities of gold and jewels, and naturally judge these to be her treasure. The witch was expecting the adventurer to bring back some of this, and would find such a thing to be of value. The Queen herself, however, appreciated her gold but loved her animals—and it was these that she considered to be her treasure. If the adventurer brought back gold, the witch would gain, and could also claim that he had failed the challenge.

The girl explained all this, and gave the adventurer two more pieces of advice: he must not attempt to steal an animal, for the Queen had laid powerful magic on them to prevent it. One of her pets could only be obtained if freely given. And the best way to charm the Queen was to offer her flowers from the valley, for she was said to live in the highest peaks of the mountains, where nothing green could grow.

The adventurer thanked the girl, and promised to pay heed to her words—because only a fool ignores advice while on a quest. Every story attests to that.

In the morning the adventurer set out, riding north. More direction than this he lacked, as the girl's book had not told her precisely where the Queen of the North was to be found. Still, he rode forth hopefully enough; directions have a way of developing on quests.

Around midday, the adventurer stopped to eat and rest his horse. It was an easy matter, too, to collect an armful of flowers from among those growing in the woods. While he was halted, the adventurer met an old woman who begged to share his meal. The adventurer shared what food he had willingly, and when the meal was over the old woman thanked him and asked if she might do anything for him in return. The adventurer laughed, and said that she could help him only if she knew the way to the castle of the Queen of the North. The old woman told him that she did not know the way herself, but that a clever man would do well to climb to the top of the nearest peak and seek an audience with the North Wind, who surely could help on such a quest.

The adventurer left his horse in the valley and climbed up the nearest peak. At the top he met the old North Wind, who nearly blew him off the mountain demanding to know how the adventurer had known to seek him there. He explained about the old woman on the road, and then the North Wind's attitude changed. The old woman, as you may suspect, was no ordinary old woman, and the North Wind knew her well. For the sake of the adventurer's kindness to her, the North Wind agreed to blow him to the castle of the Queen of the North.

Being blown about by the North Wind is not an easy trip, and as he was carried up and down and altogether too close to mountain slopes, the adventurer wished more than once that he had found a less hazardous route. At length the North Wind set him down, unharmed if very windblown, before the castle of the Queen of the North. He held on to most of the flowers.

The adventurer saw no point in skulking about, so he entered boldly through the gate, made his way to the throne room of the Queen, and set his flowers and his story before her.

The Queen studied him for what felt like a very long time, and it is said that the gaze of the Queen sees more than mere mortals. When her study was finished, she nodded in assent to his request, and led him herself to a vast room where she kept her pets. She bade him choose which he would take.

The adventurer looked at the menagerie before him—animals of all sorts and sizes, magical and ordinary, a unicorn and a firebird, a lion and a dog, an eagle and a hundred more. He looked at the animals and hesitated. He didn't want to bring the witch something which she could turn to a purpose, harming it or others. He thought to choose something ordinary, but how could he tell if what seemed to be a simple dog was really as it appeared? He hesitated for a second reason too, for he could see the affection between the Queen and her pets, and he didn't want to pain her by taking a favorite.

In the end, he asked the Queen to choose for him. She saw both the caution and the kindness behind the decision, and led him to a basket half-hidden in a corner. She reached into the basket and brought out a ball of orange fluff, which unrolled itself with a yawn into a tabby kitten. The Queen told him the kitten was rather conceited but sweet for all that, and that she would cast her own spells to see to it that the kitten could not be harmed by the witch.

The adventurer tucked the kitten inside of his cloak as the North Wind blew them back. He collected his horse and returned to the witch, to present her with the treasure of the Queen of the North.

The witch looked at the kitten and knew that he had passed the challenge, and that she could do nothing with the treasure he had brought her. She dropped the kitten with disdain into her daughter's lap, who was delighted by him, and the witch set herself thinking furiously of the next challenge. She thought that the adventurer had proved himself too clever by half, and perhaps it would be best to have him disposed of quickly.

For the second challenge, she ordered him to bring her the tooth of a dragon.

The witch's daughter could think of no way to help with this task, and so she worried. The adventurer did not. He rode out the next morning, and this time he knew his direction. The witch had made a mistake with this challenge, because the adventurer knew a dragon. It's a sad misconception that dragons live to fight humans; most are perfectly willing to be amicable if a person doesn't come charging at them with a sword. The adventurer had once rescued a baby dragon confronted by just such a person, and earned the gratitude of the baby dragon's mother. Obtaining a dragon tooth proved to be no challenge at all—the baby dragon was in the process of losing his first set.

The adventurer returned with the dragon tooth, to the fury of the witch and the relief of her daughter. The witch was doubly angry because the magic of a dragon's tooth is only as strong as the dragon it came from, and the tooth of a baby dragon would be of very little use to her. The witch had proposed the second task in haste and in anger, but it had given her time to think about the third task, anticipating that he might be successful again.

For the third task, the witch ordered the adventurer to steal the Mirror of Gemacdo from the Goblin King's Hall of Mirrors. The Goblin King was known to have hundreds of mirrors, and only the right one would do. It would be easily identifiable, for its name was said to be written on its frame.

Then the adventurer's heart sank. He was not alarmed by the prospect of stealing from the Goblin King, but he didn't see how he could get the right mirror, because he couldn't read. Somehow—and there are means available to witches that aren't possible for other folk—the witch had divined this fact, and tailored the task accordingly.

The witch made sure, too, that her daughter had no opportunity to speak to the adventurer before he was to go. But the girl was present when the adventurer was leaving, and she contrived to slip a note into his hand. The adventurer regretted his inability to read all over again, expecting that he wouldn't be able to read whatever she had meant to tell him. When he opened the note, after he was beyond the castle, he found that it only contained a single word, written large and in careful block letters. He wondered what she could possibly have to say that would require only one word, and then it occurred to him that there was, after all, only one word he really needed to read. He couldn't read "Gemacdo" to save his life (as he quite literally needed to do), but he could match the symbols on the paper against symbols on a mirror.

The adventurer snuck into the Goblin King's caverns in the early morning, knowing that goblins sleep through the day. He found the hall of mirrors, and searched through them until he found one with writing that matched that on the note from the girl. By the time he found the mirror, the goblins were beginning to awaken. Getting out of the caves involved a few fights and a great deal of running, but he made it back to the witch's castle, mirror intact.

Bound by her vow, the witch was forced to release the spells she had trapped him with. He was entirely free to go, but now that he could, he realized he was not so certain he wanted to.

He proposed a new bargain with the witch: one more challenge, not for his freedom, but for her daughter. Provided, that is, that the daughter agreed to the idea.

The girl did agree, and so did her mother. The witch by this point cared little about gaining anything except revenge on the adventurer for defeating her earlier challenges. Risking her daughter seemed to her like a very small thing.

The challenge the witch proposed was straightforward. The adventurer must choose the witch's daughter from a group the witch would provide; if he chose correctly he could take her away with him. Confident of his ability to recognize the girl, the adventurer agreed.

And then the witch summoned up four demons, who transformed themselves into the perfect likenesses of the witch's daughter, with blue eyes and long red hair. She mixed the girl in among them and presented all five in a line to the adventurer, for him to choose.

The adventurer looked at the row of girls, and could see no differences between them, in face or form or expression. He thought of speaking to each one, but whatever answer one of them might give, he feared it could be a demon's trick. Besides, he had a better idea.

From the depths of his cloak, he brought out the sleepy-eyed orange kitten, which the girl had given back to him earlier in the day. The adventurer set the kitten down on the ground before the row of women. The kitten yawned once, then trotted directly over to the second girl from the right, who knelt down and gathered up the purring ball of fur. The adventurer at once chose that girl as the true one.

The demons howled in fury, for he had chosen correctly, and they had hoped to seize him once he belonged to the witch. They couldn't take him now, and they had no power over the girl. The witch's long practice of the dark arts had left her vulnerable, and the demons fell on her instead. The witch disappeared in a swirling black vortex, and has never been heard from again.

The witch's daughter and the adventurer escaped, and took the orange kitten with them. The adventurer asked the girl to marry him, and she gladly said yes. He supposed, less gladly, that now they'd have to settle down somewhere. The girl rejected that idea entirely—she was far more interested in going out to find more monsters to fight. And so the adventurer and the girl, with the orange kitten perched on her shoulder, rode off together in search of new adventures.

Chapter Twenty-Six

Finally the afternoon ended and we sat through an equally interminable dinner. Father was looking pleased with himself. It scared me.

Two more nights. We just needed two more nights and then it was all going to be over. I tried not to add "one way or the other," to that sentence. There was only one way this was going to end. Our way. It had to.

The evening went much the same as the one before. I didn't try to talk to Julie. I was back hidden among my sisters, and it felt safer to stay that way. We gave the wine to Julie and Jasper, and they took it into the adjoining room to drink it. After enough time had passed for it to take effect, we changed our clothes and went below.

I tried to stop worrying and relax. There was nothing I could do right then except dance my shoes apart, just like usual. And the dancing, the music, the colorful dancers and, yes, Das too, should have been enough to make me feel better for a while. But one of the dancers worried me.

I'm not sure when I noticed her. By halfway through the evening I was—well, sure about absolutely nothing, except that I was suspicious.

"Das, do you know that woman with the red hair?" I asked.

"No, I like blondes," he said easily, spinning me through another step of the dance.

"That's sweet," I said when I was facing him again, "but I'm really asking. I want to know if you know who she is."

"Which one?" he asked, and looked where I nodded.

The woman was wearing a gold dress set with rubies, and had red hair falling over her shoulders. Her face, frustratingly, was hidden behind a red and gold cat mask. She was dancing with a man wearing a silver cloak and a black and silver mask.

"I don't think I know her," Das said. "We're not that small of an island. I don't know everyone. Why?"

"Our new champion, his wife has long red hair." I bit my lower lip. "I don't know. It *could* be them…or I'm being paranoid."

"Can you think of any way for them to have got here?" Das asked, the voice of dismissive reason.

There was that third tunnel, the one that connected the forest and the castle. But getting from the forest to the castle had always been a secondary obstacle. The real trick was getting through the Gate, and I couldn't see how they could have done that. "Other than the invisibility theory, no." In retrospect, it all seems obvious. At the time, I was too aware of how worried I was, how likely I was to be jumping at shadows. "I suppose I'm just nervous. You're so calm; aren't *you* worried?"

"I hide it well." He pulled me closer in the steps of the dance. "Besides," he whispered in my ear, "if everything goes horribly wrong before tomorrow, we shouldn't ruin our last night dancing together."

"It won't go wrong." If I said it enough times, if I only told the version of the story that I wanted, surely that would make it true.

"Hopefully."

This was no time for him to stop believing it would all go right. "If something does go wrong…I mean, if we can't come tomorrow, or something, then we could begin again." I clutched at the idea, and flashed a smile. "Spending another year dancing with you wouldn't be the worst thing." My feet didn't like the idea. But I could think of much worse 'worst things.'

Das didn't look at me when he said, "Right. We could do that."

I studied his face, trying to make him meet my gaze. "You're not a good liar."

He looked at me then, with deliberately wide eyes. "Why would I be lying about anything?"

"You don't think it would work," I said, mouth dry. "Trying again."

He gave up pretending otherwise. "I think this is something we only get one chance at. It works the first time, or not at all. We can all feel it, something's going to happen tomorrow night. Either the curse lifts, or...my guess is we all fade away, and probably the island goes with us."

I remembered the one time I had seen Das disappear in front of me, and it became harder to keep up with the dance steps. Even though he wasn't really saying anything I didn't know. Even if I hadn't *really* believed we could try twice. I'd never yet read a story where someone had a second chance to break a curse. Sometimes it all goes in threes, but not in circumstances like ours.

"I want you to do something for me," Das broke in on my thoughts, "if it does all go wrong—"

"Can we stop talking about it going wrong?" My throat was tight, I couldn't get the picture of Das disappearing out of my head, and this conversation was not helping.

"We can after I say this. If it all goes wrong, find some way to get away anyway. Take your sisters if you can, and if you can't, don't. Just find some way to get out of that castle and go out into the rest of the world, and..." He shrugged, looking over my head. "I don't know, find an orchard and some new stories and whatever it is about yourself you think you need to know about. And...listen to some new songs, all right?"

He was blinking rather hard, and I was definitely about to cry. So I hid my face in his shoulder and whispered, "All right."

It was hard leaving Das on the shore that night. I couldn't say good-bye, not a *real* good-bye, when everything in me was clinging to the hope that it would all turn out well. But if something did go wrong, if we couldn't come back the next night, if we couldn't break the curse…how could I *not* say good-bye, knowing I might never see him again?

In the end, we didn't say anything. Just one last, long kiss.

After that, a red-haired woman at the dance was no longer uppermost in my mind. I didn't mention her to my sisters on the way back. Not only was I distracted, I was still trying to believe that positive thoughts could make a difference. I don't think I was the only one. We talked about wedding plans on the way up the stairs. Because nothing was going to go wrong.

I checked on Julie and Jasper again. If they had left, they had got back before I went into their room, with enough time to manage a convincing semblance of sleep.

The next day, the last day, felt like years as it passed. It isn't worth much time in the telling. We all put on our dancing slippers in the morning, as if taking that first step could guarantee that everything else we wanted would follow. With our long skirts, it was hard for anyone to see we weren't wearing normal shoes.

We spent the day in an anteroom just off the court. People passed through there constantly, many of them important people, like advisors and diplomats. We all knew that Father would try to stop us from going through the Gate that night. Our theory—Vira's, really— was that placing ourselves where there would be witnesses, especially important ones, would limit what Father would be willing to do to us. It's harder to imprison or kill your daughters when people are watching.

I spent the day reading. Perhaps I should have been thinking about the situation, about plans and ideas, but I knew myself, and if I thought, I was just going to fret myself sick. Better to read. Better to not think about the curse. I read the book of stories I had found in my mother's room. By this time I had read it a dozen times; they were wonderful stories, and more importantly, they made me think of

Mother. I needed that, on this of all days. Better to think about Mother than about Father, or curses, or champions.

Besides, for all that I railed about wanting my independence, there were times when I took advantage of having eleven sisters. I didn't need to think, because I had sisters who were thinking. Vira spent hours staring into space. Mina reread Great Grandmother Eleanora's journal. It had mostly been residing at the princes' castle, but she had brought it back and forth occasionally when she wanted to study it, and had it hidden inside a larger book now. She went through it three times that day, as though she had any chance of finding something new after all the times she'd already studied it.

Since we were in public, we barely talked. There wasn't anything left to say anyway.

By supper, my fingers hurt from clenching Mother's book all day and I was hungry. At least, until we got to the dining hall. Father's smile as we came in killed my appetite.

It only got worse from the smile. The servants had barely served the first course when Father began. "Now that it has been two nights," he said, the hall falling silent at his voice, "I wonder if our latest champion will fill us in on his progress in solving my daughters' mystery."

After the vague non-answers from our very first champion, he hadn't demanded reports from any of the other 110 champions, at least not anywhere we could hear. I exchanged a covert glance with Mina, then looked at Julie and Jasper in time to see them exchanging similar glances.

Whatever their glances communicated to each other, all Jasper said out loud was, "I'd rather wait the full length of time before saying anything, Your Majesty."

The full length of time would be long enough. I didn't care in the slightest what he wanted to do tomorrow.

"Come, come," Father said, in a terrifyingly jovial tone, "don't waste my time being modest. Claim success."

Jasper raised his eyebrows. "I don't think I know what Your Majesty means."

I so hoped that was true. I so very much hoped that Father had completely lost his mind and Jasper had slept through the last two nights and knew nothing at all. And I so wished that I had grabbed that red-haired woman in the cat mask.

I watched Julie, trying without success to read anything in her face. She had been so nice in the library. Surely I didn't really need to be afraid, surely it was all going to be... My stomach went hollow and my lungs forgot to work. In the library, Julie had wished me luck with my *demon prince*. I had made the demon reference. I had not said anything about a prince. How had she known?

If I had thought of it sooner, maybe it would have mattered. As it was, I had thought of it only moments before events went galloping out of control anyway. Even as I was trying to remember how to breathe, one of Father's attendants was bringing out a small bundle wrapped in cloth. He laid it on the table before Father, who unwrapped it with loving care.

The metal twigs sparkled and shone in the light: silver, gold, diamond. I could see golden leaves, a spray of diamond flowers. There was no denying where those twigs had come from. Julie knew about more than Das' royalty.

"One of my men found these in your bag," Father said, picking up the diamond twig and turning it slowly between his fingertips. He gazed at it with the eye of the obsessive. It made my stomach turn, wondering if he had once looked at my mother similarly. It had been romance, then. It was something far more twisted now.

I barely heard Father ask if Jasper had any more proof. I was turning to look at our champion and his wife. They had no idea what they were meddling in, and they were going to ruin everything. For once I let myself have an expression in my father's castle. I let all my fear and fury show in my glare, and I didn't worry that it would mark me out from my sisters. I knew they were all looking the same.

Jasper kept his gaze on our father. "I have nothing to say until the completion of the agreed-upon time. I have a right to three nights. I also have to object to this invasion of my possessions—"

The whole table shook when Father slammed his fist on it. "This is my castle, and all that goes on in it is my business! I own everything here! There is nothing here which is not mine!" He glared around the room for a long moment. Finally, he leaned back in his chair, back in control. "Very well. One more night. I can be patient."

He had a plan. He did not have time to wait another night, so he had to be planning something.

He also had one more piece of nastiness in hand. "By the way," he added, tone very casual, "does your wife know you're carrying around a portrait that isn't of her?"

Jasper's shoulders went tense. "That's no one's business—"

"You told me you got rid of that!" Julie interrupted, palms flat against the tabletop, glaring at him almost as fiercely as I was. "I know you were in love with her for years, but why do you have to carry around her stupid picture? You said it was all over with her!"

Jasper looked completely shocked by this turn of events. "It is!" he protested. "I'm really not in love with her."

Julie pushed away from the table. "If that was true, you wouldn't need her picture." She turned on her heel and stalked out of the room.

So much for that fairy tale romance I'd been imagining for them. Life is more complicated than happily ever after. But I couldn't care about their happy ending just then, when they were on the brink of destroying mine.

Chapter Twenty-Seven

We didn't wait for the end of supper, or even for the next course. Father dropped all of his horrible announcements, Julie stormed out, Jasper followed her a minute later, and we were scant moments behind him. There was obviously no point in trying to keep up any semblance of normalcy. Normalcy had kept everything in balance long enough for us to spend a year dancing. Normalcy was over.

Father said nothing as we left. Just watched us, smiling.

Without discussing it, we went to our bedroom. We got only as far as the hallway.

Vira stepped forward to confront the four guards in front of our door. She drew herself up and gave her most imperious glare and somehow seemed taller. "What do you mean by barring us from our own bedroom?" There was the wrath of nations in her voice.

Three of the guards turned terrified expressions to the fourth, who had the highest rank. He looked scared too, but was holding up to it better. "We have orders from the king, Your Highness. You're not allowed in." A tremble entered his voice. "It's worth our lives, letting you in there tonight."

Vira tried a little more thundering, but the guards were more afraid of Father than of her, or even of all twelve of us together. In their place, I'm sure I would have been too.

Barring us from our room was such an obvious solution. So simple, and maybe that's why we hadn't expected it. Father hadn't tried this in the entire past year. Besides, his smugness at supper had suggested a more impressive plan.

Not for the first time, although close to the last, I regretted how very little power we actually had. Our defenses were good for protecting ourselves, but that didn't help when we needed to act.

We could see no point in hanging around the hallway, so we went to the library. It was as good as anywhere, when nowhere would be useful. Perhaps if we could have left the castle, and tried to find the other end of the tunnel the champions had been taking…but the castle guards had had orders for fifteen years that we weren't to leave. That wasn't an option, so we went to the library.

The library only had one door and we could lock it from the inside. We barely all fit. I sat on the floor by one of the windows and Talya curled next to me, with her head on my shoulder. Vira and Mina each took a chair, Rayna sat on top of the table, and everyone else fit themselves wherever they could. We tried to figure out what to do.

Mina went back to hunting through Eleanora's journal, which I think was an act of desperation at that point. Mina has always been happiest when she's gathering information, and likely she was falling to that now in much the same way that I had taken refuge in stories earlier in the day.

Rayna thought we needed to do something to Jasper. Drug him (except that he definitely wouldn't take any drinks from us now) or tie him up somewhere (though how exactly we would manage that, she didn't know).

Laina thought we should attack the guards. They were stronger, trained and had weapons, but we did outnumber them. No one can accuse Laina of lacking courage, though sometimes there isn't much thought behind it.

We were all surprised when Vira gave a nod to Laina's idea. "It's very probably the only thing we *can* do. Father took the direct approach in stopping us, so we'll have to act just as directly to counter him."

"But we don't know anything about fighting," Sasia protested, wringing her hands together.

"True," Vira agreed, "and if they really try to stop us, they'll succeed. We have plenty of willpower but no skills." She lifted her chin into the air, and some of that outraged majesty was still clinging to her. "However, if we pick up anything we can find—knives, heavy candlesticks, anything—and make a good show of willingness to fight...we'll find out if they're really willing to fight back. We're twelve delicate-appearing girls, and we're their princesses. It wouldn't be shocking if they decided they couldn't bring themselves to harm us."

That was no guarantee. I tried to imagine confronting those guards, with their armor and their swords. Part of me desperately wanted to hit out at anything trying to stop us. Part of me just as desperately wanted to crawl inside the pages of a nice, safe story and never come out. Excitement and fear were both making my heart pound.

"So let's go try it," Laina said, already on her feet. She had been pacing in the tiny space available. "We get past them, Mina picks the lock on the door if necessary, we go through the Gate. It's early, but so what? We move before Father expects it."

That idea Vira vetoed. If Jasper could get Father through the Gate, he could come after us into the forest. Even if Jasper had been uncooperative at supper, it didn't mean he couldn't be persuaded. Father's smug confidence made it clear he believed he could make Jasper help him. All we would be doing then would be choosing the place for a confrontation, and if there was anywhere we didn't want it to be, it was in the magical forest.

Vira's opinion, which we all came around to, was that we should try at sundown. Sundown was the crucial moment, not for us but for our princes. Sundown was when they became solid. If we went into the forest before then, they wouldn't be able to help us, even if they were there.

A horrible thought I didn't say out loud was that if it came down to a confrontation that ended with Father killing any of us, I didn't want it to be where Das and the others would have to watch. I don't know how many of my sisters were thinking the same thing.

If Father had a new way into the forest, he didn't need us anymore. And if he didn't need us...I had had fifteen years to convince me that Father would do anything to get that forest, and there was nothing I thought he'd balk at now.

He only needed to get in once, just enough to get water from the lake. If Eleanora was right, then he could destroy the Gate. So he just had to stop us from breaking the curse, and then he'd have all the time in the world to take all that wealth out of the forest.

He must have believed all that, but I wondered if it was really true. If Das was right, that not breaking the curse meant they would all fade away, maybe the forest and the Gate would go too. Without the curse, what would be the point of them? Somehow, telling Father that didn't seem likely to convince him to stand back and let us go ahead.

We discussed all of this and more. There were two hours of sunlight after supper. We couldn't find a plan that was any better than Laina's idea of storming the guards.

Myself, all I had was an idea. At some point since seeing those twigs unwrapped on the table, I had calmed down—sort of. I was calmer about that part of the situation, though it might be most accurate to say that I was too occupied being upset about other things. Whatever the case, I didn't feel as venomous towards Julie and Jasper. I thought it might be worth trying to talk to them.

"What good will it do?" Rayna asked, when I proposed the idea. "There's no reason they shouldn't help Father. We can't threaten them or promise them any reward, and he can do both."

"If we explain it all to them," I said, "maybe that will convince them to help us. Not everyone's motivated by greed." I remembered Julie saying that Jasper fought monsters for the sake of the money, but I was clinging to the memory of her also saying that she didn't believe that was his real reason.

Laina grimaced. "Just because you told a story about them, that doesn't mean they're noble and heroic."

I put my chin in the air and tried to look as though that notion was perfectly ridiculous. "It has nothing to do with the story. I talked to Julie yesterday, and she seemed…nice. And she said they try to help people."

"She didn't tell you that her husband had a way to get past the Gate," Vira said.

I hesitated. "No…" There had been a lot we hadn't said, it was true. But still. We could use a couple of allies on this side of the Gate, and they were the only prospects.

Looking around at my sisters' faces, no one else seemed to think they were a prospect at all. Vira put it into words. "We can't trust them. We've never been able to trust anyone, and that hasn't changed."

And that was the final word—or it would have been. In a story, we would have been the only ones who counted because we were the leads, and if we decided against a partnership, that would have been the end. In life, everyone gets to make decisions, and Julie and Jasper had their own ideas.

It wasn't immediately after we were talking about them—that's also how it would have been in a story—but soon enough after, there was a knock at the door.

Hands were clasped, girls shivered, and we all stared at the door, silent. I wasn't sure how afraid I should be. I didn't think it was Father. He wouldn't have knocked. Pounded, maybe, knocked, no.

There was a second knock, and a man's voice, sounding uncertain as he asked, "Princesses? Are you there?"

Vira cast a stern look at us. No one spoke.

There was a second voice behind the door, a woman's this time. "They must be there, why else would the door be locked?" That voice I recognized—Julie, which meant the man could only be Jasper. She raised her voice to call, "Please let us in; we just want to talk."

I ignored Vira's look and answered, "About what?" There was an aggravated hiss from Laina, but I ignored that too. Even if I had been overruled, I still thought it could be worthwhile trying to enlist them on our side. Jasper must know how to fight, and it wouldn't have surprised me if Julie did too. She'd said something about knife-throwing.

"About your father, mostly," she answered from the far side of the door. "And your slippers. And—whichever of you is Lyra, I *meant* it when I said we try to help people."

Laina looked like she wanted to throw something at me. "You told her your name?"

"It seemed all right at the time." I spoke louder to answer Julie. "You didn't tell me you had got into the forest."

"And you deflected every question about your slippers," Julie countered, "so I think we're even. Let us in, and let's talk about all this."

I hesitated, and most of my sisters looked doubtful.

"I understand, really," Julie continued. "You don't want to trust us. It's a risk. If you won't risk it to help yourself, will you risk it to help that man you think you might want to marry?"

"Did you tell her everything?" Rayna demanded.

"Of course not," I said, and took a deep breath. "But I think we should. It can't be a bigger gamble than attacking the guards, and what do we have to lose now, anyway? Everything's already going all wrong. If they didn't want to help, why would they even be here? They could just go straight to Father with whatever trick they're using to get through the Gate, but they're here."

"She does have a point," Vira said quietly, and once you have Vira on your side, you can win most arguments with my sisters.

When no one raised another objection, I crossed the room and unlocked the door, carefully. I opened it a crack to make sure there wasn't a whole contingent of guards lurking, and was relieved to see only Julie, Jasper, and the orange cat sitting by their feet. I let all three of them in, and then locked the door again.

When I turned back to face the rest of the room, Jasper looked like he was trying not to flinch in front of my sisters' hostile stares. Tom wound once around Julie's feet, then wandered farther into the room. Julie was looking at me.

She smiled, if uncertainly. "Taking a guess here, but I think you're Lyra?"

I nodded.

She looked relieved. "Oh good. You really do all look impossibly alike."

I shrugged one shoulder. "We try."

Meanwhile, Jasper had squared his shoulders and was staring back. Laina spoke to him first, saying, "I'm sorry we can't offer you any wine." Her voice was at its coldest. "But you haven't been drinking it anyway. Have you." It wasn't really a question.

Jasper didn't back down. "Only an idiot would drink something you gave him in this situation."

Laina arched one eyebrow. "111 champions drank the wine before you."

"Then 111 champions were idiots."

"You talk about it so calmly!" Talya burst out. "You have no idea what you're meddling with. You're ruining everything!" She broke off as the cat put two paws on her lap and arched his neck toward her. Tom apparently had a remarkable instinct for finding the one most likely to scratch his head.

"We have some idea," Jasper said, and leaned back against the nearest wall, arms crossed. "Now we want you to tell us more."

"Why should we?" Laina demanded, arms crossed as well and projecting an equal level of defiance.

Jasper had the nerve to shrug. "Because I'm half-inclined to tell your father everything I already know. Unless you convince me I shouldn't."

"*If* we tell you anything, tell us one thing first," Vira said. "How did you reach the enchanted forest?"

"I should tell you my most valuable piece of information first? I don't think so."

"You already know too much about us," Laina broke in, "why should we tell you more?"

"Because with what I already know, I can—"

"This isn't getting us anywhere," Julie interrupted. "Someone's got to be the first to tell something, so I'll do it. We're not really married."

Of all the secrets I might have guessed at, that wasn't one of them.

Julie gestured at the air between them. "We're not even together. Romantically, I mean."

So that fairy tale romance was even more imaginary than I had thought. I felt entirely too disappointed, and betrayed into the bargain. "You lied to me." So we hadn't told each other everything, I knew that. I had thought we'd been telling the truth with what we did say.

Julie at least had the grace to look guilty. "Sort of. I mean, what I said was real, it's just, instead of a reason for marrying Jasper, it was the reason I'm traveling with him."

Other people, like Laina, were still fixated on the larger issue. "But why would you say you're married when you're not? What was the point?"

"Don't take this the wrong way," Jasper began, which is never encouraging, "but the point was that I didn't want to marry one of you."

"We don't want to marry you either," Rayna said at once.

This didn't seem like the largest issue either. "Then why are you here at all?" I asked.

Julie sighed. "It's complicated."

"It's not that complicated," Jasper countered, "it's just stupid."

"We met this old woman on the road," Julie continued, "and she wanted Jasper to apply for your father's challenge. He didn't want to marry a stranger or to be killed—"

"Finally, someone else sees it that way!" I said. It was so refreshing to hear someone from the outside look at it rationally.

"How else *could* you see it?" Jasper asked.

I shook my head. "I don't know, but 111 champions thought it was a good idea. If you see it for what it is, how did you end up here?"

"The old woman cursed me," Jasper said flatly. "Apply for the challenge, or stop breathing. So here we are."

Mina, who had long since put away Eleanora's book, had her skeptical expression on. "Why would some random old woman on the road do that?"

"I think it was Marj," Julie volunteered, shooting a glance at Jasper as she said it. "She's my fairy godmother too—"

"I mentioned it," I said, to forestall a longer explanation. Although now that she put that idea together with the fact that she and Jasper weren't married… "She must be appalled that you're traveling with him."

"Gee, thanks," Jasper said.

"Don't take it personally," Julie said, pushing his shoulder lightly. "It's just that they know Marj. And yes, she is. That's why I think she was the old woman. Lyra, you told me that Marj wants one of you to marry a champion. I know she wants to get me away from Jasper. Drag him into your mess…"

"And she solves both her problems," Mina concluded. "To Marj's twisted logic, it makes sense."

Only to Marj would Jasper be suitable for one of us but not for Julie. It all had to do with circumstances and tradition and How Things Are Done, and it all did sound very much like Marj—almost. "It makes sense except for one thing," I said slowly. "Marj clings to that Good Fairy business, and even when it's completely mad, she always justifies everything as helping people. She wouldn't just curse you. She'd have to do something that she could at least claim was to your benefit."

Julie and Jasper were looking at each other, and I'm sure I couldn't see half of what they were saying—it was that kind of look. All I got was that he was reluctant and she was pushing him on.

Finally he turned back to us and said, "She gave me an invisibility cloak."

"I knew I wasn't imagining things!" Talya exclaimed. "You were walking behind us! Invisibly!" Tom bumped his head against her hand, and she resumed scratching between his ears.

Julie nodded. "We followed you both nights."

"You made the boat heavy." Rayna folded her arms over her stomach. "And I skipped dessert last night."

Meanwhile, I was skipping on to the more important part. So was Vira, because she said it first. "If you followed us, does that mean you came through the Gate when we opened it?"

Jasper looked surprised. "How else would we get through? That thing doesn't open for *anything*. I tried."

Have you ever heard twelve girls exhale in relief in unison? It was one harmonious moment followed by a babble of conflicting voices, although the theme was all pretty much the same. If they couldn't get the Gate open, that changed everything. We just had to get through, and Father wouldn't be able to follow us.

"Does your father know you're going to break this curse tonight?" Julie asked, when the voices had subsided somewhat.

Apparently they had overheard that crucial piece of information. By this point I was past being surprised and just answered, "Yes. And it's probably going to destroy the magic forest, so he'll do anything to try to stop us." We already knew he had put guards on the bedroom. None of us really believed he'd leave it at only that.

Julie nodded. "We can try to help—"

"Maybe," Jasper interjected.

She frowned at him and continued, "But we have to know more about what's going on. We know you're trying to help those princes, but what's the rest of the story?"

A great many looks flew around among my sisters. Finally Vira said, "Very well. We'll tell you the story. Lyra?"

Because I, of course, am the storyteller. So I began with once upon a time when a queen fell in love with her chief of guards, and wove in our princes' story, and told our own story of the past year too, all the way up to tonight, the four guards at the door, and our hopes that they wouldn't really fight back if we tried them.

"It's not much of a plan," Mina said with a worried frown.

"That's good, I don't like plans," Jasper said. "And we don't know enough about the King's plans to make an adequate one in response anyway. Storming the guards'll do. We'll go with you, and we'll deal with whatever comes when it comes." He glanced at his hand. "And hopefully we'll find a way to get out of here afterwards."

"Oh, that's no problem," I said. "After we reach the boats, you can take the alternate tunnel."

"The what?" Julie said.

My description of the past year had been sketchy, and had focused mostly on the curse and the princes. The champions' escapes hadn't come up. "After we get to the boats we should be fine, and you can take the other tunnel. We can point you towards it. We've been hauling all our champions down there on the third night."

"And a lot of trouble it was, too," Rayna put in, "getting them down those stairs. We could just about get them to walk themselves, although the wine made them groggy. We've been dumping them all at the tunnel, and so far they've all managed to find their way out. At least, we haven't met anyone wandering around down there."

"Then your father hasn't really been killing anyone?" Julie said.

"He would have," Vira said. "If we had let him."

"Didn't we tell you we try to be nice to our champions?" Rayna said.

Stories told, secrets revealed, and everyone apparently understanding each other reasonably well, there seemed no good reason to wait any longer. Besides, it was nearly sundown anyway.

Mina and I were the last two out the door of the library. We both stopped to look back, and she took my hand and squeezed it. I didn't know if I should want to see this room again or not.

Chapter Twenty-Eight

The four guards still stood in front of the bedroom door when we arrived. They still looked nervous, which would have been more reassuring if they hadn't looked determined too. My sisters and I hung back a few paces and let Julie and Jasper try first. The cat trotted along with them, just as though he considered himself part of their team.

If Julie and Jasper couldn't get past the guards by themselves...the rest of us had picked up whatever candlesticks and vases we could lay our hands on. Not very effective weapons, maybe, but with twelve of us they might count for something.

First, we'd see what the professionals could do. As an opening volley, Jasper began with, "Listen, why don't you just make everything easier for everyone and let the princesses into their room? Can't you just do that?"

The lieutenant gaped at him in horror. "But we're under orders!"

"Yeah, I know," Jasper said with a shrug, "because everyone wants to follow orders given by a sadistic madman."

The horror multiplied. "He's our *king!*"

"Sorry, a royal sadistic madman. I don't know, I think those may be worse." Jasper looked back over his shoulder at Julie. "What do you think?"

"Oh, definitely," she agreed, "I'll take a commoner sadistic madman any day."

"This isn't getting us anywhere," Laina said, an unpleasant edge entering her voice.

"She's right," Jasper acknowledged with a nod in her direction. "It's like this. I have a rule that, if I can, I'll talk rather than fight. However..." He raised one hand and gestured toward Julie.

She threw a knife I hadn't seen her draw. It stuck, point-first, handle quivering, in the door just to the left of the lieutenant's head. "...we can fight if we need to," Julie finished Jasper's sentence.

The lieutenant's eyes had grown much bigger, and his men were in a hurried, whispered conference.

"And then of course, if you fight us," Jasper continued, in a friendly tone, "you also have to fight *them*." He nodded back towards the cluster of myself and my sisters. "Can you really see yourselves swinging swords at them?"

The guards looked at us, already wide eyes growing larger.

Jasper pressed the moment. "Not to mention, when it's all over, you have to go home. And what are you going to tell your mothers or your sweethearts when they ask what you did at work today?"

The guards decided a retreat was in order. The locked door was no real obstacle, since Jasper also knew how to pick locks, and was faster at it than Mina.

"You know, we could have done that without them," Laina said, meaning Julie and Jasper, as we passed through the doorway.

I shrugged. "Maybe, but that trick with the knife helped."

I saw Julie grin. "I told you I know how to throw knives."

"I want to learn how to do that," I said, and meant it. I was so *tired* of not being able to do anything.

"Survive tonight, and maybe you can," Vira told me. "Right now, let's just get through the Gate and—"

"What about changing clothes?" Nila asked.

"We don't have time for that," Vira said. "We need to go, now, before—"

"What if we don't come back?" Talya asked, voice quavering. "Shouldn't we pack?"

"No. We're already wearing our dancing slippers, and that's all we really need. We have to leave before Father gets here, so we go now before it's too late."

"It's already too late."

That cold voice cut across our talk, and everyone turned silent as Father stepped out of the shadows in one corner of the room.

He looked around at us, and laughed. "As if I'd leave those fools at the door as the only protection for my forest."

"Your forest?" Vira said quietly.

"Yes, *mine!*" Father was far from quiet. "Mine because I'm the only one who sees its value. The only one who knows how to make proper use of the fortune under our feet. And you absurd girls want to throw it all away to break your silly spell with your ridiculous dancing."

Vira met his gaze levelly, back straight, slipping into her customary stance when confronting Father. "This is something we need to do, and you're not going to stop us."

Father went back to laughing. "Oh, that's grand, Avira, just grand. No one can say you don't have courage. Sense, on the other hand, that's a different matter." Suddenly he wheeled towards Jasper. "But you—you're not a foolish girl like them, surely you see my side of this? You've seen that forest, and a man of the world like you can appreciate wealth. They want to make it all vanish into smoke by breaking their silly spell. But we stop them tonight, and then tomorrow morning you open that gate for me. I'll give you, say, five percent."

I knew Jasper couldn't really open the Gate, so he couldn't agree to Father's offer even if he wanted to. I still felt a shiver of fear. If he wanted to betray us, if he still had any way to do it, this was his opportunity.

All Jasper did was shake his head.

Father's expression, briefly friendly, darkened again. "I can have you killed."

Jasper grinned. "You can try."

I thought I heard Julie groan.

Father flipped back over to friendly. "Another one with courage. Perhaps you haven't thought this through. Five percent of unimaginable wealth is itself pretty near to unimaginable."

"I wouldn't want that kind of wealth," Jasper said. "There's something wrong with that forest."

"You've been talking to my daughters, haven't you?" Father said with a dismissive gesture at the group of us. We had scattered a little when we first came into the room, but regrouped instinctively as Father spoke. Strength in numbers, after all.

Jasper was standing apart from the rest of us, and didn't move as Father walked closer to him. "There's nothing wrong with the forest," Father said. "It's everything a man could ever want. Is the percentage too small? I'll give you ten percent. Think of what you can buy your wife with that."

"I don't want anything," Julie said at once.

Father barely flicked her a glance. "Everyone wants something. I know what I want, and one way or another, you will help me get it."

"I can't," Jasper said, posture giving every indication of being perfectly at ease. "You're wasting your time with this. I can't open that gate. All I did was follow your daughters."

Father went white. I couldn't tell if it was shock or rage, but either way it made me want to run and never look back. "You followed them. You can't open the gate. All you did was follow them."

Jasper just shrugged. "Sorry, Your Majesty. Looks like you're still trapped on the wrong side."

"That makes you useless!" Father roared, and lashed out with one fist.

I would have expected Jasper to have instincts for this sort of thing, but he must have been caught unprepared. Father hit him across the face and he overbalanced to fall sideways. It wouldn't have done him much harm, except that he crashed into Mina's bedside table and hit his head on the edge. He slumped to the ground, eyes closed.

I heard Julie scream his name. She slipped past me as she ran across the room, ignoring Father to drop to her knees next to Jasper. She took his head in her hands, brushed her fingers through his hair, murmuring, "Don't be dead, please don't be dead..."

She had said there was nothing romantic between them. All of a sudden I wasn't sure I believed that.

Only I would have taken that moment to wonder whether my fairy tale imaginings for them weren't so far off and just needed some tweaking, and in the space of two seconds I got halfway to a new story before I reined myself back to the immediate situation. I'm going to say it was an unconscious attempt to escape the present moment, where Jasper might be dead and Father was dragging Julie up to her feet and I knew that any moment he was going to be looking at us again.

"Do you have anything to say that he didn't?" Father asked Julie, hand closed around her arm.

She wrenched against his grasp and somehow she got a knife into her hand. It didn't do any good; he just laughed and wrestled it away from her before she could stab him.

"I'll take that as a no," he said, and flung her towards us.

I reached out to steady her, then kept one hand on her shoulder. She didn't object. I felt fur brush past my legs and looked down to see the orange cat dart past me and wind himself around Julie's ankles. He had followed us all evening, even though I hadn't seen Julie or Jasper give any thought to making sure that he was coming.

In more important matters, Father had returned his gaze to us. "So we're back where we've always been, my dears. You're going to open the gate for me."

Vira was still our spokesperson, and she answered. "What if we came to an agreement? We'll let you through the Gate tonight, provided you don't interfere with our breaking the spell. You'll still have a few hours to take whatever wealth you can."

It wasn't a perfect solution, but it could have worked. The damage he could do with only one night's gathering was comparatively limited. Too bad Father didn't like the idea.

"I'm to be satisfied with a few petty armfuls of branches, when I could have an entire forest of wealth? And I don't need to make a deal with you."

"You need us to open the Gate," Vira said.

"Yes. But you're going to do that for me without needing a compromise. You think you're so clever, but I know more than you think I do." He nodded towards Jasper, who still hadn't moved. "I know Marjoram helped him. I suggested it to her."

"We knew that too," Mina said, which was half true. We hadn't known that he had suggested it, though it explained that recent evening when I thought I'd seen sparkles on his sleeve. He really had been talking to Marj.

Father's eyes narrowed. "But did you know she helped me too?" He reached into a pocket of his coat and brought out a thin rod, perhaps as long as my forearm and a few inches around. "It's all about putting things to Marjoram the right way. I just told her how I was concerned about not being able to reach the wealth down below, for the good of the country of course, and wouldn't it be grand if we had another way to obtain gold and silver. She was more than happy to provide me with a tool for mining. At least, that's what she thinks it is."

Father aimed the rod at a vase sitting on Vira's table. He twitched his wrist and a ball of flame spat out, hit the vase and exploded, spraying shattered ceramic everywhere.

Talya screamed and Laina muttered curses and I stared at fragments of the vase and tried not to think about other things that could explode.

"Don't worry," Father said in jovial tones, "I won't use this to stop you from opening the gate tonight. I *want* you to open the gate tonight. Because if I stop you going through, I don't know but you might be able to break your little spell tomorrow or the next night or next week. I won't take a chance on the spell ending and my forest disappearing with it. So we put a close to all this tonight, because I also know you must be dancing with someone down there, and it must be very particular someones. Did you really think I wouldn't notice when my daughters fell in love? Maybe one of you could hide it, but all twelve? I think you need to dance with those particular someones to break your spell, so all I need to do is make sure they aren't there to be danced with." He smiled at that horrible thing in his hand. "Ever again."

I did not not *not* want to imagine one of those fireballs hitting Das. So of course that was all I could think of.

It was after sundown by now, so if Father had proposed going below with a knife, a sword, anything normal…then by all means, let's go through the Gate, and rely on the idea that twelve able-bodied young men ought to be able to get a knife away from one man without anyone getting too badly injured. We might have been able to attack him ourselves, if it came to it. But shooting flames…that was another matter entirely. He could have killed all our princes and all twelve of us too, before anyone could get close enough to lay a hand on him.

Vira found her voice first. "If you really think we'd agree to that, you don't know nearly as much as you think you do."

"I think you don't have a choice," Father snapped.

I had moved to the front of our group when I had caught Julie. Maybe that's why it was me that Father reached out and grabbed now. Before I could take a breath Father had a grip of steel around my upper arm and his flame weapon pressed against my temple.

"You open the gate," Father said, "or your sister dies."

Chapter Twenty-Nine

"You can't kill her," Mina said, voice too tightly controlled to shake. That's what happened when she was *really* upset. "It takes all twelve of us to open the Gate."

The rod pressed against my temple and my arm hurt where Father was holding it. I wanted Mina to be right, I so desperately wanted Father to believe her and to just let go.

He didn't. "I don't think so," he countered. "I don't think there's anything so magical about the number twelve. Eleanora used to open it alone. So did your mother. I don't think it needs twelve, it just needs all of you who are alive. So it'll open if there are only eleven of you. Or ten, or nine."

I knew what I was supposed to do. I had read so many stories. Ideally I was supposed to somehow get the flame rod away from him. At the very least, I was supposed to tell my sisters not to worry about me, and make a defiant speech telling my father that my life was less important than stopping his plans. I knew that it *was* less important. Stories had always been my area, not arithmetic, but I could do the math to balance my life against our twelve princes, their thousands of subjects, the hundreds of thousands whose lives would be destroyed if Father took that wealth from the forest and used it to conquer the world.

I could see all of that, and I knew that I was supposed to look my own death bravely in the face and consider it worthwhile.

The truth is, I had death pressing against my temple and shards of pottery filling my vision and I was just too scared to be defiant. In that moment, all those other lives felt much more abstract than my own.

I didn't cry or beg either, which was worth something, but I didn't tell my sisters not to give in. I just said nothing.

My sisters couldn't bring themselves to accept the arithmetic either, so they opened the trapdoor and began to descend the stairs on Father's direction. Father put his weapon back in his coat pocket, still very accessible, and with one hand holding me, he used the other to haul Julie along too.

"You're coming with us," he told her. "I still think the two of you know more than he admitted."

I had never liked going up and down those stairs. It had never been as bad as when I had Father dragging me down them. I stumbled and banged my toes and the arm he was gripping was going numb. The walking, at least, was easier when we reached the flat tunnel, and all too soon we were standing in front of the Gate.

"Open it," Father ordered. "Now." He let go of Julie and took the flame-thrower out of his coat.

My sisters looked to Vira, and I saw her hesitate. I could see it on all their faces, the uncertainty. In a strange way I was almost glad that Father had grabbed me, because at least it meant I didn't have to decide. Who to save? Who to let die?

"You'd really do this? All of that…" Vira gestured towards beyond the Gate. "…is really worth this? It's worth killing for?"

"All of *that* is everything!" Father growled. "Everything I've wanted for all these years, everything I can do once I have that money. You think I'd stop now? You think I'm afraid to get my hands dirty? Maybe I'll just prove it to you."

I tensed, expecting to feel a burst of flame. Would I *feel* it or would I die too quickly? But Father swung the rod around to point at Julie instead.

"We know we don't need her to open the gate," he said. "She might know something, but once the gate is open, who cares? So why not use her to prove—"

He never finished. At that moment the rod flew out of his hand, under its own power for all that I could see. It disappeared into the shadows, making a skittering noise as it hit the rocky ground.

Father only got an inarticulate expression of surprise out before he had a new problem: a hissing, spitting orange cat who materialized directly above his head, and dropped down with claws extended.

The answer to Father's question, about why not to kill Julie, turned out to be 'because she had friends.'

Julie and I both sprang away from Father when Tom appeared. I dived back into the welcome circle of my sisters, and at once had Mina on one side and Talya on the other. Julie nearly fell as she pulled away; I saw her somehow straighten up again, getting support from something I couldn't see.

Meanwhile, the cat was yowling and Father was cursing with equal strength. Then Father fell abruptly silent, back arching as though something was pressing him there. Tom leaped away, landing neatly on his feet.

"Let's reconsider a few plans, shall we?" Jasper's voice said, and a moment later he appeared behind Father, one hand holding the clasp of a silvery cloak that draped his shoulders, the other pressing a knife into Father's back. I had forgotten the invisibility cloak he had mentioned. There was blood on the side of Jasper's head, but he seemed steady enough on his feet.

Visual evidence wasn't enough for one of us. "Are you all right?" Julie demanded.

"Head hurts, otherwise fine." I could see Jasper's grin behind Father's shoulder. "Lots of monsters before this one have found out that I don't die easily."

"I'm fine too, thanks for asking," an unfamiliar male voice put in, and it was only after a confused moment that I realized it had come from Tom.

"The cat talks!" Even in the midst of it all, I was delighted by this revelation. "I *knew* there was something special about him."

"That's just my natural specialness," Tom said, arching his back proudly.

"Conceited," Julie said, bent down and picked Tom up, hugging him against her chest.

I stared at the tabby, mind spinning. He met my gaze and winked one green eye at me. Now I understood why Julie hadn't been worried about the cat going off on his own into the castle, and why he had come along with us all evening with no human guiding him. I wanted to know how he had learned to talk and if he did anything else magical and if he might really *be* a cat who had belonged to the Queen of the North—and now was not the time to ask any of that.

I tore my attention away from the cat to the discussion about what we were going to do next. Jasper had ideas on that. He suggested that he, Julie and Tom guard Father, while my sisters and I went through the Gate, and set about to break the spell.

"Couldn't we just leave him on the far side of the Gate?" I asked. "You could come with us…"

Jasper shook his head, then winced as though he regretted the movement. "That would mean taking the chance that he doesn't have some other trick hidden in his sleeve. I'd rather take a chance on the gate disappearing when you break the spell, so we can get out the second tunnel. If it all goes wrong and we have to get out through the castle, we can use the invisibility cloak. Anyway, we'll come up with something."

It was a vague plan, but then, Jasper had said he didn't like plans.

"Good luck," Julie told me with a smile.

"You too," I said, and impulsively hugged her. As I looked over her shoulder my eyes landed on Jasper, and I remembered Julie's expression when he had been hurt. I thought I was wishing her luck on more than one front. "You too," I repeated.

Then I was lining up with my sisters, each grasping one bar of the Gate, until it swung open in front of us. I looked back as I stepped through, to look at Father. I didn't know if I was ever going to see him again. I think I wanted to feel some sadness, some regret. Even with all that he had done, he was still my only living parent, and I wanted to feel something about that.

But he was glowering at us with so much fury that all I could feel was fear. It was a relief when the Gate closed behind us, and I followed my sisters through the cursed forest.

Have you ever seen twelve men try to pace on the same beach? Neither have I, but seven of them were pacing, two were throwing pebbles at the nearest diamond tree, and three, including Das, were leaning against the prows of their boats with worried expressions.

I *have* heard twelve men try to ask the same questions all at the same time. For just once in my life I had a story I didn't want to tell, so I let someone else answer—Vira, I think, although I had my face pressed against Das' shoulder at that moment so I didn't look to see who was talking.

Explanations didn't last long, whoever gave them. Even with Father on the far side of the Gate, under guard, none of us felt comfortable lingering.

I didn't feel much better even once we were in the boat and underway. "You're staring at me," I pointed out to Das, some minutes into the ride. A stare wasn't unusual, but his concerned expression was. Either it was the story my sisters had told, or my unease was showing.

"Are you sure you're all right?"

This was the third time he had asked that since we arrived on the beach, and it was not helping me in my efforts to keep calm, to not let all the hectic adventures of the last few hours catch up to me and send me collapsing into tears. "I would be better if you would stop asking me that."

"Sorry. I just…worry." He gave a particular vicious turn to the oars. "And I hate always being on the wrong side of that gate to *do* anything!"

There wasn't anything to say, so I didn't try to say it.

He brightened after a moment. "But it's over now. Your Father's on the wrong side of the gate this time, we're here, it's the last night…just some dancing left and it's all settled and done."

I tried to smile, and match his hopeful tone. "Right. It's practically as good as finished."

His smile faded. "You're saying that, but you don't believe it."

I shrugged helplessly. "Maybe I'm not all right after all. I just…can't shake the feeling that something could still go wrong. I'm not really going to be sure it's over until it *is* over."

"What could happen now?"

A misinterpretation of the Rhyme? Slippers that mysteriously refused to wear out? Father impossibly still following us? Maybe it was all irrational fear, or maybe any of those could happen. "I don't know. It's probably just…lingering dread, left-over, or something." I summoned up another smile. "An overreaction, probably."

It might be an overreaction, but I couldn't really believe it was just a left-over fear of events that were done. This feeling wasn't about the past. It was about the future, a kind of awareness of the pattern. Stories have patterns. Life rarely arranges itself so neatly, but recently our lives had been playing out rather according to the shape of a story. I had read so many stories, and even if I couldn't quite put it into words, I had a sense that the hard part of the story wasn't over yet.

My fears didn't play out as anything during the boat ride, and we arrived at the dock without incident. After everyone had gathered, we made our way up the path to the castle.

I couldn't have been the only one still afraid, because it was very quiet. It had been quiet the first time we walked this way too. Everything else was different. Then, it had all been so strange and new and wondrous. It still felt wondrous sometimes, in a different way and for different reasons. It all felt so familiar by now. And the people I was with—the same people, but what a difference a year had made. Das and I had come over together the first time too. Then, he had been a near-stranger who I had only just decided wasn't a demon and I only half-trusted. Now...

And I didn't know what was going to happen with the two of us. Even if everything went the best we could hope, we defeated the curse and it was all a success—what then? I still wanted to get out on my own, go away and see something new, just me, by myself, alone. I was sure about that, but it was not unmixed happiness in anticipating it.

We reached the top of the path and entered through the wide doors, the usual sea of masks and elegant figures in the room beyond. We had all of us, the rest of the court included, become so accustomed to the nightly routine that it had been months since our entrance had created any great stir. Everyone knew that tonight was special. Tonight the movement stilled, the conversation died away, and everyone turned toward us. There was a ripple through the crowd, and then applause.

That nervous feeling that there was more to come made me want to tell them not to applaud, that we hadn't really done anything yet—or at least, we hadn't done enough.

You can't tell a crowd of clapping people that, so instead I whispered to Das, "What do we do?"

"You curtsy, I bow, and then we dance."

I curtsied, my sisters dipping around me, while Das and his eleven brothers bowed with all the training of a royal court. Das and I were already holding hands. Now he extended his other hand, I took it, and we swept off into the dance.

Rayna wore through her shoes first that night, and never were holes in dancing slippers greeted with such excitement.

"Feel any different?" I asked Das, as we continued the steps of the dance.

"No," he said, "but I don't usually *feel* cursed."

The signs of a change turned out not to be with our princes at all. Someone in the crowd chanced to glance out the window, cried out, and then everyone was looking. Usually, with the bright lights within and the darkness without, the windows showed only reflections. Suddenly there was a brighter light outside too—the curtain of fog encircling the island was shot through with silver. It still loomed, gray and oppressive, but it shone too. And right through the center of the wall, there was a ragged hole, very like the holes we'd been wearing through our slippers all year on a larger scale.

I felt Das' hands tighten on mine, and I looked up at him, smile more genuine than it had been all night. Something was really *happening*.

Laina wore her slippers out next, then Sasia, Vira, Dalia and me. As soon as I found a hole in my second slipper, Das and I joined the others who had finished, standing at the largest window to watch the fog. It was torn by dozens of holes now, large and small and growing. More appeared as Mina, Cacia, Mara and Drina wore their slippers through, until the fog was a tattered web, stars shining in the gaps.

Das stood behind me, his arms around my waist. I covered his hands with my own, fingers wrapped around his wrists, and I could feel the excited beat of his pulse. I felt the same excitement from my sisters, and inside myself too. I almost believed we were going to make it, a smooth slide to the end.

Only almost. I wasn't really surprised when I heard shouting from the door leading to the docks. I think I had been listening for something like it all evening.

Chapter Thirty

We turned to look at the disturbance, and I wasn't shocked to see Father in the doorway. I had known who it would be as soon as I heard the first sound of alarm. Who else could it be? I wasn't surprised by the rage on his face or in his stance. Only the livid red burn marks splashed across his face were unexpected.

"He *can't* be here," I heard Sasia say.

"He must have found the third tunnel." I felt strangely calm. Almost detached. Like I was reading a story.

I knew suddenly what had seemed wrong before. Julie and Jasper had stopped him at the Gate, and that wasn't the way it was supposed to go. The heroes always have to face the villain in the end, and it's no good hoping someone else will do it for you. Now it was time for us, and my strongest feeling was that this was simply how it was supposed to be.

Das had stepped in front of me, some kind of chivalrous impulse, well-meant but badly placed. I stepped around him. "Don't, I want to see."

Father was yelling. "Stop! Everyone stop dancing. I know what you're doing and I won't let you!"

Everyone present knew that there needed to be dancing, had to be dancing. There was protest from the crowd, and more than one person started towards him. Father raised his hand, and I saw that somehow he had got the enchanted rod back. He pointed, and a jug of wine on a nearby table exploded in a ball of flame.

Everyone stopped then, including Talya and Nila, the last two of my sisters left dancing.

"That's better," Father said, smug satisfaction in his voice. "I knew you could be reasonable."

"Father, don't do this," Vira said, taking a step forward from our cluster. "This is important, so much more important than a little wealth—"

"It's not a *little* wealth," Father contradicted. "It's enough wealth to buy the world and I won't let you take it from me. I've sacrificed too much. I thought it was all over when you abandoned me on the far side of the gate, but that absurd adventurer turned out to be useful after all, with his bottle of lake water. He fled and now I'm here. And I'm stopping you."

At least that explained how Father had got through the Gate; Jasper had water after all, and Father had used it to burn through. I wondered if that explained what had happened to his face too. They were the kind of burns that could have come from being splashed by lake water. I couldn't imagine Julie and Jasper fleeing, but if they had thought our father was giving up and that we were already safely away—had we ever mentioned the third tunnel to them? It was hard to remember what had been said. I didn't think so. It made a horrible kind of sense. If they had thought it was all over and left through the alternate tunnel, then Father had found the third tunnel after they were gone and come after us...

I lost my train of thought when Talya suddenly cried out. "The fog!" She was pointing at the window behind us. "Look at the fog!"

I looked back, heads turning all around me, and clutched Das' arm. The fog was reforming. It was less tattered than it had been only moments before, and even as I watched I could see holes shrinking.

"It's because we stopped dancing," Talya said, and raised her chin in a defiant gesture. "That means we have to keep dancing." She dragged Dathan through two steps before he caught up and started following her.

"Stop it," Father ordered. "*Stop it.*"

Talya, my little sister who was always afraid of everything, completely ignored him. After a moment, Nila and Dagan picked up the dance as well.

I checked the fog. It wavered, and then the holes began spreading out again.

"I'm not bluffing," Father shouted. "If I have to kill one or all of you, I'll do it!"

He wasn't that sure about it. If he had been, he would have done it by now. He was hesitating. I would have found that more reassuring if I wasn't sure that he wouldn't hesitate forever. It was just that he needed to work up to murder. Unless, that is, we could encourage him to keep hesitating.

Feeling that strange, 'reading a story' calm, it was all perfectly clear. Someone had to distract Father. Someone had to keep him talking, or looking in the wrong direction, or thinking about something else, anything as long as it didn't mean blasting people with flames, anything to distract him long enough for Nila and Talya to wear through their slippers. It couldn't be long now. We just needed a few more minutes. A few minutes of distraction.

I stepped out of the group, out of the protective circle I'd been in all my life, and began the walk across the hall. I heard Das call my name. I knew that if I looked at him I was going to run back to him, so I didn't look back. I looked forward and kept walking.

"Father, I want to talk to you."

He turned his glare on me, rage-filled, all the more horrible for the shiny burns marring his face. "About what?" he growled. "More stupid pleading? Or ridiculous moralizing about the wickedness of wealth?"

His gaze landed on me and my calm detachment evaporated. My stomach curled up and my heartbeat grew loud in my ears. Apparently I was not one of those heroines who faces danger and feels no fear—far from it. Now I wished I hadn't stepped forward, wanted desperately to run back. But I couldn't, because in the same moment that the fear came crashing over me, I also saw exactly what needed to be done. Arguing, trickery, it wasn't going to work. He'd see through it too quickly.

Something else was needed, and I couldn't run because I was the only one who could do this. I licked dry lips, hoped he couldn't see my hands shaking, and said, "I want to tell you a story."

He stared at me as though I was mad. "You ridiculous child, why would you tell a story now?"

"Because that's what I do. That's who I am." Maybe I *was* mad, to be telling him that, to be trying this.

Father sneered. "I don't know who you are. All twelve of you, you're all so alike. Do even you know who you are?"

"Yes," I said, and then I said something I had never thought I would ever say to my father. "I'm Lyra. I'm Lyra, and I tell stories, and I like raspberry tarts, and I'm in love with Dastan over there. And now I want to tell you a story about once upon a time, when a queen fell in love with her chief of guards."

"This is pointless," he hissed.

Maybe. I dragged a breath in past my tight throat, pushed words out. "It's said that the guard was handsome and very skillful, yet when people spoke about him it was usually his charm they mentioned first. He had a talent for making everyone feel that he was deeply interested in them, that he understood them in a way no one else did."

I wasn't telling the same version of the story that I told to you, back at the beginning of my own story. This was a version that I had never told before. It was full of details that had been mentioned here or there throughout my life, pieces of the story that I knew but didn't usually include. I suppose most people have trouble imagining the romantic lives of their parents. Considering the situation with my father, I had never wanted to think about those parts of the story, the ones that made him out as the hero of the tale.

"Because of his skills, the guard ended up spending much of his time personally protecting the queen." Thinking about my mother nearly shattered my fragile control. I dug my fingernails into my palms. This story, it had to be *this* story, so I had to keep telling it. "She was a young queen, very beautiful, and much beloved but somehow very alone. The affection of a country is not the same as the bond of a close friend. The queen's parents were dead, she had no siblings, and she spent her life surrounded by advisors, not family or friends."

"I don't know what you think you're going to accomplish," Father said, "but this is a waste of time."

A waste of time was exactly what I hoped desperately to accomplish. Time was what I needed, enough time for two more girls to dance through their slippers.

"The guard saw his queen's beauty and loneliness, and the queen saw her guard's charm and understanding, and each one thought that perhaps together they might find answers to all life's questions. But queens don't marry guard chiefs, and so neither spoke of what they were feeling." If I died in the next few minutes, at least Das already knew I loved him.

It was a dark and fleeting comfort, a tiny reassurance to set against the waves of fury coming off of Father. I wanted to look away, but I had to stay focused on him, to keep his attention on me. As I stared at his face, I thought I could see a new strain there. There was something different in his eyes. He looked...trapped. I didn't know if that was good for us or not.

"They might have gone on this way forever, but then one day the queen met an accident while out riding. She was captured by a giant, a renegade who had wandered north from the Fallaron Mountains."

Father raised the carved rod a few inches, the end wavering in his hands. "Not this story," he said through gritted teeth.

I stared at the fire rod, breath hitching. I swallowed hard, lifted my chin and tried to imitate Julie's confident stance. Just keep *talking*. "The court was thrown into despair for their queen, with wild talk of rescue attempts. Except no one knew how to fight a giant. In the midst of the chaos, the queen's fairy godmother arrived, shedding pink sparkles and consoling comments. She was hopelessly oblivious generally, but she had a sharp eye when it came to love, and she quickly saw that the chief of the guards was in love with his queen."

"I said, *not this story!*" Father shouted, and extended the hand holding his weapon.

I threw myself down instinctively, hit the ground with my palms and heard glass shattering. The sound told me Father must have aimed at one of the chandeliers above me and I hunched my shoulders, throwing my arms over my head and expecting a rain of glass.

A few pieces smashed on the black floor around me and I curled tighter, but didn't feel anything strike me. The magical fire seemed to have consumed most of the glass entirely.

"No one move!" Father yelled, and pointed his weapon again, this time towards the group at the window.

I turned my head, and saw that Das had run forward a few steps; he was halted, balanced with one foot forward, poised to move again. "Don't, I'm all right," I said, holding up one hand. It was mostly true.

Behind Das and beyond the window, the fog suddenly blazed out golden. It was down to mere wisps now, threads of golden gauze. My gaze darted to Nila and Talya, and saw them checking their shoes. Nila sank down in a crumple of skirts, expression mingling relief and exhaustion. Talya tugged Dathan's hand and started dancing again.

One more down. Everyone still alive. And if Talya could keep going, I had to keep going too.

"The fairy godmother," I said, pushing myself up to my knees and trying to pick up the thread of the story. "She gave the chief of guards a magical sword, which she said would have the power to kill a giant. So the guard set off into the hills, and found the cave where the giant was holding the queen. Since giants leave a very large trail, this wasn't difficult."

Father was silent, gaze locked on my face. Since he didn't lift his weapon again, I kept on. It was a story just like any other story, and I could keep telling it.

"The cave reached far into the earth and the giant, for his own reasons, had descended into a deeper section, leaving the queen closer to the entrance. At first the guard thought that the giant had made a mistake, because now it would be easy to escape with the queen. He quickly discovered a problem, though—the giant had enchanted the queen, giving her a potion that made her forget who she was, and everyone she had ever known." Magic that could steal a person's identity, sunder all relationships…even in this moment, the thought of it gave me a thrill of terror, a thread winding through the much larger tapestry of my fears.

"The guard now had to use all his charm to convince the queen that she could trust him, and should come with him. The effort took too long, and the giant returned before they could get away. The giant was willing to negotiate, and offered the guard a share of the wealth from the ransom of the queen. The guard refused."

It was impossible to imagine my father refusing wealth today. He stirred now, when I got to that part.

"Because he was a fool," he ground out, "an idealist, a romantic, and what did it ever…" There was a pause, a pause that made me hold my breath and hope that maybe, just maybe, this was doing something besides stealing time. "Maybe for a while. But in the end…in the end…" He pressed one hand to his face, voice trailing away.

I picked the story up again, talking faster now because there was a part I wanted to get to, the part that before I had avoided with the most dedication. "The giant and the guard fought, and the giant had more magic ready to use. He threw another potion over the guard, burning him badly. The guard knew he was dying, but with his last strength he threw the sword the fairy godmother had given him. It struck the giant, and because it was magical, the giant vanished in a cloud of smoke. The queen ran over to the dying guard. And then— because he had charmed her, or because there was something between them that even the giant's potion couldn't bury completely—and then..."

"What?" Father said in a low voice. "Then what?"

I swallowed. "She kissed him. And a kiss, with love behind it, can break the most powerful spells. The guard was healed and the queen's memory restored, and they returned to the castle together, where the difference in rank didn't seem to matter so much anymore, and so they were married.

"They had twelve daughters. Twelve beautiful princesses with blond hair and blue eyes, just like their mother." If only the story could end there. So many stories would have ended there, concluding they had all lived happily ever after. Not ours. "But their mother had a secret." The words felt heavy on my tongue. "And their father wouldn't leave it alone."

Back at the mention of the kiss, Father's gaze had dropped to the ground and stayed there. Now he looked up again, eyes burning with intensity. "No. Not this part of the story."

That stare had always terrified me, and it still did. But it needed to be turned on me, had to be on me. As long as he was looking at me, he wasn't looking at Talya. It was Talya who mattered, because it was Talya who still had a slipper to wear out. My shoes had holes. My part of breaking the spell was done, and if it was me who died now...I wasn't needed anymore.

Besides, Talya was my little sister and I had always watched out for her.

"It was a magical forest." I tasted salt as a tear rolled down my cheek and touched my lips. I didn't know when I had started crying.

"The queen's secret was a magical forest of riches. But it was a forest that twisted the mind, and when the king saw it, it made him forget. He forgot what mattered. He forgot that when he had rescued the queen from the giant, it wasn't wealth that helped him succeed, or fighting, and I don't think it was even charm."

"No," Father whispered.

"It was love."

"*No...*" Face twisting in pain, Father fell to his knees, still muttering words I couldn't hear clearly. I stood up, took a step towards him, to do what I honestly didn't know.

Before I could do anything, the ballroom was flooded by a flash of light. I looked back at the window just in time to see the last traces of the fog flare up in a blaze of sparkling white light, like a web made of millions of diamonds, and then dissolve into air, leaving nothing but water and stars.

Talya had finally worn through her slipper.

There were hundreds of voices exclaiming, crying out, even cheering. One rose above the rest, one furious shout.

"No! *No!* It's gone, it's all gone, you've taken it away!"

My head snapped back to look at Father. There was murder in his eyes, and no hesitation left. He raised the carved rod toward me, and this time there was no chance he was aiming above my head.

Das crashed into me and knocked us both to the ground, Das covering me. Beneath his arm I could still see Father, and I saw when he released the ball of flame. I gasped some kind of protest and pushed at Das even though there was no time to get out of the way. He wrapped his arms tighter around me, burying his face in my hair.

The flames hit us—and I felt nothing. There was a flicker of light, nothing more.

Then Father screamed. I caught a glimpse of him, engulfed by flames, before I shut my eyes. But I heard the screams, horrible and with only one intelligible word in them—Anna. It was my mother's name.

When the screams stopped, and the flames went out, there was nothing left. Fairy fire is very strong.

I couldn't think about Father yet, so I thought about Das instead. "You shouldn't have done that," I said, as we both sat up.

"Fine, I won't do it again," Das said, and kissed my forehead. "Does throwing myself in front of fire for you mean that I come in ahead of the raspberry tarts?"

I remembered my self-description to my father. "It wasn't in order of importance," I said, and hid my face against his shoulder.

Chapter Thirty-One

It took a long time to sort out everything that had happened, and what all the effects would be. Most of them we didn't know right away, though that didn't prevent the crowd from carrying on a hundred conversations about the possibilities.

I had a couple of cuts on my arm from when that chandelier had burst. I hadn't even noticed them at the time. Sasia had wrapped them up, and now I was sitting on a bench near a window with my head on Das' shoulder, listening to all that conversation swirl around me. Everything felt unreal, as though any moment someone was going to announce it was all just an illusion, and we'd better be going home for some sleep before another day in my father's castle, another night of dancing.

One of the first questions, of course, was what exactly had happened to Father. That was the topic Mina and Das were discussing somewhere above my head. Every witness agreed that he had pointed his weapon at Das and me, and then been consumed by flames himself. The weapon itself had been destroyed in the fire.

Mina, unsurprisingly, had a theory. "It's possible Marj built the weapon so that it wouldn't work on a person. But I think it's more likely it didn't work because of you."

I felt Das shift as he shook his head. "Me? I don't have any magical ability."

"I don't mean you did anything magically. What you *did* was throw yourself in front of the fire to protect Lyra. That's classic hero behavior, and Good Fairies like heroes. Marj may have built a safety into the weapon, in case it was used on…well, for lack of a better term, the wrong person."

"You're suggesting she designed a 'mining instrument,' gave it to a madman, was not at all concerned if it killed Lyra, or you, or a random bystander—but because I was a little more dramatic in my sacrifice, I somehow attained protective status?"

His tone was disbelieving, but Mina nodded. "Exactly. *That's* classic Good Fairy behavior."

That could mean Marj had also built a protection into the weapon so it wouldn't harm me or my sisters. We couldn't know that, though, and the possibility didn't make the evening seem any less terrifying in memory.

"Maybe that's what happened," Das said, still sounding doubtful. "So why cause it to bounce back? Why not just have it fail whenever it pointed at anyone? Aren't Good Fairies supposed to be *good*?"

I sighed. "You obviously haven't met many Good Fairies. They go on about sweetness and light, but sometimes they decide someone deserves punishment too. And then they're ruthless." At least, Marj was, and I had read enough stories about Good Fairies to believe she was typical.

"And attacking a hero," Mina resumed, "would clearly make someone a villain. According to a Good Fairy, anyway."

For the first time it occurred to me that life must seem very simple to Marj.

Nothing seemed simple to me that night, or to my sisters. Too many conflicting emotions happening all at once to know quite what to feel.

For most of the crowd the mood was celebratory. The spell had been lifted. For the first time in two hundred years, the fog was gone from around the island. Everyone was still awake at dawn, and no one turned insubstantial when the sun rose, a fact that brought on a renewed round of celebration.

There was one lingering piece of magic from the curse, and it proved to be a very useful one. There was the problem of getting back and forth between castles now. Rowing out into the sea seemed obviously pointless, but the third tunnel had survived. Our countries were hundreds of miles, two other countries and much of a continent apart. They were also a thirty-minute walk by tunnel.

We didn't try it until the afternoon after we broke the curse. All of my sisters and about half of the princes (all the ones who could get away from the suddenly expanding affairs of state that had cropped up now that they were a normal country again) walked through the tunnel together. Das came; he cheerfully said that he had never had a flair for governing and didn't plan to start now. It was really a good thing that neither of us were anywhere near the oldest in our families.

There was nothing about the tunnel that felt magical, no looming gates or metal trees. If I hadn't known we were arriving in a place that we couldn't be in, I wouldn't have known there was anything strange. We came out by a lakeshore that was only familiar from the shape. The forest was gone as though it had never been. Even though it was darker without the forest's light, the water in the lake looked more natural, without that shiny black quality. We found the tunnel we had gone through every night for a year, but we came up with nine different opinions about where in that tunnel the Gate had been. We were lucky that the carved stairs were still there, and the trapdoor still opened on our bedroom.

We came out on a castle that was in an uproar, with their king and all their princesses gone missing in the night. There was enormous relief to see us, although I didn't know if it was personal, or just that we were a better alternative to anarchy. Nasty things happen when you have no one at all in line for a throne. It became personal quickly enough, as Vira stepped immediately into the role she'd been waiting for all her life. I'm her sister so I'm biased, but she really was meant to lead, and she's good at it.

No one knew what had happened to Julie, Jasper and their talking cat. There had been some wild theories that they must be with us.

Once we returned, no one had any information on where they had actually gone. I hoped they had slipped off through the alternate tunnel, to go fight other monsters.

After years and years of everything being exactly the same, suddenly everything began to change. I had to catch my breath every so often, but mostly it was wonderful. And I cut my hair. Two days after breaking the curse, I sat down in front of a mirror, picked up a knife, and lopped off most of my golden ringlets. When I was done, it was chin-length and uneven and I loved it. For the first time I didn't look like my sisters. I didn't even look princess-like. It felt like taking off a mask I had been trapped under forever.

Nila cried about it. Talya was doubtful but came around quickly, Mina took the whole thing as a matter of course, and Das swore he liked it. He said it looked more like me, which I think was getting at the same thing as my mask analogy. It was still long enough to be played with; we tested it.

Marj arrived in a cloud of sparkles a week after the curse was broken. She was utterly convinced that it had been her idea all along for us to break the spell and marry the princes. We didn't bother arguing. We did ask her about Father, and the way he had died. She looked at us with wide and innocent eyes and avowed with apparent sincerity that Father had brought the entire affair onto his own head and she simply wasn't to blame. She was deeply saddened and never would have expected it, etc., etc. She never apologized for misjudging Father for fifteen years.

Everyone was finding their own place in this very changed world. Mina was having a wonderful time learning everything she could about Marileigh; within a month she knew more than people who had lived there all their lives. I don't know how much Daemyn planned it when he fell in love with her, but he made a good choice. He took over proper ruling as soon as the curse was over, and he was officially crowned soon after. Between him, Vira and Mina, there was lots of talk about alliances and trade agreements and shared resources and plenty of other words I couldn't recognize as easily. The details put me to sleep, but I knew they were good things, when I got a grasp on the overall idea. One princess getting involved with one prince is always good for tying two countries together; get twelve involved with twelve, and you find yourself with two countries ready to hail each other as brothers—or sisters, whichever gender countries are.

There was also a wedding. One wedding and several marriages. Vira, Mina, Laina, Rayna and Sasia had a joint wedding. Das, to my eternal gratitude, didn't make any comments about how we could have made it an even half-dozen. Leading up to the day, I had wondered how I was going to feel. When it came, I was glad I hadn't changed my mind. There was plenty I still wasn't sure about, but I did know I didn't want to spend the rest of my life solely as one of a circle of sisters, and lining up with them to be married was no way to start that new life. I don't mean it couldn't be perfect for them. It just wasn't at all right for me.

I spent some time exploring Marileigh. It was a beautiful country, and it didn't hurt that I had a beautiful man who wanted to show it to me. But, like the maiden who followed the birds, I was still dreaming of going farther, of seeing new places, and new people. Like the witch's daughter, who maybe had a few things in common with Julie.

I had no desire, however, to end up like the maiden without hands, alone, stranded and hungry. Laina and Dacien had plans to travel, and I made plans to go with them as far as Ryvideau. Ryvideau was where clumsy Sam's inn was, and I was hoping to find a position there. I could think of no better place to have new experiences than an inn in the capital city of Perrelda, our neighbors south of the Fallaron Mountains.

It was on a fall day, after the summer's heat had gone but before any of winter's chill had arrived, that we planned to set out. Das and I took a walk in the orchard in the early morning; thanks to the magic tunnel, I could take a walk in Marileigh with plans to leave from my own castle an hour later.

We walked without talking for a while, and finally stopped to stand under an apple tree. It could have been the same one that had knocked me into Das' arms, once upon a time, but I honestly couldn't tell. I looked up at him now, trying to read his expression in the half-shadows of the tree's leaves. "So...you're sure you're good with me leaving?"

"Good? No, I wouldn't say *good*. But..." His mouth twisted into a humorless smile. "...I'll manage."

I did not feel reassured. "It's just, I need to—"

He put two fingers over my mouth. "I know. You need to do this." He pulled me closer and kissed my forehead, then said, "I do know, and I think I understand. I still say you know yourself better than you believe you do. Maybe you just need to find that out. And I wish I could come with you, but I know that's not what you need right now. Which I suppose puts me still on the wrong side of the Gate. When you decide to open it—let me know."

I sighed and leaned my head on his shoulder. "You're really wonderful, you know that?"

"Yes." There was a pause, and then I could hear the grin in his voice. "So wonderful you couldn't ever dream of leaving me?"

I lifted my head. "Don't ruin it."

"Sorry, wishful thinking," he said, without any sign of repentance. "And I don't suppose either that this is one of those tests where you really just want to see if I'll come after you?"

"That's it," I said, backing up a step. "You ruined it."

Das laughed, and caught my hands in his. "Don't be angry. I didn't really think so. And I don't think I'd be willing to go after a girl who'd set up something stupid like that anyway."

"I wouldn't do that."

"I know. One of the many reasons I'm willing to wait for you."

That should have been reassuring. Instead, I felt guilty. I wanted him to wait, but I felt like I shouldn't want that. Not when I wasn't willing to make any promises myself. I couldn't imagine not loving Das, or loving someone else, only that was the whole point—I couldn't imagine what would happen once I got on my own. That's why I needed to go. All of which meant there was something I knew I should say, however hard it was.

I looked down at our hands clasped together, which didn't help but was better than looking at his face. "Maybe you...I mean, if you didn't want to, you...that is, we never really promised exactly..."

Mercifully, he interrupted me. "Are you trying to give me my freedom?"

I scuffed my toe along the ground. "Something like that. If you want it."

"I don't, so that's settled."

"I don't even know..."

"I do," he said, freeing one hand and lifting my chin to look in my eyes. "We're right, you and me. It's just our timing that's wrong. Don't get upset with me for being presumptuous about it, I don't mean it that way. I just know what I feel."

I didn't get upset. I kissed him instead.

We were late getting back to the castle, though not really any later than everyone had expected us to be anyway.

It was just as hard saying goodbye to my sisters. Vira had mountains of advice. Mina had a thousand questions about Ryvideau and wanted me to write to her with answers. Talya cried.

I promised Vira I'd follow her advice (while privately thinking I'd pick and choose what to follow, since thinking for myself was the whole point). I promised Mina to send her all the information she could want about Ryvideau. I told Talya she was going to be just fine, because she was so much braver than any of us had ever known; the last night of dancing had proved that.

I didn't wear Das' ring when I rode away. Our engagement was still too 'conditional' for that. But I did wear a scarf he had given me as a farewell gift, dyed the special shade of blue they only made in Marileigh, accented with white bands at either end that were seven rows wide; Das said they were lucky.

The scarf lay around my shoulders and I wrapped my fingers in one of those white stripes and didn't cry until we were on the road. Laina didn't, but Laina never shows any emotion if she can help it.

It's a problem, when you love the people you also want to get away from.

Chapter Thirty-Two

Once I had got over the initial sting, the journey to Ryvideau was exciting. It took us a week on horses to get there, and in that week I felt like I saw more new faces than I had seen in the rest of my life combined. And everywhere we stayed, I found someone (or many someones) happy to tell me their stories, tales they had heard or the most important parts of their own lives.

Ryvideau was every bit as big as I had imagined it, and then some. I had new respect for the heroes of my stories, who went venturing into places like this all on their own. There seemed to be endless people, rushing about their own business, buying and selling and traveling and talking and arguing. For the first time, I worried that it might not be so easy to find one person in all this throng—especially a man we knew only by the very common name of Sam, with no distinguishing characteristics apart from clumsiness.

Luckily, Sam had mentioned the name of the inn where he worked, and it was much easier to ask for and receive directions to The Nightingale. We found it down a quiet street, and walked into the common room, where I approved of the cleanliness of the tables and the smell of food coming from the kitchen. Coming out of the kitchen was a man carrying a basket piled with far too many apples.

Sam didn't recognize me. That haircut made a considerable difference. He did recognize Laina. The apples, not surprisingly, went everywhere.

"Hello, Sam," I said with a grin, bending down to scoop up an apple. "So you remember us?"

Fortunately, he remembered us gratefully. Sam wasn't in a position himself to give me a job, so we talked to the innkeeper's daughter, Catherine. That woman was more sure of who she was and what she wanted to do than anyone I had ever met. Inside of ten minutes I wanted to be her—except that I wanted to be *me*, so I guess I should say I wanted some of her qualities. Anyway, she thanked us for helping Sam when he went on that absurd quest (her phrasing), and pretty quickly I had myself a job.

Laina and Dacien stayed two days, then they went on and I finally had my chance to try life alone. I worked at The Nightingale, and learned about cooking and making beds and all sorts of things princesses never do. On my days off I went to the marketplace, walked by the river, and one day took a public tour of the castle. I sat by the river with books for hours, with no one to interrupt me just when I was at the good part. I talked to Sam, and Catherine, and everyone else who worked at The Nightingale, and I talked to the travelers and met people from places I'd only ever dreamed about. I heard new stories, and I told my own. After Catherine heard me a few times, storytelling became part of my job.

To put it briefly, I lived. It was perfectly ordinary life, but to me it seemed wondrous. I was like the girl who left her mountain village and found everything around her to be strange and new, while the people who had known it all their lives saw nothing to remark about.

I wore whatever dress I felt like in the morning, without needing to put it to a committee. I ate whatever I wanted, including many, many raspberries. I made all kinds of decisions without needing to consult anyone. Whenever I wasn't working, I could come and go and never need explain it or fit my schedule to anyone else's.

I was lonely for the first time in my life. With eleven sisters, and then Das, there had always been someone. I certainly wasn't lonely all the time, and I enjoyed the people I met at The Nightingale. There were other times when I desperately wanted to tell Mina something, and a letter just wasn't good enough, or when I thought wistfully of Talya and her eager attention to my stories.

I missed all my sisters.

And I missed Das. I missed him when I heard a song he would like or when I had a new story I wanted to tell him. I missed him when I unthinkingly made a remark about demon princes and no one around me understood. I missed his smile and his laugh and his easy way of understanding things even when I only half-said them, and I missed his arms around me when we danced. The Nightingale held a dance one night and I had to abandon my confused partner halfway through the first set, to run to my room and cry into Das' scarf. Then I dried my eyes and went back and only watched the rest of the dancing.

I couldn't lean on Das' shoulder, so when life got hard I had to pull myself together and go on anyway. I couldn't rely on Vira to be the strong one, so I had to be strong myself. I couldn't rely on Mina to have all the answers, so I had to find them myself. I couldn't rely on Talya to look up to me, so I had to prove my worth to the people I met.

I had difficult moments and I had beautiful moments, and for either one they were *my* moments. I was finally me, instead of we. I finally got to see who *I* was, just me, by myself.

Did I find out I was someone different? Or that there were deep, important things about myself that were completely unexpected?

No. Which doesn't mean that I hadn't been right that I needed to do this. There were plenty of things about myself that had always been true but I had never quite known, or realized I knew. Like the way I enjoyed being alone sometimes. All that time I had spent running off to the library should have told me that. It wasn't until I was *really* alone that I saw clearly how much I liked it. Or saw clearly how much I liked having the people I loved around too.

Ultimately, maybe I needed to be alone for a while to find out one more story. I'm sure I read in some story somewhere the idea that if you can't imagine your life without a certain person in it, then you really must love them. I had never been able to imagine my life without my sisters, and once Das arrived, he was so *there* and so sure that I hadn't really been able to imagine life without him either.

And that had always scared me. Because how could I know that I really wanted them in my life, if I had no idea what my life would be like if they weren't there?

Julie had said she traveled with Jasper because she was better with him than alone. I hadn't been sure about that in my own life. But after six months at The Nightingale, I finally had some idea.

Speaking of Julie and Jasper...now and then at The Nightingale, someone came through who had a story about a wandering adventurer, one who was traveling with a red-headed woman and a talking cat. I was always particularly pleased to hear those stories.

So the winter went by with work and fun, new stories and new people. And then one warm day, the first day that felt properly like spring, a young man came to The Nightingale looking for the storyteller. I was in the kitchen helping to prepare supper when Catherine came in to say someone was asking about me.

It wasn't an enormous surprise. I had been telling stories in the evening at The Nightingale for months, and I was beginning to be known for it. "Was he anyone you recognized?" I asked Catherine, which was as good as asking if he had ever been at The Nightingale before. Catherine knew everyone. If she didn't, that would mean someone who hadn't ever been here himself had heard of me. That would be exciting.

"No, I think he's new," Catherine said, pausing to stir the stew. "You'll like him. Seems nice. He said he's a minstrel."

I stopped chopping herbs. "A minstrel?"

"Mm-hmm. He must be a good one, he's not as ragged as some who come through." She frowned at me; I can't imagine what my face looked like. "Is something wrong?"

"No." I scooped the chopped herbs into the pot. "I'm about done here, do you mind if I...?" I gestured toward the common room.

"Sure, go ahead. Maybe you can work out some related songs and stories for this evening."

"Right," I said, and bolted.

It wasn't *necessarily* him. I told myself that, firmly. And I was not going to be crushed if it wasn't. Because there were plenty of minstrels, and there was no reason some other minstrel couldn't have heard about a storyteller at The Nightingale, and I couldn't be sure.

Until I saw him, that is.

"Das!" I ran across the empty common room to throw my arms around him. He laughed, and swung me around twice. When he finally set me down, he asked, "So you're not upset that I came after you?"

I shook my head, grinning up at him, eyes pricking. "Not upset. Very, very not upset," I said, and kissed him. I would have been, if he had come right away—but after six months? Not upset at all.

We talked about a hundred things that evening, some of them important and some of them not, but none of them *the* important thing. That finally came up the next day. Catherine gave me a holiday, and Das and I went walking by the river.

We talked about other things too, until finally the conversation came around to Das asking, "So do you think you've found out yet what you needed to know?"

"I found out...all sorts of things. And most of them were already true about me, but I didn't know it. Or I didn't know I knew it, which is practically the same thing."

Das already had hold of one my hands, and now he stopped walking and took the other one, turning me to face him. "And did you find out that anything very important is different?"

"*Well...*" I said slowly, "I still tell stories."

"So I gathered."

"And I still like raspberry tarts."

"Very important, that," he said, tightening his hold on my hands. "And…?"

I looked up into his dark eyes, and smiled. "And I still love you."

I had wanted to know who I was alone, and one thing I had found out was that I was someone who would desperately miss Das if he wasn't in my life.

I had missed my sisters too, but it was a different kind of missing. Our shared story was over, or nearly. While we would always be part of each other's stories, we each had our own story to live. There was wistfulness in that knowledge, but it felt right too.

And I felt sure now that *my* story, whatever story I ended up living, was going to be a much better one if I shared it with Das.

So in the end I did marry Das. You probably aren't surprised. No one else was. We went home to be married, because I wanted my sisters there—I just didn't want a joint wedding.

After we were married, Das and I went traveling, to find out who we were together, and to look for new stories and new songs. We stopped in inns and campsites and marketplaces to go about our own particular kind of trade. I heard so many stories, and I told my own, about girls who found out who they were, or overcame challenges, or fell in love—or who did all of those things.

Sometimes, on evenings when I was in a special mood and the audience seemed right, I'd tell a story about twelve sisters. Twelve sisters who most people thought of as one, because anonymity was their strength, and their curse. Once upon a time they danced their shoes to pieces—but that was just one part of their story.

Looking for more tales?

For more about Julie, Jasper and
talking cat Tom, read

The Wanderers

Find out how much of Lyra's story about them
was true, and read Julie's perspective on the
twelve dancing princesses.
Currently available in paperback or ebook!

For more about Catherine, Sam and The Nightingale, read

The People the Fairies Forget

An unusual fairy named Tarragon clashes with Good Fairy Marjoram,
by championing the people who live on the edges of familiar fairy tales.
Look for it in Fall, 2015!

For more information, visit
http://marveloustales.com/novelnews

Never miss an update! Email letterstothecat@gmail.com with
"Subscribe" in the subject line to join the newsletter list.

A Note on the Stories Within the Story

Besides being a character who originated (more or less) in a Brothers Grimm story, Lyra has also grown up reading the Brothers Grimm. The story in Chapter 9, of the girl who frees her cursed brothers, is based upon "The Six Swans." The story in Chapter 19, "The Maiden Without Hands" is inspired directly by Grimm, with added commentary. The story Lyra tells to Talya in Chapter 2 is, of course, "Beauty and the Beast," which the Brothers Grimm did not tell. Most likely Lyra knows the version from Jeanne-Marie LePrince de Beaumont. Lyra's other stories are original, although inspired by elements found throughout fairy tales.

Daemyn couldn't really have read Oscar Wilde, but that's still who he was thinking of in Chapter 7, and the relevant quote from the 'philosopher' is "Man is least himself when he talks in his own person. Give him a mask, and he will tell you the truth."

A version of Lyra and her sisters' story may be found in Grimm as "The Shoes Which Were Danced to Pieces" or "The Twelve Dancing Princesses," though you'll find it's not quite the way Lyra tells it!

Acknowledgements

This book would not have been possible without the support of friends, family, and everyone who believed me when I told them I'd publish novels someday. A big thank you to early readers, Kelly, Lynn, Karen, Ruth, Dennis and Meaghan, for their invaluable feedback. As always, thank you to the entire writing group at Stonehenge—you continue to make me a better writer every week!

I owe thanks as well to Juliet Marillier, whose *Wildwood Dancing* first brought "The Twelve Dancing Princesses" tale to my attention; to Gail Carson Levine, who wrote about her fascination with the three forests in the story, and inspired me to look at that part myself; and to Margaret Hunt, for translating a crucial sentence from the original German as "each prince danced with the girl he loved" and setting me off thinking about a whole new way to read the story.

About the Author

Cheryl Mahoney can't remember when she began her love affair with stories. She never goes anywhere (including the grocery store) without a book and a pen. She is not any good at dancing, but she does share Lyra's love of raspberries and, as you might imagine, of story telling.

Cheryl also writes a book review blog, Tales of the Marvelous (http://marveloustales.com), and is on Goodreads (MarvelousTales) and Twitter (@MarvelousTales). Her first novel, *The Wanderers*, was published in 2013. She has also been published in *The Ignatian*, and has completed NaNoWriMo twice.